The Corner Shop on Foxmore Green

Lilac Mills lives on a Welsh mountain with her very patient husband and incredibly sweet dog, where she grows veggies (if the slugs don't get them), bakes (badly) and loves making things out of glitter and glue (a mess, usually). She's been an avid reader ever since she got her hands on a copy of *Noddy Goes to Toytown* when she was five, and she once tried to read everything in her local library starting with A and working her way through the alphabet. She loves long, hot summer days and cold winter ones snuggled in front of the fire, but whatever the weather she's usually writing or thinking about writing, with heartwarming romance and happy-ever-afters always on her mind.

Also by Lilac Mills

A Very Lucky Christmas
Sunshine at Cherry Tree Farm
Summer on the Turquoise Coast
Love in the City by the Sea
The Cosy Travelling Christmas Shop

Tanglewood Village series

The Tanglewood Tea Shop
The Tanglewood Flower Shop
The Tanglewood Wedding Shop

Island Romance

Sunrise on the Coast
Holiday in the Hills
Sunset on the Square

Applewell Village

Waste Not, Want Not in Applewell
Make Do and Mend in Applewell
A Stitch in Time in Applewell

Foxmore

The Corner Shop on Foxmore Green

LILAC MILLS

The Corner Shop on Foxmore Green

ꟍ CANELO

First published in the United Kingdom in 2023 by

Canelo
Unit 9, 5th Floor
Cargo Works, 1–2 Hatfields
London SE1 9PG
United Kingdom

A CIP catalogue record for this book is available from the British Library.

Print ISBN 978 1 80032 880 8
Ebook ISBN 978 1 80032 879 2

Cover design by Rose Cooper

Cover images © Shutterstock

Look for more great books at www.canelo.co

Printed and bound in Great Britain by Clays Ltd, Elcograf S.p.A.

1

Chapter 1

Rowena Lloyd stepped out of her front door, pulled it shut behind her and turned her face up to the sun, feeling its warmth on her skin. The day was shaping up to be a glorious one, and she couldn't wait to dive right into it.

She took a steadying breath, the scent of the wisteria which grew around her front door filling her nose. Bees hovered over the cascading purple flowers before settling, and their busy drone made her smile. She'd thought she'd lost the plant as last winter had been such a harsh one, but it had gamely rallied and was now in full bloom. It looked marvellous growing up and over her porch, and it was just a pity it didn't flower for longer. Maybe she could grow some honeysuckle through it, or jasmine, so there would be flowers well into the summer.

Rowena cast her eyes over the rest of her tiny front garden with satisfaction. At this time of year it was a riot of colour. Orange, red, and yellow tulips stood to attention in their pots, although they'd be past their best shortly, and the lilac bush growing on the other side of the window sported many pink flowers. The lavender was out, and the sweet peas that scrambled through the hedge separating Rowena's garden from next door's added their fragrance to the heady mix. It was a bee's paradise and Rowena was immensely proud of it.

She allowed herself a few more moments of indulgence, thinking that her granny would have approved of what she'd done with it. Granny had died when Nia was only seventeen-moths old, leaving the cottage to Rowena (plus a small inheritance which Rowena guarded closely) and although she didn't have a great deal of spare cash, she had spent it wisely on the flowers and shrubs that she'd planted in the garden.

Tearing herself away, she focused her mind on what she needed to do today. 'Rallying the troops', she called it in her head. Another term was 'guilt tripping' them. For Rowena, this meant knocking on doors and trying to drum up interest.

She wasn't religious and only went to church for weddings and at Christmas, but the lovely old building was in danger of falling down if something wasn't done about it. It would be a shame for it to be deconsecrated and sold off, either to be demolished or turned into a house or flats.

It's not like she was asking anyone to put their hands in their pockets – what she was asking was for people to sign a petition to keep the church going, and maybe donate a few things to the bring-and-buy sale that Betsan was organising in order to raise funds. It wasn't much to ask, surely?

Foxmore without its lovely, rickety old church would be unthinkable. Although it was no longer a cornerstone of village life in terms of religious attendance, it was as much of a feature as the green with its ancient Celtic cross in the middle, and Betsan was determined to ensure it carried on. Actually, Betsan wanted more than for it to continue in its present capacity – her friend wanted it to *thrive*, and she didn't care who she roped in to ensure that happened. Which was why Rowena was about to traipse the streets this morning asking villagers and visitors alike to sign the petition that Betsan intended to present to the local council. If the bishop wasn't prepared to stump up the funds to save the old building, Betsan had no qualms about seeking funding elsewhere. Rowena had to admire her drive and dedication. The vicar's wife was a force to be reckoned with.

Turning the corner at the end of her road and hugging a clipboard to her chest, Rowena's pace slowed as she took in the familiar view. The heart of Foxmore consisted of one main road running through the village, with shops and businesses to either side, and a green at the far end.

She intended to work her way along one side of the high street towards the green, which was flanked by the fifteenth-century church and an olde-worlde pub, as well as a couple more shops and a busy cafe (she should be able to acquire a few signatures from there) and back down the other side of the main street. It would probably take her most of the morning, but after she had finished work in the local primary school where she was a lunchtime supervisor, she would fan out into the side roads and see how many signatures she could collect before she had to pick her daughter up from school. She was wondering just how many people would be at home on a Tuesday morning, but there was no way she was going to leave it until this afternoon and drag a four-year-old around with her, as Nia would soon get bored and cranky.

Rowena quickly glanced along the main road and thought of all the shops and businesses she'd shortly be entering. The butcher's shop boasted that it had been trading since 1905 and had been owned by the same family throughout that time. The corner shop, which until recently had been run by Ewan Evans, used to belong to his father and his father before him – although Rowena's mam claimed that both ancestors would turn in their graves if they knew that he'd sold it. Apparently, it had once been the heart of the village, together with the post office, but the corner shop was now a convenience store of sorts and the post office had become an estate agent, run by Dee and Vaughan Pritchard.

There was a florist and an antique shop which had some lovely bits and bobs in the window, although Rowena couldn't afford the prices they charged. And the pretty shop selling home-made cards, which had only opened last year, was always busy. A couple of premises lay empty and she thought it such a shame, though to be fair, empty buildings didn't stay empty for long in Foxmore; the village had its fair share of hikers, climbers and assorted outdoorsy people to make it an attractive proposition for new businesses.

A Cut Above was the first place she came to, and as she opened the door Rowena put a self-conscious hand to her hair. It flowed down her back almost to her waist, thick, caramel coloured, and utterly straight – not even a kink at the ends. She only ever had a trim, and a dry one at that. No wash and blow-dry, no highlights or lowlights, no drastic restyle. She never made an appointment, either.

Lowri glanced up from teasing out curlers from the hair of an elderly lady and gave a warm smile when she saw who had walked into her salon. 'Hiya, my lovely, take a seat. If you give me ten minutes, I should be able to fit you in.'

'I'm not here for a trim,' Rowena replied, sheepishly.

4

'You aren't?' Lowri's tone implied that she should be, and once again Rowena's fingers crept to her hair. It wasn't that bad, was it?

'Erm, no… I wanted to ask you something.'

'About time! I'm thinking light blonde to lift your natural colour, with some darker tones underneath to give it depth.' Lowri's expression was one of satisfaction.

'Pardon?'

'Your highlights,' Lowri said impatiently, as she unwound the final curler out of Mrs Moxley's lavender-tinted perm. Mrs Moxley had her hair washed and set every week without fail. With the last curler removed, the old lady risked turning her head to give Rowena a smile and a nod.

'Good grief, no!' Rowena cried as she understood what Lowri meant. 'No highlights, or lowlights. Sorry.' She didn't care how much her locks needed lifting or deepening; she didn't want to go down that route, because it wouldn't stop at one visit to the salon, would it? She would have to get those highlights re-done and touched up over and over again, and she simply didn't have the money or the patience for it.

'Knickers! I thought I'd finally convinced you,' the stylist sighed, then her eyebrows shot up and she let out a gasp. 'You're not thinking of having it all chopped off, are you?' There was a gleam in her eye that Rowena didn't care for.

'Most certainly not. I love my long hair,' she retorted.

Lowri deflated. 'In that case, what can I do for you?' She ran her fingers through Mrs Moxley's hair, gently pulling and patting the curls into position.

Rowena was conscious that most of the salon's staff and clientele had paused to hear what she had to say so, angling the clipboard away from her chest, she whipped a pen out of the rear pocket of her jeans, clicked the top, then took a deep breath.

'I'm asking people if they would be kind enough to sign a petition,' she said, wincing internally at the officious tone she'd suddenly adopted. She cleared her throat and tried again. 'To save the church? Terry says that the diocese doesn't have the cash to do all the repairs needed, but Betsan reckons it does and the bishop is just being mean. It's such a feature of the village and it dates back to the year dot, so it would be a shame to lose it.'

Rowena didn't add that it would also be a shame if Betsan and Terry had to move to another parish. But the vicar and his wife loved living in Foxmore, and Terry had been a vicar in the village since before he and Betsan had married. Their wedding had actually taken place in the very same church she was trying to save.

'Give it here, I'll sign.' Lowri held out a hand and Rowena passed the clipboard to her. 'I got married there,' the hairdresser added, 'although saying that, maybe it should have been torn down years ago, because if it had been I'd have saved myself a lot of aggravation.' Lowri pretended to glower, earning herself a ripple of chuckles.

'Get on with you; you love your Lewis to bits,' one of the other stylists said.

'He has his moments,' Lowri conceded. 'I just wish he'd have more of them and spend less time following the rugby. Ball mad he is. If it involves a ball, he'll watch it – tennis, footie, netball... although I get the impression he watches that because of those little skirts the women wear. And don't get me started on beach volleyball – the dirty sod!' She bared her teeth and shook her head.

One of the juniors who had been tending to a woman at the bank of sinks turned the tap off to better hear the conversation.

'Get on with rinsing your lady's colour out,' Lowri told her. 'She'll be orange if we're not careful.'

The woman, who must have been uncomfortable lying there with her head tilted back at an unnatural angle, let out a squawk and Lowri hastened to reassure her. 'Just joking, love. It won't really be orange.' She caught the junior's eye and made a face.

Rowena hoped the lady's hair would turn out the shade she wanted, otherwise Rowena would feel responsible.

'It's better they keep themselves occupied,' Mrs Moxley said. 'If a man's got a hobby, he's less likely to get up to mischief.'

'I wouldn't call sitting on his backside watching the rugby with a family-sized packet of crisps in one hand and a beer in the other, and yelling at the screen because Wales has given the other side a penalty, a hobby,' Lowri retorted.

'Yes, but at least you know where he is,' the elderly lady countered. 'Now, are you going to sign that petition or are you going to take it home with you and give it some dinner?' She jabbed a finger at the clipboard.

Rowena grinned. Mrs Moxley certainly was a character. She was in the same league as her granny had been, God rest her soul: not afraid to call a spade a spade – and her turns of phrase were often amusing and unusual.

She watched as the petition was passed from hand to hand, everyone willing to sign. When it was returned to her, she straightened her shoulders for the next part of her mission. Despite it being for a good cause and not for herself, she felt as though she was begging, and it made her a little uncomfortable.

'Go on, spit it out – what else do you want?' Lowri asked, turning to face her with her hands on her hips.

'A donation? To the bring-and-buy sale?' Rowena plastered an ingratiating smile on her lips. 'Please? It's for a good cause.'

'I'm still not so sure about that,' Lowri said, continuing with her 'I hate marriage' act before relenting. 'Oh, go on, then. I suppose I'd better do my bit. Where else am I going to get the baby christened?'

A sudden hush descended on the salon, then the junior plucked up the courage to ask, 'Are you… *pregnant*?'

'Uh huh.' Lowri nodded, a huge grin on her face.

'That's marvellous news!' Rowena cried, amid the squeals and the congratulations, and for a while she forgot the reason she'd come into the salon in the first place. There was nothing like the prospect of cuddling a new baby to bring joy to her heart, and everyone was equally as thrilled.

Eventually the excitement subsided and Rowena made to leave, her head full of little booties and snuggly soft blankets, when she suddenly remembered and slapped a hand to her forehead. 'Donation?' she reminded Lowri.

'If you're holding a raffle, I'll chuck in a free colour and cut to the value of eighty quid,' Lowri offered. 'I'll print out a voucher this evening – you or Betsan can pick it up next time you're passing.'

'Thank you so much,' Rowena gushed. 'That's very generous of you.'

'Yeah, well, you caught me at a weak moment.' Lowri winked. 'Just don't expect this every time you come in. And you might want to hope you'll win it – you could do with a makeover, if you don't mind me saying.'

'You know what they say: new look, new man,' Mrs Moxley piped up.

Charming, Rowena thought wryly. That was another phrase she hadn't heard before. 'I don't want a man,' she retorted. 'New, or otherwise.'

'Nonsense. Everyone wants a bit of love. It's what makes the world go round,' Mrs Moxley chortled.

'I thought that was supposed to be money? Anyway, I've got enough love in my life – there's Nia, my parents, Betsan, my friends...'

Mrs Moxley gave her a narrow-eyed look. 'That's not the kind of love I mean, and you know it.'

'I'm perfectly happy as I am,' Rowena retorted.

But as she wandered out of the salon and made her way to the card shop next door, she began to wonder. Was she really perfectly happy?

If she was being truthful with herself, she had to admit that she wasn't as contented as she might be. But – and here was the thing – it wasn't a man she needed. It was a new challenge. Now that Nia was in school full time, Rowena wanted to do *something* with her life, but she wasn't sure what.

Chapter 2

Huw Morgan hadn't expected to fall in love, but from the minute he had driven through the pretty little village of Foxmore three months ago he had been captivated.

As he approached the turnoff to the village today, his chuckle was ironic. It served his sister right for nagging that it was time he settled down – Ceri's face when he'd told her he was in love had been a picture, and he'd laughed so hard his sides had hurt when she'd realised he'd been referring to a place and not a woman. The strange thing was, he couldn't put his finger on why he felt this way. All he knew was that as soon as he'd set eyes on Foxmore, he'd had a sense of coming home.

The love affair had begun the minute he'd seen the place. He had been aiming for Aran Fawddwy, a mountain which was an impressive 900 metres above sea level and the highest peak in the southern range of the Snowdonia national park, and had been looking forward to exploring the walking trails in the area. He had also planned on taking a gander at the glowering craggy buttress near the village of Foxmore, made up of bare rock and heather-covered terraces. Mountain climbers loved it, and he wanted to see for himself what all the fuss was about. Not that Huw was a climber – if a hill needed a rope in order to scramble up it, then it wasn't for him

– but he did enjoy a good hike and a spectacular view. But when he had neared the turnoff to the village, a break in the trees lining the side of the road having given him a glimpse of his destination, he'd had the strangest feeling.

Lying in a flat-bottomed glacial valley with a meandering river running through it, Foxmore was surrounded by patchwork farmland, and above it were mountains whose lower slopes were clothed in pristine native woodland. If Huw hadn't known any better, he might have thought he was in the Alps.

Only five miles from the A470 which ran north to south through the unspoilt heart of Wales, the village was off the beaten track but close enough to the trunk road so as not to be totally isolated. Like many people, he had driven past the sign to Foxmore many times and had never thought to explore it. He suspected that most visitors sailed right past as they headed further north to the impressive peaks of Mount Snowdon and her rugged sisters, or to the beaches and coastal resorts. He'd done the exact same thing on numerous occasions.

However, once he'd found Foxmore, he had been smitten.

So much so that he had bought a house there. He'd been smitten with that, too.

And today he had a car full of possessions and was ten minutes away from picking up the keys.

He couldn't wait!

How ridiculous to feel like this about a village and a house, he thought, as he found a parking space on the edge of the green and got out of his car; but even as he was telling himself not to be so silly, he was once more gazing around in delight.

As it had done on the very first time he'd visited Foxmore, the centrepiece of the green caught his attention. A four-metre-tall Celtic cross was carved out of what appeared to be a single block of light grey stone, and his gaze lingered on it for a moment as he wondered how old it was and what its original purpose might have been. Gradually his eyes were drawn to the rest of the green, and he couldn't help smiling. A rickety old church stood on one side, with a graveyard surrounding it and a lychgate at its entrance, and next to the church was a whitewashed pub with a grey slate roof. The pub looked just as inviting as it had done the last time he'd visited Foxmore, with its large wooden planters filled with flowers, and window boxes and hanging baskets galore. He'd stayed there a couple of times, enjoying the landlord's real ale and full English breakfast. The first time had been when he'd discovered Foxmore, and the second had been when he'd arranged to view a couple of properties, before putting down an offer on one of them.

His gaze roved around the rest of the green, seeing the cafe with tables outside on the pavement, a dress shop, another store selling baby things, an antique shop and the estate agents, which Huw now made a beeline for.

Inside, two women were chatting, one sitting behind a desk, the other standing in front of it. Both of them glanced at him when he walked through the door and he gave them a smile. The one standing in front of the desk was holding a clipboard, so he waited patiently for her to finish her business, and while he did so he studied some of the listings displayed on the walls.

He was in the middle of reading some particulars when a voice said, 'Can I help you?'

Huw turned to see the two women staring at him. 'I've come to pick up the keys for Rosehip Cottage,' he said.

'Ah, yes, Mr Morgan, isn't it? Welcome to Foxmore! I'm Dee. I think you've been dealing with my husband, Vaughan.'

'That's me,' he confirmed. 'Huw Morgan.'

'Vaughan is out on a viewing, but I'm sure he'll catch up with you soon, probably in the pub,' she chuckled.

'I'll look forward to it,' he said, wishing she'd get on with it, anxious to hold the keys to his new home in his hand.

'I'll just fetch the paperwork, as there are a few bits that need signing,' she said.

She rose and as she did so the woman holding the clipboard said, 'Thanks, Dee. Your support is most welcome.'

Dee waved a hand in the air. 'We can't let an historic building like the church go to rack and ruin, can we?' She opened a filing cabinet and brought out a thick envelope. 'Here we are,' she said to Huw, before turning to the woman with the clipboard once more. 'Actually, why don't you ask this gentleman to sign your petition?' She tilted her head to the side and before the other woman had a chance to open her mouth, she said to him, 'What do you think about the church falling down?'

'Erm, I've only just arrived, so...' He shrugged helplessly. The building was lovely, but it did look rather in need of some major repairs.

'Leave the poor man alone,' the woman with the clipboard said. She met his gaze, and he was struck by how pretty she was. 'Sorry,' she added, pulling a face at Dee.

'She's asking people to sign a petition to save the church, aren't you, Rowena?' Dee said, then shoved a sheaf of documents at him, none of which was a petition, he noticed. 'Right, if you can sign here, and here…' She pointed to the documents, which Huw duly signed, then she held the keys to the cottage out to him. 'I'm sure you'll find everything in order.'

He took them with a smile. 'I'm sure I will. Is that everything?'

'It is. Enjoy your new home.'

'Thanks.' He stepped towards the door, hefting the satisfying weight of the bunch of keys in his hand, and feeling like doing a little hop, skip and a jump. The house was finally his, and excitement washed over him.

Rowena was blocking the exit and she hastily moved to open the door for him.

'Thanks,' he repeated with a smile, and as he stepped through it, he looked at her again, and was struck by how gorgeous she was. Briefly he entertained a vague hope that he might see her around at some point, before pushing her to the back of his mind. He had a brand new home to move into!

Although Huw was eager to settle into the cottage, he needed something to eat and a coffee first. He'd been too excited this morning to bother with food, and he knew that once the small removal van which he had hired eventually arrived, he would be too busy unpacking to stop for a break.

His tummy rumbling in anticipation, he paused outside the cafe and peered through the window to see if there was an empty table inside because the ones on the pavement were occupied. There was, and he was just about to go in when he paused again. There was something about the woman with the clipboard… something that very much appealed to him, and no matter how hard he tried to shove it away, her face kept popping into his mind. He felt as though he knew her, but not in a 'we've met before' way. He couldn't describe the phenomenon, and as he was trying to make sense of it, he suddenly wondered what she would feel like in his arms.

Shaking his head at his fancifulness (he was never usually like this) Huw went in search of a sandwich and an Americano. Gosh, Foxmore must seriously be getting under his skin. In a good way.

–

'Flippin' heck, did you cop a load of that!' Dee fanned her face with both hands, her eyes sparkling. 'If I wasn't happily married…!' She stared through the window with a dreamy expression.

Rowena hadn't been able to avoid staring, either. It wasn't often a man as good looking as this one pitched up in Foxmore and she wanted to make the most of the view without appearing to be ogling him – although that was precisely what she was doing as she continued to gaze at him out of the estate agents' window. He was hovering outside Pen's Pantry as if wondering whether the food was any good.

It was – she could vouch for that. Should she pop outside and tell him? Maybe not: he probably wouldn't appreciate her interference.

'Behave yourself,' Rowena chuckled, secretly agreeing with Dee.

'I didn't see you averting your eyes,' Dee countered, with an arched brow.

'I'm young, free and single – I'm allowed.'

'I'm allowed, too! A girl can look, can't she? There's no harm in that, and you've got to admit, he was an absolute dish. Did you see his bum?'

'Dee! You can't say things like that!'

Dee nudged Rowena with her elbow. 'But did you see it, though?'

'I saw.' Rowena was trying not to giggle. Dee was right, he did have a nice behind. Other bits of him had been equally as nice, if not nicer – his face for one. She had a weakness for clean-shaven men with blue eyes and dark hair. Especially hair that was brushed back from his face with unruly bits flopping over his forehead. She quite liked broad shoulders and a flat stomach too, and from what she'd seen Huw Morgan appeared to have both.

'He's got a rugby player's bum,' Dee continued. 'All muscly and shaped nice. If I was a few years younger, and not married…' She sighed wistfully and fanned her face again.

'I'd better get a move on!' Rowena suddenly realised the time. If she didn't hurry, she was going to be late for work. Collating signatures had taken rather longer than she'd anticipated, and she'd only made her way along one side of the street, and around less than half of the shops and businesses surrounding the green. At the rate she was going, it would take a week to knock on every door.

Pushing thoughts of handsome strangers out of her head, Rowena hurried off home to change. There were 130 hungry children wanting their lunch, and if she wasn't careful she'd have a riot on her hands – and that would be from the teachers.

The cottage was possibly the quaintest cottage in the world, Huw suspected. Mind you, he was somewhat biased.

His new home was in the middle of a row of five on a road tucked away down the side of the churchyard. All were built of stone, not brick, and had grey slate roofs. Most of them still had chimney pots, and when Huw had first been shown around the cottage, he'd been thrilled to discover a wood-burning stove in the small living room. A pile of logs was stacked neatly beside it and he decided to light a fire later, regardless of whether it was chilly enough.

There were original floorboards in the sitting room and two of the walls were exposed stone with cream wooden panelling on the lower halves. Lining the top part of the walls were a haphazard arrangement of shelves on which a wide range of books sat. The vendors had agreed to sell him the contents of the house, as it had formerly been used as a holiday let and his request had probably saved them from having to dispose of all the bits and pieces. Which was the reason why he'd only hired a small van – he hadn't particularly wanted to bring much in the way of furniture with him from his old place in Cardiff. None of his modern flat-packed stuff would have looked right in a cottage oozing with so many original features.

As he walked through the ground floor, he ran his fingers across the scarred wooden table which sat in the dining area on the other side of the stairs, along with four equally old chairs. They rested on top of stone quarry tiles, and there was an imposing oak dresser up against the far wall. Beyond the dining area a kitchen lay through a low door.

When Huw walked into this part of the house, he gazed around in wonder once more. He felt like he was stepping back into the early part of the twentieth century, with the kitchen's terracotta floor, whitewashed walls and low ceiling. His head just about cleared the ceiling, and if he'd been an inch taller than his six-foot-one, he'd have had to have kept his neck permanently tilted to the side whenever he entered the room. There wasn't a fitted unit in sight, either. Every cupboard was free standing, and the Belfast sink was possibly original.

However, some concessions had been made to the present day and the comfort of the holidaymakers who had rented it in the past, and Huw was grateful to see that the modern cooker in the nook where a fireplace and a bread oven might once have stood was still there, and so was the washing machine next to the sink. There was also a fridge, thank goodness. Pots, pans, plates and bowls were hidden behind curtains attached to the tops of the cupboards, and another dresser showcased teacups, mugs and glasses. True to their word, the vendors hadn't removed anything, and as he returned to the living room he grinned when he noticed a flat-screen TV still propped up on an artist's easel. How much nicer than standing it on a generic piece of flat-packed furniture, he thought.

Another concession to modern living were the old-fashion-style radiators underneath the windows, and he guessed he'd be grateful for those come the winter, despite the wood-burning stove.

A flight of steep stairs took him to the upper floor and yet more artistically bare stone walls. There were also fireplaces in the rooms up here, even in the bathroom, and he was looking forward to lying in the claw-footed tub with a fire roaring in the grate and a glass of wine in his hand. The view from there was pretty good too, looking out at a majestic mountain. What a wonderfully relaxing place to soak the cares of the day away!

He walked across the creaking wooden floorboards and hung his jacket in the wardrobe standing in the larger of the two bedrooms, the one with the double bed. As he gazed out through the sash window at the same view that he had admired from the bathroom, he couldn't stop grinning to himself. The previous owners had thought of everything while continuing to retain the character of the place, and he still had trouble believing that this gorgeously quaint and quirky cottage finally belonged to him.

After the moving van left and he had found places for the few bits of furniture that he'd decided to bring with him, Huw unpacked the rest of his things, stowing his suits, shirts, and more casual clothing in the creaky-doored wardrobe, and placing his toiletries in the bathroom. Then he set up his laptop on the little dining table – he'd yet to arrange for a Wi-Fi connection but he could do without it for a week or so by using his phone as a hotspot – and he also connected a small printer and put his mobile on charge. Only once that was taken care of did he turn his attention to the subject of food.

He'd brought some essentials with him, bread, butter, milk, coffee, eggs and so on, which would see him through until tomorrow without having to go shopping, and he had planned to pop into the pub on the green for dinner, so there was no immediate urgency to stock up. Besides, there was only one small convenience store in the village and they didn't have a particularly good selection, so one of the first things he'd do tomorrow was to pay a visit to the nearest supermarket, which was around ten miles and a twenty-five-minute car journey away.

Huw decided to check his emails, then go for a walk to re-familiarise himself with the village before calling in at the pub for some supper, and he had just settled down at the dining table with a cup of coffee when a knock on the front door made him jump. Expecting it to be a neighbour, possibly coming to introduce themselves or to check that he was settling in OK, he got to his feet and went to answer it.

Standing on the path was one of the women who'd been in the estate agents earlier, the one with the clip-board. The gorgeous one, with the long golden hair and the arresting face.

'Do you want me to—?' he began, assuming she wanted him to sign her petition.

'Sorry to—' the woman said, as they both spoke at the same time.

'You go first,' he said. 'Rowena, isn't it?'

The woman blushed and looked away for a second. 'That's right.' Her gaze met his. 'And you're Mr Morgan?'

'Call me Huw.'

'Huw,' she repeated. 'Nice to meet you.'

'You, too. Still collecting signatures, I see?'

'Sorry, I know you've only just moved in...' She ground to a halt.

He thought she looked cute with her pink cheeks and flustered expression, then he almost blushed himself. Cute was a word used for kittens and puppies, not for women, and he'd never thought of a woman in such a way before. But, damn it, this one *was* cute. Heart-shaped face, big brown eyes, upturned nose and a generous mouth with full lips. Kissable lips.

Oh, heck! Where did that come from?

Giving himself a mental shake, Huw tried not to stare at them, concentrating on her eyes instead.

Big mistake...

Luminous and liquid, they drew him in, and he found he couldn't tear his gaze away.

With an effort he cleared his throat and nodded, although what he was nodding at was anyone's guess.

'Anyway, I'm sorry to disturb you,' she said, and as she spoke his attention dropped to her delectable mouth once more.

He swallowed and tried to get a grip. First Foxmore, then the cottage, and now this woman. Was there something in the air in this part of Wales?

'That's OK,' he croaked, huskily. Dear God, he sounded like one of those American voiceovers for an action movie trailer. He cleared his throat again and gestured at her clipboard. 'How is it going?' Ah, that was better – he no longer sounded as though he was trying to advertise the latest thriller. 'Something to do with the church, wasn't it?'

'That's right.'

'How are you getting on?'

'Good, I think. Most people have happily signed. It's been a bit harder getting them to donate to the bring-and-buy sale, though.'

'I'll sign the petition,' he offered, 'but I might struggle with a donation. I had a good clear out when I moved out of my old house, which left me with not much more than the essentials. I could make a cash donation, if that's all right?' He held out a hand and she passed him the petition and the pen.

'That's most generous of you, but please don't give any money to me: pop into the church and give it to Terry, the vicar.'

'No problem.' He'd do it on the way to the pub later, if the church was still open at that time in the evening.

'Thank you so much. I appreciate it.' She beamed a smile at him, and his heart did a funny little flip.

Without thinking, his eyes dropped to her left hand, the one holding the clipboard.

She wasn't wearing a ring, but that didn't mean anything.

His gaze crept back to her face and he drank her in, thinking she really was gorgeous.

'I'd better leave you to it,' she said abruptly, and he realised he'd been staring. 'Welcome to the village. I hope you'll be happy here.' The smile she gave him was a little more reserved and he prayed he hadn't been too obvious in showing how attracted he was to her.

'I'm sure I will be. It seems lovely,' he said.

'It is! It's a fantastic place to bring up children. There's a real community spirit, and don't forget all the fresh air and outdoor activities. Anyway, sorry again for intruding. I'd better get a move on.' She held up her clipboard.

'Of course. Nice to see you again.'

'You, too.'

Huw watched her turn away and walk down the short path, then he went back inside and closed the door. But as he returned to his cup of coffee and his emails, he couldn't help glancing out of the window, and his eyes followed her until she was out of sight.

He wondered when he'd bump into her again and hoped it would be soon.

Gosh, he really *did* think there must be something in the air...

Chapter 3

Foxmore's little primary school was situated at the far end of the village from Rowena and Nia's house, which meant running the gauntlet of the high street every time Rowena either took her daughter to school, or collected her from it.

It didn't help that the village's main thoroughfare was filled with lovely shops which were irresistible to a four-year-old. Correction, almost five, Rowena amended: Nia was very keen to tell people that she was nearly five whenever anyone asked her age, as though being older was a badge of honour. Rowena's heart bled as she thought of how desperate her little girl was to grow up. Nia was growing fast enough as it was, without wishing the time away.

This afternoon, her daughter skipped next to her, hanging on to her hand and chattering about her day. She was in the reception class and simply loved it, which Rowena was relieved about, because some of Nia's classmates howled every time they were dropped off at school.

As she walked along the pavement, Rowena steeled herself to pop into the convenience store. It was always touch-and-go whether they stocked what she wanted and, if they did happen to have it, it was usually ridiculously expensive. However, she needed bread for tomorrow, so it was a choice of either buying a loaf from the bakers or buying a bag of flour from the convenience store. As she preferred to bake her own whenever she could, she decided to bite the bullet and buy the flour.

She should have called into the shop before she had picked Nia up from school, but she had been running late (she shouldn't have stopped to have a chat with Foxmore's newest resident, but she hadn't wanted to be rude – at least, that's what she was telling herself) so Rowena was now forced to take her daughter into the store with her. The problem was that Nia wanted everything she saw, and since the shop placed those items that would directly appeal to kiddies at child height, Nia saw a lot – sugar-laden cereals, garishly coloured bottles of additive-filled drinks, cartoon-plastered yoghurts, and primary-coloured sweets, to name but a few.

The worst sinners, in Rowena's opinion, were the cookies. They were sold as oatmeal and raisin, to try to appeal to the more health-conscious parents, but the list of additives in them made Rowena cringe. They were stuffed so full of ingredients she couldn't even pronounce that it made her stomach churn. Not only that, but the cookies came in a plastic tray, covered in plastic wrapping, and inside a cardboard box, to give the impression that the pack contained more cookies than were actually there. And don't get her started on the amount of packaging that ended up in the bin. Nia adored them and so did her classmates. Rowena's refusal to buy them was a bone of contention between mother and daughter. If Nia wanted a cookie, Rowena would either bake some, or buy the occasional one from the baker's shop over the road, where the list of ingredients was mostly pronounceable and generally recognisable, and the cookies came wrapped in a single plain paper bag.

'Mammy, look!' As soon as Nia stepped through the mini-market's door, she spotted something she wanted, and Rowena's heart sank.

Maybe she should have bought a loaf from the bakers after all and avoided the hassle. But she also needed some fruit and veg, and this shop was Foxmore's only option, even though the range was small and the quality was often dire.

Nia was pointing to a display of snacks aimed specifically at children and their pester-power. In an attempt to appear to give a damn about children's diets, the shop had placed a range of healthier snacks near the door, fully aware that parents popped in with their children on the way to and from school. Rowena had no objection to most of the snacks – she applauded the sale of apples and grapes over sweets and chocolate – but what she did object to were the tiny plastic packets they came in, and the price.

Nia wanted some apple slices, but when Rowena grabbed a six-pack of whole ones from the fruit and veg aisle instead, her daughter folded her arms across her skinny chest, stuck out her chin and stamped her foot. 'You said apples are good for me.'

'These *are* apples,' Rowena replied, holding the packet up for Nia to see.

'I don't like them. I like *those*.' She stamped her foot again.

'You're not having them.' Rowena put the apples in her basket.

'You're mean. Skye's mammy buys them for her.'

'I'll cut your apple into slices when we get home,' Rowena offered. 'It'll be just the same.'

'Won't.' Yet another stamp, this time accompanied by a glowering frown.

Huh! This parenting malarkey wasn't easy, was it? Rowena scowled at the apples in her basket, wondering why on earth they too had to be packaged. Why did they need to be in a cardboard tray with plastic over the top, instead of loose? They were probably sold in a pack just to get the customer to buy more she thought snidely, wishing she had room for an apple tree in her garden. Considering she barely had room for a sandpit and a bench out the back, it was wishful thinking. Maybe she could squeeze one into her front garden...?

'Remember what your teacher said about reducing the use of plastic?' Rowena said, crouching down in front of her disgruntled daughter. Nia adored Miss Caldicott and hung on the teacher's every word.

Nia nodded reluctantly, her eyes narrowing.

'This is only one apple in this plastic bag,' Rowena explained, holding up the little bag of distinctly unappetising-looking slices of Granny Smith. 'There are six apples in this one. And these are much prettier, see? They're pink.' Calling them pink was stretching the truth a little, but Nia loved pink, and as far as Rowena was concerned all was fair in love and supermarkets.

'Criminal, isn't it?' Bronwen Jones grumbled, appearing at her side and glaring at the packet of apple slices that Rowena was still holding. Rowena hastily put it back on the shelf.

'I only want a couple of tangerines,' Bronwen was saying, her eyes huge as she peered through her varifocals.

'Yet they want me to buy a whole bag of them. What Foxmore needs is a proper greengrocer, where you can buy as much or as little as you want.'

'And where it's not all encased in plastic,' Rowena added, smiling at the elderly woman. She also wished Foxmore had a greengrocer; preferably one stocking locally grown produce and not items that had been flown halfway across the world.

'My mammy says plastic is killing the planet,' Nia declared in her high piping voice, and Rowena was grateful to the pensioner, even if side-tracking her daughter away from a public meltdown hadn't been Bronwen's intention.

Bronwen bent down to speak to her. 'Your mam is right. There's no need for it. Wasteful, that's what it is.' She straightened, addressing her next comment to Rowena. 'There's plastic in everything these days.'

And that, Rowena thought, was the problem. Something had to be done about it, but she had no idea what.

–

'How has your day been? Get many signatures?' Betsan rested her backside against the kitchen table as she spoke, a cup of herbal tea in one hand and one of Rowena's home-made flapjacks in the other.

Rowena picked up a flapjack of her own and bit into it, hoping Nia didn't come in from the garden and catch her indulging in an illicit treat when she'd already told her daughter she would have to wait until after tea to have one.

'A few. I did both sides of the main street, the green, Church Lane, Oak Street and Bluebell View.' She glanced at the chopping board which had a pile of veg on it waiting to be peeled, and sighed. She was going to have a fight on her hands to get Nia to eat her vegetables – maybe she'd make soup instead? That way she could blend everything together and Nia would never know...

'Nearly everyone I spoke to signed the petition,' she added, 'and many pledged to give a donation to the sale. Lowri, bless her, said she'd donate a colour and cut to the raffle.'

'That's great. I noticed some things have started to trickle in. They were piled up in the porch.'

Rowena finished her drink and went to fetch the clip-board. Betsan had printed her out a map of the village and as Rowena had trawled the streets earlier today, she'd marked them with a highlighter to show the ones she'd done. 'Here you go. That's how far I got this afternoon.'

'I'll do some this evening. Thanks for helping.'

'Any time,' Rowena said warmly, meaning it. She'd do anything for Betsan. She began to tackle the vegetables with grim determination.

'What are you making?' Betsan asked. She always took a keen interest in whatever Rowena was cooking or baking.

'Vegetable soup.' Rowena rolled her eyes. 'Smooth, not chunky.' She chuckled as she threw a few generous handfuls of diced onion into a saucepan, having decided to make enough for several portions and freeze what they didn't eat today.

'Is Nia still being fussy?' Betsan sympathised. 'I remember when mine went through that stage.' Betsan was fifteen years older than Rowena and her children were now teenagers. Rowena found her support, advice and friendship invaluable.

'How did you cope?' she asked.

'I ignored it,' Betsan said, licking sticky flapjack crumbs off her fingers. 'The more fuss you make, the fussier they get. At least you're able to hide the vegetables. Mine used to sniff out a floret of broccoli at a hundred paces. They still can, but the difference between then and now is that I've stopped trying. It's impossible to force a fifteen-year-old to eat cabbage if he doesn't want to.'

'Did a man call into the vicarage today to give you a cash donation?' Rowena asked abruptly, her mind darting to the guy who had just moved into Rosehip Cottage, and she cringed internally. She would dearly have loved to have had a proper chat with him: instead, she'd come across as a total idiot prattling on that Foxmore was a nice place to bring up kids. No wonder he hadn't been able to wait to get rid of her.

'No, no one today. Who said they wanted to donate cash?'

'Um, er, a guy who's bought Rosehip Cottage. He said he'd call in with some money.'

Betsan shook her head. 'Maybe he'll call in later. What's he like? Young? Old? Single? Married?'

'Erm…' she hedged. 'About my age, maybe a bit older.'

Betsan cocked her head to the side. 'What is it? What's wrong?'

'Nothing.'

'Fibber— Ah ha!' Betsan slapped her hand on the table. 'You fancy him, don't you?' she crowed.

Rowena blushed and bit her lip. 'No. Yes. A little.'

'From the look on your face, I'd say you fancied him a lot.'

'OK, a lot. But that doesn't mean I intend to do anything about it.'

'You should – let your hair down. It's been yonks since you had some fun.'

'The last time I had some "*fun*" Nia was the result,' Rowena said dryly.

'Finn was hardly a fling,' Betsan pointed out. 'You were in love with him.'

'It was a shame he wasn't as in love with me as I was with him,' Rowena retorted. 'He had his fun, then he moved on.'

'He mightn't have moved on if he'd known about the baby.'

Rowena sucked in a slow breath.

She had been living and working in Cardiff when she'd met Finn. She had been twenty-three, fresh out of university and keen to stay in the city she'd studied in. She'd found a job working for a logistics company and had earned enough to pay rent on a minuscule flat that she shared with one of her university friends.

Then she'd met Finn Bowen and her world had been turned upside down. She'd fallen head over heels in love with him, and from the way he'd behaved he had led her to believe he felt the same about her.

Until one day he'd told her he was moving to Birmingham, that they'd had fun and he'd always think fondly of her, but they were over.

Finn had been gone seven weeks before Rowena realised she was four months pregnant. Maybe if she had been showing the usual signs, she might have realised sooner, but her periods had always been irregular, so with everything else that had been going on, she hadn't given it a second thought.

Heartbroken, she'd returned to Foxmore, and had refused all attempts by her parents and her friends to get her to contact her baby's father. She had been such an emotional mess that she simply couldn't have coped with having him in her life again, knowing he would only be there because she was having a baby and not because he wanted to be with her. After she'd given birth, she had been trying so hard to deal with being a mother that she couldn't face any more complications in her life, and she'd kept telling herself that she'd contact him soon, when she felt stronger emotionally. She'd been heartbroken and her hormones had been all over the place, and it had taken her months and months before she was able to think clearly enough to try to get in touch with him. Once or twice she'd got as far as dialling his number, but each time she had heard a message that her call couldn't be connected, and she'd had the feeling he might have blocked her or even changed his number.

In hindsight, Rowena wished she had told him she was pregnant as soon as she had found out – he had a right to know, and Nia might hate her for not telling him when she was old enough to understand – but it was too late now. She could hardly track him down and say, 'Hey, Finn, remember me? By the way, you're the father of my four-soon-to-be-five-year-old daughter.'

'Can we not talk about him? It's water under the bridge,' she said to Betsan, as she continued to peel and chop.

Betsan's lips narrowed into a thin line. It was the only thing Rowena and her friend had disagreed on in the four and a half years since Rowena had returned to Foxmore. Before Rowena had left for university she'd not had much to do with the vicar's wife – they were too far apart in age, lifestyles and interests for them to mingle in the normal scheme of things. But when Betsan, who had been visiting the elderly gent next door, had discovered Rowena in tears in the garden, a cross and grizzly Nia screaming her head off in a bassinet next to her, she had offered to mind the baby for a few hours for the new mother to get some rest. And with that, the two of them had become firm friends. The only bone of contention between them was that Betsan thought Rowena should have told Finn he was a father.

'Seriously, you need to have some fun,' Betsan said. 'You need to live a little.' Eyes gleaming with mischief, she asked, 'What's this new bloke like?'

'Tall, dark, handsome, and his name is Huw.'

'Handsome, eh?' Betsan smirked, and Rowena snorted in disgust. She was about to put Betsan straight and tell her that just because the guy was good looking it didn't mean she wanted to jump his bones, when Nia bulldozed through the door, her face and hands covered in dirt.

'I've been making mud pies, and Terror has been helping me. Hello, Aunty Betsan. What's for tea?' She drew a breath. Terror was her cuddly toy cat.

'Soup and cheesy bread. If you're hungry you can have an apple to tide you over.'

'Cut up?'

'Yes, I'll cut it up for you, and I'll even put it in a little bag.' The bag was a reusable one, naturally. 'You'll have to wash your hands first, and your face could do with a swill. I hope Terror isn't as dirty as you.'

'Cats don't get dirty, do they Aunty Betsan?'

'They certainly don't get as dirty as little girls,' Betsan replied with an indulgent smile.

'I'm not dirty,' Nia said.

'Oh, yes, you are. Have you seen your face?' She tickled the little girl's ribs, making her squeal.

'Is Nia going to your mam's tomorrow?' Betsan asked, after Nia had settled down to watch one of her programmes and munch on one of the apples that she'd made so much of a fuss about.

'She is. Why? Do you need me for anything?' Betsan had a habit of reeling Rowena into her madcap days out. The last one had been to accompany her on an archaeological dig. It had rained constantly, and although the dig had been under cover to a certain extent, Rowena had still managed to get cold and completely soaked. It had been an experience though – one she had thoroughly enjoyed but probably wouldn't want to repeat. Betsan was so full of enthusiasm and get-up-and-go that she put Rowena to shame.

'If you're offering,' Betsan began, and Rowena quickly leapt in with, 'You haven't told me what it is yet. And even when you do, I'm not promising anything, especially if it involves muddy fields and getting wet.'

'How about a trip to a nice city centre?'

'What's the catch? I'm assuming we aren't going for the shopping.' Betsan, Rowena knew, didn't like shopping all that much, especially not for clothes or shoes.

'Erm, no, not really. There's this rally—' Betsan saw the look on Rowena's face and hurried on. 'It's a protest against single-use plastic. The organisers are trying to persuade the government to make food and other

35

suppliers do more to reduce it. It should be right up your street.'

It certainly was. Even before Nia was born, Rowena had been making a serious effort to reduce the amount of plastic she used, and since her daughter had come along she'd become positively manic about it. That, and obsessively switching lights off in an effort to conserve energy. She was horribly conscious of the state of the planet that her child would inherit if something wasn't done about it now. So Rowena was trying hard to do her small bit, and one of her bugbears, besides unnecessary packaging, was the prevalence of plastic toys, plastic toothbrushes, and anything else that was plastic and disposable.

'Will I have to make a placard?' she asked. Nia had some finger paints and Rowena could use one of the large pieces of cardboard that she had rescued from school when they'd had a delivery of exercise books.

Betsan smiled. 'Placards will be supplied at the start. It'll only be for a couple of hours and it's for a good cause.'

It *was* for a good cause, and it was a subject close to Rowena's heart. 'Go on, then, count me in.' All she hoped was that the protest was successful enough to offset the fuel they'd use in getting there!

It's time I stretched my legs, Huw thought, after he'd spent longer answering emails than he had intended. Although today – moving day – was supposed to be a day off, he hadn't been able to resist checking in. And once he'd logged on, he might as well reply… and before he knew it an hour had gone by and he was starting to get hungry.

Before descending on The Jolly Fox for a well-earned supper, he wanted to detour to the church and make the donation he'd promised Rowena, so he made his way to the green and entered the graveyard via the lychgate.

Once beyond it, he stopped, gazing around in pleasure. There was a paved path constructed out of old cobblestones with moss growing between them leading to the church's door, and on either side of the path higgledy-piggledy gravestones and tombs seemed to grow out of the long grass, leaning drunkenly this way and that. From a quick scan of the nearest, he saw most of them were dated well before 1900, and he noticed one or two folk that had been buried in the eighteenth century. Dotted among the graves and growing beside the low stone wall surrounding the churchyard were several large trees, casting their soft shade, their leaves rustling gently in the faint breeze. Wildflowers bloomed in the grass, and although the graveyard should have looked unkempt and uncared for, it actually looked peaceful and well loved. The people who were buried here must be happy with their lot, Huw mused: when his time came, he'd love to be laid to rest in such a serene and picturesque place.

The church looked as though it had been there since the beginning of time, or at least for the greater part of the last thousand years. It might be ramshackle and crumbling, but its ancient charm spoke to him, and he wondered how many pairs of feet had walked along this path, how many births, marriages and deaths it had seen, what joys, what sadness.

It was sobering yet reassuring to think that he was one in a long line of people to enter this church, stretching backwards and forwards in time. There would be more

37

generations to come after him, and it anchored him, giving him a sense of history and his place in the world.

Remembering the reason for his visit, he glanced up at the roof and saw that it did indeed need some repair. In fact, the whole of the outside of the building could do with some attention, as the pointing between the old stonework was in dire need of replacing.

He wasn't a religious man and never ventured inside a church unless it was to attend a wedding or, God forbid, a funeral, but he appreciated the history of old buildings such as these and how at one time it would have been the focal point of the village. It would be a shame to let it fall into decay, and Huw was more than happy to make a donation towards its upkeep. After all, Foxmore was his home now, and he had a vested interest in everything that went on in it.

As he strolled towards the porched entrance, he noticed that the pitted oak door was open, and he went inside, calling 'Hello?' and hearing his voice echo back to him.

Wow, the interior was even more impressive, and he almost cricked his neck gazing up at the wooden vaulted ceiling with its massive beams reaching towards the heavens. Grey flagstones lay under his feet and bare wooden pews lined both sides of the aisle, leading towards a marble pulpit. A stained-glass window at the far end let in coloured beams of light that bathed everything in rainbow hues.

'Can I help you?' A man in his mid to late forties, wearing a pair of brown corduroy trousers and a checked shirt, emerged from a door at the rear of the church. A clerical collar was just visible at his neck.

'You must be the vicar,' Huw said, striding forward and holding out his hand. 'My name's Huw Morgan, and I've come to give you some money.'

'Terry Pritchard.' They shook hands. 'Well, now, money is always welcome.' He was staring at Huw with a questioning expression on his face, so Huw explained.

'A woman called at my door asking if I'd sign a petition. She was also collecting for a bring-and-buy sale, but I've only just moved to Foxmore – today actually, I've bought Rosehip Cottage – and I had a good clear out when I left my old place so I haven't got anything to donate, apart from good hard cash. I promised her I'd pop in with a donation.'

'Good hard cash will do just fine,' the vicar said. 'I'm pleased to hear that my wife's fundraising efforts are bearing fruit.'

His *wife*? Oh... so Rowena was married? That was a pity. Huw had rather fancied getting to know her better. He rather fancied her, full stop. But that would have to end, now that he'd discovered she was none other than the vicar's wife. He might have felt a little less disappointed if she had been wearing a wedding ring because he wouldn't have got his hopes up, but perhaps she was a modern clergyman's spouse and didn't see the need for it, or there might be any number of other reasons why she didn't wear one. However the vicar, Huw noticed, did have a wedding band.

'Welcome to Foxmore,' the man was saying, as Huw pulled himself together and dragged his wallet out of his pocket.

He handed some notes over and the vicar's eyes widened. 'That's very generous, I must say! Thank you.'

'I love old buildings like these. It would be such a shame if it fell into disrepair.'

'I totally agree. Try telling that to the bish—' He stopped and glanced around the church guiltily. 'Best not to speak out of turn. I'm sure there are perfectly good... God moves in mysterious...' He trailed off, waving a hand in the air. 'Enough about my troubles. Is there a Mrs Morgan?'

'No, just me.'

'Pity, my wife would have loved a fresh face to rope into her causes. Perhaps I'll rope you into mine instead?' Terry chuckled.

Huw was mildly alarmed, but he tried not to show it. He was all for integrating himself into village life, but he wasn't sure he wanted to be involved in the vicar's good causes, whatever they might be. 'If I can do anything to help...' he replied vaguely.

'You've done enough for today.' The vicar patted his shirt pocket, where Huw's donation had been neatly folded and placed for safe keeping. 'Thank you again.'

'My pleasure.' Huw turned to leave.

'Maybe we'll see you in church sometime?' The vicar's voice was hopeful.

'Maybe.' Huw thought it unlikely. 'Nice to meet you Father... Reverend... er...'

'Reverend is fine, although most people just call me Terry.'

'Terry it is,' Huw said. He gave the man a nod, then headed for the door. His supper was calling, and he quite fancied a pint, too. He felt he deserved one after the busy and exciting day he'd had.

The Jolly Fox looked very inviting from the outside, with its whitewashed walls, window boxes and swinging sign depicting a grinning red fox with a bushy tail. It was also busy, and delicious cooking smells wafted through the open door. Huw debated whether to sit in the little beer garden which abutted the churchyard because it was such a lovely evening, but he decided he'd leave that for another time.

The pub was equally as inviting on the inside, and the bar was lively, which was what he'd expect for a Friday evening, with couples and families tucking into meals or simply enjoying a drink and a chat. He ordered a pint and sat down at one of the few free tables, clutching his drink in one hand and a menu in the other.

He had taken a welcome swig and was perusing the menu and feeling spoilt for choice, when someone brushed against his chair as they walked past.

'Aled, you old duffer! How the devil are you?'

Huw glanced up to see an elderly gent making his way to the bar to join a group of men who were propping it up.

'Not so bad,' the man called Aled said. 'And you?'

'So, so.' The other fella made a sawing motion with his hand. 'I think I'm ready to retire.'

'I've been ready to pack it in for years. Pint, please, Dai,' Aled motioned to the barman, then turned around to face his mates and tapped his nose. 'I've got an iron in the fire that might help things along, but I can't say nothing yet. Not till the deal is done.'

'What deal? Come on, Aled, you can't drop ruddy great hints like that then leave us hanging.'

'I can and will. Ta.' He accepted his pint, took a long swallow, then wiped foam from his upper lip with the back of his hand. 'You'll hear about it soon enough, if I can pull it off.'

'You're not going to breed alpacas or anything daft like that, are you?' another fella asked.

Someone else piped up with, 'Oi, don't knock it until you try it. I've got a mate down Carmarthen way who's been farming them for years. Easier than sheep, he said, and people pay to come and take 'em for walks. Imagine that! You don't see people wanting to take a Texel for a walk.'

Huw was wondering what a Texel was when another bloke grumbled, 'I shouldn't bloody think so. They might be good lambers and produce lean meat, but they're the ugliest feckin' sheep I've seen in my life. Give me a nice Herdwick any day.'

'Too small,' came a call from further along the bar, and this prompted a heated and in-depth discussion about the merits of certain breeds of sheep over others, which Huw listened to with amusement and a degree of interest. Wales, especially the part he was now living in, was renowned for its sheep farming, and he'd come across many of the woolly creatures on the hillsides and mountaintops when he'd been hiking.

Dai appeared at his elbow with a notepad and a pencil in his hand. 'Ready to order?'

Huw made a face. 'I don't suppose you've got any lamb on the menu?'

'Not today—' The landlord stopped and rolled his eyes. 'Ha, very funny. Haven't I seen you in here before?'

'Huw Morgan. I've stayed here a couple of times.'

'I thought I recognised the face. Where are you staying this time?'

'Rosehip Cottage.'

'I didn't think it was still a holiday let? I'd heard it had been sold.'

'It has. I'm the new owner.'

'We'll be seeing a lot more of you, then?' Dai looked pleased at the thought.

'You definitely will.' Huw ordered and settled back to listen to the debate at the bar, which had moved away from sheep and on to tractor matters.

When his phone rang, he hastened to answer it before the strident notes annoyed the pub's clientele.

He didn't have a chance to say anything before his sister demanded to know if he was in a pub.

'Yes, I've just ordered chicken in a wine and mushroom sauce.'

'Don't,' Ceri groaned. 'All I've had is a sandwich. I'm still at work.'

'At this time on a Friday? You ought to tell them to shove it and go home.'

'I might just tell them to shove it period. Why garden centres need to stay open until eight in the evening is beyond me. Who needs to buy a forsythia that urgently?'

'What's a forsythia? Actually, never mind. When are you coming to see my new pad?' he asked.

'Listen to you! *New pad*, indeed…' Her laugh tinkled down the phone. 'Actually, that's why I was calling – what are you doing next weekend?'

'I thought I might go for a stroll up Aran.'

'Would you like some company? And while I'm there, I can take a look at your garden for you. You said it needed a bit of TLC.'

The garden was functional but uninspiring. 'Brilliant! I'll see you next week.'

He couldn't wait to show Ceri around his lovely cottage and Foxmore, and it was a bonus that she had such green fingers.

He'd definitely made the right decision to move to the village, he thought. He already felt as though he'd been here for ages. The only thing marring his contentment was that he wished he had someone to share it with other than his sister.

But when an image of the woman with the clipboard floated through his mind, he hastily shepherded it back out again.

There was no point hankering over what he couldn't have.

Chapter 4

The noise was deafening, and if Rowena hadn't been hoisting a placard (made from repurposed wood and cardboard, naturally) she would have put her hands over her ears. There were at least five thousand people on the march, maybe more, and they were all chanting in unison. More or less. And singing 'Mae Hen Wlad Fy Nhadau', although what good singing the Welsh national anthem was going to do at a protest about the indiscriminate use of plastic was anyone's guess. Still the atmosphere was incredible, and she felt honoured to be part of it. Surely the government had to sit up and take notice after this?

If she was honest, Rowena wasn't convinced that the protest would do any good, but it had to be better than doing nothing. Nothing simply wasn't an option.

'There's a lovely tearoom just around the corner,' Rowena said hopefully, remembering it from her student days. 'It's just inside Bute Park.'

She and Betsan were roughly in the middle of the snaking mass of protesters, and were just winding their way past Cardiff Castle. Beyond the castle was one of the city's loveliest parks and as a student she'd spent many a happy afternoon sitting on the grass with a bottle or two of something alcoholic and a sandwich from Greggs.

Someone would be blasting a Spotify playlist and everyone would be chilled and slightly merry.

They had been such good times…

Rowena hadn't frequented the tearoom often because she hadn't been able to afford it, but she used to take her mam there when she visited, and they served the most wonderful fruit pots with clotted cream.

'You can't be hungry already?' Betsan was astounded. 'You've only just eaten.'

Rowena wrinkled her nose. Trying to stuff a sandwich in her mouth with one hand and carrying a banner with the other while stomping down Queen Street hadn't been her idea of a proper lunch. And she mightn't actually be hungry, but she quite fancied a sit down, a cup of coffee and a slice of cake. They seemed to have tramped all over the city and had been on their feet ever since the train deposited them at the station this morning.

'There's a nice cafe on St Mary's Street,' a woman in front of them said. 'We'll be going past there in a minute. They do a lovely selection of home-made cakes.'

Betsan said to Rowena, 'Do you think you can hang on until then? We can go straight to the station from there.'

St Mary's Street was only a ten or fifteen minute walk away, so Rowena nodded. Coming on the march had been fun and had certainly been different to her usual Saturday pastime of chores, but she'd had enough.

With the promise of a sit down and some caffeine in the very near future, Rowena threw herself into making her voice heard, and she shouted and sang, smiling at shoppers gathered at the sides of the road most of whom were watching the protesters with bemused expressions, and waved her placard enthusiastically.

Despite the crescendo of noise, the hordes of people, the blocked-off streets and the police presence, the protest was peaceful in nature, and even when a young man deliberately threw a plastic bottle at one of the protester's feet, a sneering look of defiance on his face, all that happened was that an elderly shopper bent down to retrieve it and handed it back to him. The youth took it without a murmur.

Good for you, Rowena thought, giving the old lady a huge smile. The woman smiled back, and when Rowena relinquished her placard to a guy walking next to her just before she dashed towards the cafe that had been recommended, she thought that as a result of the protest today if just one person learnt not to casually throw litter on the ground, then some good would have come of it.

Rowena blew out her cheeks as she sank gratefully onto one of the cafe's padded chairs. 'My feet are killing me,' she announced, wishing she could ease her trainers off and give her toes a rub. She'd wait until she was on the train before she did that, because she didn't want to put people off their food, which looked delicious.

Betsan went to the counter to order, then sat down with a sigh. 'That was full on. Fun, though.' She pointed to an archway leading to another part of the building. 'No wonder that woman suggested this place,' she said. 'Through there is a zero waste shop.'

'I've heard of those,' Rowena said, 'but I've never been in one.'

'We can take a look after we've had this,' Betsan suggested, as a waitress approached with their cakes and drinks. 'The cakes are vegan, by the way, and so are the lattes. Almond milk.'

Rowena took a tentative sip. It was different, but not unpleasant. The cake, however, was delectable. 'What is this?' she asked, her mouth full of moist sponge.

'Orange and almond.'

'It's gorgeous. I wonder if they'll give me the recipe.'

To Rowena's delight, they were happy to. In fact, they had a number of recipes already printed out for customers to take, and she scanned the list of ingredients.

'They use ground almond flour instead of normal flour and… Crumbs! Carbonated water instead of eggs. Who'd have thought it?'

'If you need any ingredients, you can find most of them in our shop next door,' the assistant told her, pointing to the archway.

'Come on.' Rowena grabbed Betsan's arm. 'I'm going to try making this. Nia loves orange juice, but she wouldn't eat a real orange if she was starving, and this recipe uses two medium-sized ones!'

The pair of them hurried into the shop, then stopped abruptly. There was shelf after shelf of glass jars, all neatly labelled. Rowena spotted herbs and spices, flavoured salt and pepper, and other shelves held dispensers filled with nuts and seeds, muesli and other cereals. There were also huge steel containers in which flour, rice and pasta were kept. Black drums with taps on them dispensed washing detergent and other assorted cleaning products, and there were stacks of loo roll – made out of bamboo, no less! – hemp pads for washing dishes, beeswax food wraps, shampoo bars, and bamboo toothbrushes.

Rowena didn't know what to look at first, and she noticed that Betsan was equally as enthused.

They spent far longer than they'd intended, and too much money, but Rowena thought that the concept was one of the best she'd ever seen. She wished she'd brought some containers with her, but the almond flour was sold to her in a paper bag, so she didn't feel too bad. She purchased several brightly coloured beeswax food wraps as well, which would be useful when she and Nia went on picnics, plus some wonderful-smelling soap for Nia which had flowers buried in its fragrant depths.

'Why haven't we got one of these near us?' she demanded, as she was paying for her purchases. 'If we did, I wouldn't shop anywhere else.'

'Where do you live, and I can check online for your nearest,' the guy behind the counter offered, but when he told her she was disappointed to learn that the closest shop to Foxmore was even further away than the nearest big supermarket.

'That's typical,' she grumbled. 'I might have guessed.'

The sales assistant gave her a measured look. 'My girlfriend and I started this from scratch,' he said. 'Not in Cardiff, in Caerphilly. Then we opened a second one in Thornhill, just up the road. Now this one. This is our flagship store.'

'Can't you open one in Foxmore?' Rowena joked.

'No, but *you* can.'

'Don't be daft!' Rowena giggled and looked at her friend, expecting her to be laughing too, but Betsan was strangely silent, her focus on the man behind the counter.

'If you want something, you've got to make it happen,' he said. 'You just can't sit back and hope someone will do it for you. That's what we did, and now look at us. You don't have to start big, but you do have to *start*.'

Rowena froze, her thoughts whirling, the suggestion lit up in neon in her mind.

What an absolutely fantastically wonderful and ridiculously absurd idea!

But as one, the two women looked at each other, and Rowena knew precisely what Betsan was thinking, because she was thinking the exact same thing.

The question was – could they?

Dare they?

—

A half-hour commute to work wasn't so bad, Huw thought, as he made himself some breakfast on Monday morning, and at least he didn't have to go into the office every single day. He could work from home for some of the time and occasionally he was also out in the field, so to speak: it all depended on the needs of the business.

He counted himself lucky that Foxmore was near enough to the North Wales satellite office to make the commute feasible. He enjoyed his job in Co-Op Cymru and would have hated to have had to look for another, so it was the icing on the cake to have wrangled a transfer from the Cardiff office to the one in Dolgellau. It was incredibly satisfying helping people come together to form a co-operative, and he took immense pleasure from it. As far as jobs went, he considered himself lucky: he had one of the best.

However, having worked in the Cardiff office for the past few years, he found himself unaccountably nervous on this Monday morning to be meeting a new team of co-workers. He felt rather like a kid on his first day in a new school.

After his supper in The Jolly Fox on Friday evening, he'd retired to bed and had enjoyed the best night's sleep he'd ever had. He'd drifted off listening to the bark of a fox and the call of an owl – talk about idyllic! It was a far cry from the rumble of traffic and the frequent sirens that were to be expected when living so close to Cardiff's major hospital. Living in the country might be a novel experience for him, but he had a feeling he wasn't going to miss the city at all. Anyway, if he did find he had a hankering for the occasional bright lights and excitement, he could always pay his sister a visit, as she still lived in the capital. And not only that, the organisation he worked for was also based there, so he couldn't entirely divorce himself from the metropolis.

For now though, Huw was more than content with his lot, and he'd spent the weekend stocking up his freezer and kitchen cupboards, drinking coffee in his garden (he was looking forward to seeing what Ceri thought of it) and thoroughly exploring the village.

By the time Sunday evening had come round, he was fairly confident that he knew every square inch of Foxmore, and not just the main street and the green.

Early morning might become his favourite time of the day he thought, as he took his coffee and toast into the garden, as he'd done yesterday morning and the day before. This new penchant for rising early was a bit of a surprise because generally speaking, unless he had a long hike planned, his days often tended to begin with a nice long lie-in. However, he'd been so excited to start his new life in Foxmore on Saturday that he hadn't wanted to waste time lingering in bed, and he'd been up with the lark. And he'd done the same thing yesterday.

Now, though, as he munched on his breakfast he wished he'd not been in such a hurry to get up yesterday, because he would have given his right arm to stay in bed this morning. He didn't have to be at work until nine thirty thankfully, but if he had still been living in Cardiff it would have meant he probably wouldn't have had to roll out of bed until half past eight at the earliest. Today, though, he was facing a thirty-minute commute, factoring in the rush hour traffic.

Blearily, he let the sounds of the new day wash over him: the rhythmic cooing of a collared dove on the chimney pot, the sweet song of a blackbird high in a tree, and the buzz of bees searching for their own breakfasts.

Beyond the garden, he heard a car door slam, then the sound of bottles chinking as the milkman made his deliveries. Which reminded him – he must put in an order. How great would it be to wake up to a fresh pint of milk in a real glass bottle on his doorstep? For some reason milk didn't taste as nice out of a plastic container.

With his toast finished, Huw picked up the mug of coffee and cradled it in his hand, his gaze on a butterfly. Its orange wings flitted from blossom to blossom, and he absently tracked its progress, his thoughts on the day ahead, his mind on work.

Although he loved what he did, he would have preferred not to have to do it today. He wasn't yet ready to return to the real world, because for the past couple of days he'd felt as though he was on holiday, and every now and again he'd have to pinch himself to check he wasn't dreaming.

He had a few more minutes in which to enjoy the tranquillity of the garden before he had to get ready, though, so he determinedly forced thoughts of work out of his head. There would be time enough to think of that when he was on the road. Instead, he focused on the people he'd met over the course of the past three days. Although he hadn't actually introduced himself to anyone, people seemed to know who he was, and he wondered if Dee and Vaughan from the estate agents or Dai at the pub had been responsible for setting the local tom-toms off. Or maybe the vicar had informed his congregation that there was a new fella in town? Because when he'd popped into the baker's yesterday for some fresh bread, the woman who owned the place had asked him outright if he was the person who'd bought Rosehip Cottage.

Then the guy in the antique shop had said he'd seen him go into the house, and he had also asked him if he was the new owner. And he still couldn't get over the kindness of one of his neighbours, Pen, from Pen's Pantry, who had popped around with a bunch of flowers from her garden. She'd been incredibly curious though, and had been staring over his shoulder the whole time she had been talking to him, trying to get a look at the inside of the cottage, so maybe her gift had been more to do with nosiness than altruism.

Huw had a feeling that in a small place like Foxmore everyone knew everyone else's business, but instead of making him uncomfortable it was rather reassuring to think that such community spirit was alive and kicking in this day and age. It was a refreshing change from the relative anonymity of Wales's capital city, where he'd only seen his neighbours once in a blue moon and even then they would only exchange awkward nods if they happened to make eye contact.

There was only one small thing that niggled at him – and it really was quite insignificant in the scheme of things – and that was the vicar's wife. It wasn't any surprise to find that he was attracted to her (she was a pretty and vivacious woman), but what was causing him a smidgeon of concern was that she kept popping into his head. He'd be sweeping the kitchen floor (far easier to do that than to get the vacuum cleaner out) and suddenly her face would be in his mind. Or he'd be brushing his teeth, and her image would flash into his head.

It was rather unsettling and slightly worrying. Although he knew it was absurd, he suspected he was starting to develop a crush on her – which he wouldn't have been bothered about, if it wasn't for the fact that she was married, and to a man of the cloth to boot.

It made him feel quite uncomfortable. Never once had he harboured any longing for another man's wife, and he was concerned that he was starting to now.

Heck, he even suspected he'd walked the roads and lanes of Foxmore yesterday in the hope of spotting her. Although, he reasoned, if he'd been that determined to bump into her, all he'd needed to do was to hang around the church. He could even have attended the service yesterday morning, because he'd have been certain to have seen her then. But he hadn't gone to such lengths, which made him feel a little better about himself. He was beginning to worry that he was turning into a stalker.

Determined not to let his weird fascination with the vicar's wife develop any further, Huw finished his coffee and got to his feet. Time to go to work. He had a new team to meet, and he couldn't wait to get started.

After a shower, a quick shave and a splash of cologne, he donned a suit and tie. He wanted to make a good impression, and he also had a meeting lined up with a bunch of people who worked in a pub threatened with closure and who were considering venturing into employee-ownership. Finally ready, he picked up his keys, patted his pocket to make sure he had his wallet, then left.

The inside of the car was already warm, but instead of turning the air-con on, Huw wound the window down and sat there for a moment enjoying the sound of birdsong before drowning out his feathery friends by starting the engine.

The pavements around the green were relatively quiet he noticed, apart from several mothers with children. It was only 8:45 and the shops weren't open yet, but Pen's Pantry was getting ready for the day and Pen was putting out tables and chairs on the pavement in front of the cafe's window.

He drove slowly towards the main road and came to a halt at the junction, looked both ways, and was about to pull onto the high street when he looked again, his stomach doing a roll as he saw a familiar face.

Rowena was strolling down the street, a little girl at her side. She was holding the child's hand and her head was bent as she spoke to her. In a few strides she'd be at the junction, about to cross the road.

He fleetingly considered pausing for a moment, waiting until she had to check that the road was clear. He'd catch her eye and he'd smile, and maybe she'd smile back.

But what good would that serve? He was annoyed at himself for even thinking about doing such a thing. The last thing the vicar's wife needed was a secret admirer; he'd be better off finding someone who was unattached to set his sights on.

Yet again, he gave himself a stern talking-to, but he had a sneaky feeling that no matter how often he told himself to forget about her and move on, his tummy would turn over every time he saw her.

He'd dithered for too long and a lorry rumbled past, so he was forced to wait until the road was clear. But as he did so, he made the mistake of glancing in Rowena's direction again, and this time he caught her eye. In that fleeting moment, he registered her smile of recognition as their eyes locked in an intense stare, before he hastily looked away and dragged his attention back to the road and pulled out.

Her eyes remained seared on his mind, though, like a brand on flesh, and he hoped she hadn't picked up on how attracted to her he was. Ashamed to be having such thoughts about another man's wife, Huw tried to concentrate on the day ahead – but that was easier said than done.

–

'Mammy, why was that man looking at you funny?'

'Huh?' Rowena gave herself a shake. 'The man in the car?' she asked, buying some time to gather her scattered wits. She'd noticed Foxmore's newest resident as he waited at the junction. He'd noticed her too, but not in a good way, she'd thought. Although she'd given him a nice smile, all he'd done was glare at her.

Maybe he resented her knocking on his door on Friday and asking for a donation? Or maybe he didn't like her for some reason. Or perhaps he just wasn't a morning person.

'He was looking at you like this.' Nia tugged on Rowena's arm, making her look down. Nia glowered, her eyes boring into her. Her daughter had captured Huw Morgan's expression perfectly.

'He was, wasn't he?' Rowena agreed.

'He didn't look happy. *We're* happy, aren't we, Mammy?'

'We're very happy,' Rowena confirmed.

And she was telling the truth, sort of. She loved her daughter, her parents, her friends. She loved her little house and the village she lived in. But something had shifted over the past few days. Whether it was meeting the only man she'd had the hots for since Finn, or whether it was attending the rally with Betsan, she honestly didn't know.

One thing she was sure of, however, was that she must be mad to think about opening her own zero waste shop. What did she know about starting a business? What did she know about running one? Heck, she didn't even know the first thing about working in a shop, let alone owning one.

She said as much to Betsan when she called into the vicarage on the way home from dropping Nia off at school.

'I can't believe we're seriously thinking about doing this,' she told her friend as they drank coffee in the vicarage's large garden. It backed onto the churchyard, and was incredibly peaceful and tranquil. The trees and bushes were dressed in their summer finest, casting dappled shade over the expanse of lawn. The flowerbeds were crammed with blooms and their fragrance filled the air. Bees and other insects flew from flower to flower, and a pair of finches squabbled noisily at the birdfeeder. Partly hidden under a drooping bush with stunning red blossom was a wooden hedgehog house, and an insect hotel had been nailed to the trunk of one of the trees.

Rowena had an acute case of garden envy. She wished she lived here – she'd kill for a garden like this. Betsan even had a small vegetable patch on the far side, and a coveted apple tree. And beyond that was the remains of a disused orchard and allotment, which had been allowed to degenerate into a wilderness. It was a shame, but it was a fantastic place for wildlife.

'*You're* doing it,' Betsan reminded her, bringing Rowena's thoughts back to the matter at hand. 'This will be your baby, not mine.'

Now that the euphoria had gone and Rowena had taken a cold hard look at the idea, she was having a serious case of second thoughts. She had been on a high on Saturday when she'd got back from the march, but had cooled off considerably over the course of Sunday, and by the time this morning had rolled around, she'd all but talked herself out of it.

Rowena pulled a face. 'I'm not sure I'm up for this. It's a fantastic idea, but…'

'You've been looking for something to do with yourself – no offence to dinner ladies, but I can't see you doing that for the rest of your life, and this is a subject you're passionate about, and one that you believe in. As that guy in the shop in Cardiff said, if you want something to happen, *you've* got to make it happen: you can't sit back and hope someone else does.'

'I can't afford it.'

'What about the money your granny left you?'

'I was saving that for Nia.'

'Your gran gave it to *you*, not to Nia. And if you did go ahead with this, it would be for Nia too, so you can give her a better life – and show her that she can do whatever she wants to do if she believes in herself enough.'

'We both know that's not true.'

'It's a good starting point. If you don't try, you'll never know. If you go ahead with it you'll be showing her that her mam is willing to put her money where her mouth is. Look, Rowena, you won't be on your own with this. Terry and I haven't got any money to put in – you know he doesn't get much of a stipend – but I've told you I'll help in any way I can. I'll do a lot of the research, the ordering, the accounts, and I can help out in the shop so you won't have to employ anyone initially.'

'I wasn't thinking of employing anyone at all.' Rowena suspected she'd have enough difficulty paying herself a living wage, let alone anyone else. As soon as she became self-employed, she suspected the state benefits she received that were currently topping up her income from her dinner-lady job would cease, and it was a scary thought.

'Be realistic, you'll probably have to. You've got Nia to see to, and although you wouldn't need to open until after you've taken her to school, you can hardly shut at three thirty every day, and what about Saturdays?'

'My mam has her most Saturdays.'

Betsan chuckled. 'Are you listening to yourself?'

'What?'

'You've already set your heart on this, otherwise you wouldn't be arguing with me.'

'Setting my heart on it is one thing, actually making it happen is quite another. I don't even know where to start.'

'*I* do. You need to find a suitable premises, do your costings for the initial start-up, and you need a business plan.'

'You make it sound easy.' Rowena's tone was sour. If she did decide to go ahead with this – and it was a very big if – it was going to be the most difficult thing she had ever done.

'It won't be easy,' Betsan said. 'It'll be hard work, but Foxmore needs this – *you* need this. You need a challenge in your life, something that makes you leap out of bed every morning, eager to start your day. I know you've got Nia, but Nia won't be little forever.' There was a melancholy in Betsan's voice, and Rowena knew that her friend was acutely aware of how fast her own children were growing up. The eldest would be going to university soon, and the youngest would be starting college. Maybe Betsan needed this shop as much as Rowena did, despite her varied and seemingly never-ending duties as the vicar's wife.

Could opening her own zero waste shop fill the hole in her life that she'd only just realised was there?

A warm glow filled her chest, and she thought it just might.

Chapter 5

'Yeah, you do need to pretty it up a bit, but apart from that you've got a nice little garden,' Ceri called from the far end of it.

'Oi, less of the little!' Huw remonstrated, and his sister grinned at him.

'It is little when you compare it to Mam and Dad's,' she shot back.

Huw was forced to agree, because their parents' garden was over half an acre; big enough to warrant their dad having a sit-on mower, which Huw made no secret about coveting. He didn't want a garden large enough to make such a thing a necessity and neither did he really want a lawn, but that mower was a thing of beauty.

'So, how are you settling in?' Ceri asked, sitting at the little patio table and picking up her wine glass. 'You seem happy.'

'That's because I am. I love it here.'

Ceri gazed at him, her eyes twinkling with mischief. 'Now all we need to do is find you a woman.'

'No, we don't. I'm perfectly capable of finding my own woman. I don't need any help.'

'You're thirty-two and you haven't found her yet,' she pointed out.

'I didn't realise there was a time limit.'

'If you're not careful, all the best ones will be taken,' Ceri joked. 'Cheers!' She held her glass aloft and clinked it against his.

'Cheers,' he replied absently, failing to take the required sip of his drink, his mind on a certain woman with a clipboard who was most definitely out of bounds.

'What's up?' Ceri asked.

'Nothing.' His reply was automatic as he thought about how true his sister's words were. The woman he was thinking of was very taken indeed.

'Huw...' Ceri's voice carried a hint of warning. 'You don't fool me.' Her eyes widened. 'You're not regretting moving to Foxmore, are you?'

'Good grief, no!'

'Pity. Because if you were and you fancied moving back to the big city, I'd buy this cottage from you in a heartbeat. It's bloody gorgeous!'

'It is, isn't it? But you can't move to Foxmore — what about your job?'

Ceri was a horticulturalist and she currently worked in a garden centre. 'I can get another easily enough. Stop trying to change the subject. Now, are you going to tell me what's going on?'

'You're like a terrier, you don't give up.'

'I'd prefer to be a spaniel. You've got to love those long, floppy ears.'

'Rottweiler,' Huw muttered under his breath.

'Don't care! Mam and Dad love me the best, anyway,' Ceri retorted, and Huw gasped.

'They do not!' He feigned indignation, secure in the knowledge that his parents loved both their children equally.

'Mam might love you more if you gave her a couple of grandchildren,' Ceri teased. 'Heck, just one would do.'

'She's been going on at *you*, hasn't she?' Huw hazarded a guess.

'All the damned time.' His sister rolled her eyes.

'Is that why you keep on at *me* to settle down? To take some of the heat off you?'

'Too right. You can't blame me for trying.' She drummed her fingers on the table. 'You still haven't told me what's on your mind. Is it your job?'

'The job is fine.' The people he worked with all seemed lovely and they'd made him feel very welcome. 'Honestly, there's nothing wrong. It's been a busy week, that's all, what with the move and starting a new job.'

He wasn't lying, but he wasn't being totally honest. The move had probably been one of the smoothest in the history of moving, and he hadn't technically started a *new* job: he was still doing what he did before, just in a different location.

'And you're definitely not having second thoughts?' she persisted.

'None whatsoever.' Huw was adamant. 'I love it here,' he repeated. He'd been more content this past week than he'd been in a long time. The only thing missing was someone to share his new happiness with, and Ceri being here had suddenly made him acutely aware of the lack of a special someone in his life. Perhaps his sister was right – it might be time to settle down.

Ceri gave him a measured look but to his relief she dropped the subject. 'I'm starving,' she announced. 'What are we having for dinner?'

'Whatever is on the menu at The Jolly Fox.'

'We're going out?' Her voice was full of disbelief. 'I've come all this way, and you can't be bothered to cook me a meal?'

'I thought you might like to see a bit of the village.'

'From the inside of a pub?' she countered archly.

The pair of them were still bickering as he ushered Ceri out of the door, but Huw had a smile on his face: he loved his sister to bits and he missed her like crazy.

Linking arms with her, he led her down the road, and thought how lucky he was to have her.

—

'Hold my hand,' Rowena instructed, grabbing hold of Nia to escort her across the road. They were on their way to the vicarage this evening to help Betsan and Terry set up for the bring-and-buy sale tomorrow, and also to discuss the zero waste shop's progress. Since her chat with Betsan on Monday, Rowena had thrown herself into the project, telling herself that it was only a bit of research and that she could knock the idea on the head anytime she liked.

Having a serious talk today with Betsan wasn't going to be easy with Nia around, but Rowena wanted to have a catch-up session as she'd not seen a great deal of her friend during this past week, although they had been messaging each other constantly.

If Rowena was honest, she was feeling overwhelmed, and she still wasn't convinced she was doing the right thing. Starting up a business involved a considerable financial risk, and although she had some savings the thought of ploughing all her money into a venture like this was giving her the heebie-jeebies.

Rowena didn't believe she was cut out to be an entrepreneur. Just doing the research was freaking her out. She'd never realised how involved opening a shop could be until she'd started looking into it, and she'd not even moved beyond setting it out on paper yet! Or should she say 'tablet', because that was what she was doing all her work on.

That same tablet was currently in her shoulder bag, and she was taking it with her to the vicarage, even though she'd already shared a whole load of spreadsheets and other documents with her friend. No doubt she would refer to it several times over the course of the next hour or so.

Nia tugged at her arm, trying to persuade Rowena to walk faster. She adored visiting the vicarage, and not just because she loved Betsan. The garden at the vicarage had seen scores of children grow up there over the years, and each generation had added their own delights.

Terry and Betsan's contributions were a basketball hoop and a pair of goalposts. Previous occupants had installed rope swings which hung from the lower branches of a spreading chestnut tree, a playhouse, a pond for catching tadpoles, and a willow wigwam.

It was a magical place for children, and Nia was hopping beside Rowena in excitement. It also added to her daughter's delight that Terry had promised to keep Nia occupied by having a kickabout while Rowena and Betsan discussed business, so they might manage half an hour of uninterrupted brainstorming. Nia adored Terry – he had been a very hands-on father with his own kids and he always had loads of ideas of fun things to do.

Rowena dutifully speeded up, as anxious as Nia to get to the vicarage, but for different reasons – Rowena was hoping there might be a glass of wine on offer.

Rowena and Nia were on the opposite side of the green to the church when Rowena's tummy gave a lurch as she spotted Huw.

To her dismay, he wasn't alone. A woman was hanging off his arm and laughing up at him. They looked good together, being fairly tall, although Huw was the taller of the two, both with dark hair, and similar features. They appeared to be made for each other. They also appeared to be extremely happy and very much in love.

Rowena's heart sank, despite not holding out any hope that Huw Morgan might be interested in her. Let's face it, the spark that she'd thought had been between them when she'd knocked on his door the day he'd moved in had clearly only been in her imagination, because he'd looked right through her on Monday when she'd been taking Nia to school.

And now she knew why – he was married, or had a girlfriend. Either way, he was in a relationship.

Never mind, she consoled herself. It was just as well. After Finn, she didn't need any more heartache in her life, and Nia certainly didn't need a surrogate father. Besides, if she was serious about going ahead with the shop, she'd have more than enough to keep her occupied, without the added complication of a budding romance.

Maybe when things had settled down she could turn her attention to matters of the heart. However, she wasn't going to hold her breath on it happening anytime soon, because she had a feeling she was going to be far too busy to give love more than a fleeting thought for the foreseeable future.

'He's married, you know,' was the first thing out of Rowena's mouth when Betsan opened the oak front door.

'Who is? Hello, by the way.'

'Sorry, hello. Nia, say hello to Betsan.'

'Hello, Betsan,' the little girl said obediently, then not so obediently added, 'Can I have a biscuit?' She threw her arms around Betsan's legs and gave her a pleading look. 'Pleeeease?'

'Nia!' Rowena pulled a face. 'Sorry, she's cross because I wouldn't let her have biscuits for tea.'

'Oh dear. Maybe you can have one later,' Betsan said to Nia. 'Why don't you go and find Terry? He's in the garden, and he's got a surprise for you.'

'What is it?'

'If I told you, it wouldn't be a surprise, would it?'

Rowena watched her daughter scamper off. 'You can tell *me* what it is,' she said.

'Someone donated a bike to the church for the sale tomorrow, and Terry called first dibs. Nia will love it – it's bright pink and has glittery tassels on the handlebars.'

'You realise she's not going to want to give it back?'

'She doesn't have to. It's a present from us. Coffee?' Betsan filled the kettle.

'Betsan! You shouldn't have. At least let me pay you for it. How much is it?'

'I'm not telling, and Terry has already paid the money into the church fund.'

Rowena pursed her lips. 'You spoil that child.'

'I know, but I enjoy doing it, so indulge me, eh? Anyway, what were you saying about someone being married?'

Rowena thought about Huw and his companion, and experienced a twinge of jealousy. 'Huw Morgan is either married or has a girlfriend. I just saw him going into The Jolly Fox with a woman, and they looked very lovey-dovey.'

'Aw, that's a shame. Never mind, there are plenty more fish in the sea, as they say.'

'I don't want a fish. They're more trouble than they're worth.'

'Some of them are, I agree,' Betsan said. 'But others are keepers – look at my Terry.'

Rowena glanced out of the kitchen window and looked. Terry, bless him, was pushing Nia around the lawn on the bike, one hand on the handlebars, the other on the back of the saddle to steady her. Nia's little legs were going up and down, and she was wearing such a big smile that it made Rowena's heart swell with love.

'Terry is definitely a keeper,' she agreed. 'I'm so glad Nia has Terry and my dad.' Out of the corner of her eye she saw Betsan open her mouth and knew what was going through her friend's mind. 'Don't say it,' she warned. 'It's far too late in the day to try to find Finn. Anyway, Nia is happy as she is – she doesn't need Finn, not when she's got her grandad and Terry.'

'What happens if you meet someone? Will you let him be a father to her?'

Rowena heard the rest of Betsan's unspoken sentence – since she hadn't given Finn the opportunity, because he didn't know that he had a daughter. 'Any man who loves me will have to love Nia too, so yes, that mythical man will be her father, to all intents and purposes.' She knew she sounded cross, but honestly!

Betsan winced. 'I'll shut up, shall I?'

Rowena immediately felt contrite. 'Aw, my lovely, I know you mean well, but with this shop I think I've got enough to be going on with, don't you? Have you had a chance to look at that supplier list I sent you? And do you have any idea what insurance I'll need?'

And with that, the two of them got down to the serious business of deciding whether opening a zero waste shop in Foxmore was viable, or whether it was a complete non-starter.

But even as Rowena was trying to get her head around the complexities of VAT, she could still see the happiness on Huw's face when he gazed down at the woman on his arm, and all she felt was envy and sadness that she didn't have that kind of love in her own life.

–

Saturday afternoon found Huw whacked, yet exhilarated at the same time. Hiking did that to him, especially when it consisted of trekking up a hulking great mountain like Aran. It had been worth it, though. It was such a warm, clear day that the views from the top had been breathtaking, and it had been fun to share them with his sister.

He grinned to himself when he thought of the state she was in. If he was knackered, then Ceri was exhausted. The problem was that she didn't do enough walking uphill to build up her stamina. And by uphill, he didn't mean trotting up several flights of stairs to the top floor of St David's car park in Cardiff city centre because the lower ones were full – he meant walking up mountains. To be fair, there weren't all that many hills on that part of the South Wales coast, although not too far inland was the start of valleys, and a bit further again was the Brecon Beacon mountain range, all of which were within easy driving distance. So, nah, she didn't have any excuse – she just couldn't be bothered.

Mind you, none of her friends were into hiking, so if she wanted to go she'd have to go on her own, and he didn't blame her for not wanting to do that.

'We've got to do this more often,' he said, and laughed when she groaned. 'What you need is a hot bath.'

'What I need is a gin,' she countered.

'Do you want to go to the pub again this evening, or would you prefer a takeaway?' he asked, as they walked past The Jolly Fox. Correction – he walked, Ceri hobbled.

'Still not cooking for me?'

'I cooked you breakfast and I made the sandwiches to take with us. You enjoyed your picnic,' he pointed out. Ceri had eaten every morsel of her outdoor lunch.

'It's hungry work climbing mountains,' she argued. 'Takeaway, I think. I'm pretty sure that once my backside touches the sofa, I'm not going to be able to get up again.'

His attention was drawn to a flurry of activity in the church grounds, and when he spotted a hand-written chalk sign, he realised that the bring-and-buy sale was taking place inside. He immediately wondered whether Rowena was there, and he guessed she must be: a vicar's wife would no doubt be expected to preside over an event such as this.

'My thighs are killing me, and don't get me started on my knees and ankles,' Ceri was saying.

'I'll run you a hot bath when we get in,' he said, rounding the corner just as the words left his lips, and ran straight into the very person he'd been thinking about.

'Ow!' Rowena cried as she stumbled sideways to avoid him and nearly fell over an eye-wateringly bright pink bicycle.

'Are you all right?' His hand shot out to steady her, but before he was able to grab her, Rowena righted herself, and he let his arm drop to his side.

'I'm fine. Sorry, I wasn't looking where I was going. I was trying to keep an eye on madam, here.'

The little girl riding the bike was extremely cute, with her dark hair in pigtails and huge brown eyes. The bike had stabilisers and that was what Rowena must have tripped over.

'No harm done,' Huw said awkwardly, then immediately wished he hadn't sounded like his dad.

For a second he stared at her and she stared back, and no one said a word.

The spell was broken when Ceri cleared her throat loudly and said, 'You promised me a bath?'

Huw was abruptly brought back to himself. 'Ah, yes, so I did. We've… um… been out for a walk. More than a walk – a hike, really. To the top. Of Aran.' Lord, now he was having trouble stringing a sentence together. What must Rowena think of him? He was aware that she was giving him an odd look, and so was Ceri. 'Right. Bath. See you soon. I mean, see you around. Glad you didn't hurt yourself. Um… bye.'

Without waiting for a response, Huw strode off, feeling like an absolute idiot. He was dimly aware of Ceri hobbling behind, but it wasn't until he reached his front door that he slowed down enough for her to catch up.

'Do you want to tell me what that was about?' Ceri demanded.

'Not really.'

'Who was she?'

'Rowena Pritchard. The vicar's wife.' He went inside and bent down to untie the laces of his hiking boots.

'She wasn't wearing a ring,' Ceri observed. Trust his sister to notice something like that.

'She doesn't,' he agreed. 'I don't think it's the law that you have to wear a wedding ring if you're married.' He toed off his boots and padded towards the kitchen.

Ceri followed. She still had hers on. 'I'm going to have to sit on a chair to take them off,' she said, when she caught his pointed look at her feet. 'Anyway, they're not muddy – it was as dry as a bone up there.' She perched on one of the dining chairs, and he carried on into the kitchen to empty out his rucksack.

'She likes you,' Ceri called, through the open door.

Huw ignored her.

'I said, she likes you,' his sister repeated as she appeared in the doorway, her boots in her hand.

Huw had his back to her but when he turned around his face must have given him away, because Ceri's mouth dropped open and her eyebrows shot up.

'Bloody hell, Huw! You like her, don't you?'

He brushed past her. 'I'm going to run you a bath.'

'Huw…?'

'Leave it,' he snapped. 'She's married, so it doesn't matter whether I like her or not.' But it did matter to him.

However, what mattered even more, and what really unsettled him, was that he had the feeling that his sister was right – *he had the feeling that Rowena Prichard liked him, too.*

Chapter 6

Rowena had been in two minds about whether to join Betsan, Terry, their children, his parents and half of the congregation of Foxmore in the pub to celebrate Terry's forty-sixth birthday this Sunday lunchtime. He'd given his sermon this morning (which Rowena hadn't attended), then the whole family had descended on The Jolly Fox for a traditional Sunday lunch. They'd invited her and Nia along, but she'd hesitated.

The reason she'd been in two minds was that she didn't want to run the risk of bumping into Huw Morgan and his wife, which was silly because she lived in the village and so did they, so the chances of her being able to avoid them forever were non-existent.

The more she'd thought about her brief meeting with Huw yesterday, the more uncomfortable she'd felt, and the more embarrassed she had become. Rowena was positive that she hadn't imagined his reaction to her, and if she'd noticed then his wife had assuredly been aware of it, too. He'd stared deeply into her eyes with such intensity it had taken her breath away, so goodness knows what Mrs Morgan must think.

Rowena wondered what had happened when his wife had caught up with him. He'd dashed off, leaving his poor spouse to limp after him, and leaving Rowena with a bad taste in her mouth. Even Nia had asked why the man was behaving funny, and for a four-year-old to notice…

Despite wanting to stay at home and hide, common sense prevailed, so here she was, waiting for her meal of roast beef with all the trimmings to arrive, and trying not to glance at the door every time it opened. She was already aware of Betsan giving her odd looks, and she knew she was in for a grilling the next time her friend got her alone.

It was typical that the one time she didn't look up when someone came into the pub was the one time she should have done. She was cutting up Nia's meat for her and rearranging the child's plate so that the peas didn't touch the carrots, when she became conscious of someone staring at her.

She knew who it was without having to look, but she looked anyway. She couldn't help herself.

Huw and his wife were at the bar, waiting to be seated, but it wasn't Huw who was staring, it was his wife.

Hurriedly Rowena looked away, her cheeks flaming.

'Is everything all right?' Terry asked, and Rowena turned back to the table. The vicar, who was sitting opposite her, wore an expression of concern.

'Absolutely,' she replied, with conviction.

Terry's mam placed a hand on top of hers and gave it a squeeze. 'You do look a little flushed, dear. Mind you, it is rather warm in here.'

'Honestly, I'm fine,' Rowena protested, but before she could say anything further Nia piped up, loudly, 'Mammy, there's that funny man again.'

Nia had stopped eating and was staring at Huw.

'What funny man, lovey?' Dorothy, Terry's mam, narrowed her eyes as she scanned the room, and Rowena shrank into her seat.

Wonderful, now everyone was staring at him, and she wished the ground would open up and swallow her whole. Never had she been so embarrassed in her life. And from the expression on her face, Huw's wife also must have heard what Nia had said.

'Shh!' Rowena admonished her daughter. 'Eat your lunch.' She nudged Nia with her arm and the child stabbed at a morsel of roast potato.

Rowena's appetite had disappeared along with her composure, but she made a valiant attempt to clear her plate. Concentrating on her meal was better than brooding over how awkward she felt. But as soon as the plates had been removed, Rowena asked Betsan to keep an eye on Nia, and she escaped to the loo to splash cold water on her still-red cheeks.

Once inside the relative sanctuary of the ladies' toilets, she put her hands on either side of one of the basins, hung her head, and breathed deeply. All through the main course she'd been conscious of Huw and his wife, even though their table was on the other side of the room, and she'd continued to catch glimpses of him out of the corner of her eye. Every now and again she could have sworn that one or the other of them was looking back at her. At one point, Rowena thought they might have been having a heated discussion, and she wished they were sitting nearer so she could hear what they were saying, because she had an awful feeling they were talking about her. Hastily, she reassessed that wish, and decided it was probably better she didn't know.

Rowena raised her head. Her reflection in the wall-to-wall mirror above the bank of wash basins didn't look happy, and when she tried to plaster a smile on her face it became a grimace. With a sigh, she ran the cold tap and cupped her hands underneath it.

She was just patting her face dry with a paper towel and gathering her courage to return to her friends when the door opened and Huw's wife walked in.

Great, that was all she needed. Hoping it was a coincidence and the woman hadn't come to confront her, Rowena shot her a vague smile, scrunched the soggy paper towel into a ball, and reached for another.

'Hi,' the woman said. 'I don't know if you remember, but we met yesterday. I'm Ceri Morgan.'

Rowena really didn't want to do this, but neither did she want to be rude, so she said, 'Nice to see you again. I'm Rowena Lloyd.'

'Lloyd?' Ceri frowned. 'I thought…? Never mind.'

'That's right, Lloyd. Have you settled in yet? Finished unpacking?' Their eyes met in the mirror and Rowena quickly looked away.

She had the uncomfortable impression that Ceri Morgan wasn't here to freshen up her lipstick or to use the loo. Rowena was fairly sure the only reason for the woman's presence in the ladies' toilets right now was to speak to her, and she braced herself. She didn't blame Huw's wife for being miffed. Rowena knew she would feel the same way if she was married to him and he'd looked at another woman in the same way that he'd looked at her yesterday.

'I don't think my brother had a great deal to unpack,' Ceri said. 'The cottage was sold fully furnished, thank God, because his taste is appalling.'

'Your *what*?' Rowena was hung up on the first sentence and wasn't paying attention to anything else.

'Huw, my brother. That is who we are talking about, isn't it?'

'He's your *brother*?'

'Yes, sorry, didn't you know?'

'You're his sister?'

Ceri smiled. 'That's usually how it works.'

Rowena's mind was whirling, and she felt giddy with the realisation that he wasn't married. Oh, hang on – just because Ceri wasn't his wife, that didn't mean he wasn't married to someone else.

'Is he married?' Rowena blurted.

Ceri's eyes crinkled. 'No. He's not got a girlfriend, either. Look, I hope you don't mind me asking, and please don't take this the wrong way, but are *you* married? Huw seems to think you are, but you don't wear a wedding ring and, forgive me, but I can't see you as the vicar's wife.' She ground to a halt.

Rowena frowned at her. 'The *vicar's* wife?'

'I'm sorry, I didn't mean to speak out of turn. Ignore me. I've got a habit of putting my foot in it. I've no idea what a vicar's wife looks like.'

'I'm not the vicar's wife. I'm not *anyone's* wife.'

'You're not? Phew, that's a relief. For a moment there, I thought I'd made a right booboo. I just had a feeling, you know, that Huw had got it wrong.'

'I'm sorry, you've lost me.' Rowena was beginning to feel as though she was in the middle of a scene from Alice in Wonderland.

'For some reason, he was under the impression that you were married to the vicar.' Ceri laughed.

'Not me. I'm not married to anyone. It's my friend, Betsan, who's married to him. And she's probably wondering where I've got to...'

'Sorry, please don't let me keep you. I just wanted to check. We had a bit of an argument, you see, Huw and I.' Ceri smirked. 'I like it when I'm proved right. Hang on—' She bit her lip. 'Have you got a partner, or a boyfriend?'

'Neither.' Thoroughly bemused, Rowena couldn't help smiling.

'Neither has Huw! That's good, isn't it?'

It was very good indeed, Rowena thought, but only if Huw was interested in her. If he wasn't, it didn't matter whether he had a girlfriend or not.

'Anyway,' Ceri continued, 'it was lovely meeting you, and I'm sure I'll see you again. Very sure,' she added with a wink, and with that she turned on her heel and marched out of the door, leaving Rowena stunned and nonplussed in her wake.

Had that really happened? It hadn't simply been wishful thinking on her part? Because if he really was single...?

Suddenly, Rowena's heart lifted – she had a feeling that her life was about to become a great deal more exciting.

–

Huw was furious. 'You just had to, didn't you!' he hissed when Ceri slid back into her seat. 'Why couldn't you leave it alone, like I asked?'

'Because it might have taken you ages to find out the truth and, let's face it, you aren't getting any younger.'

'What *are* you talking about?' He didn't look at his sister – he was too busy waiting for Rowena to appear. She'd been gone ages, and he prayed his interfering, annoying sister hadn't said anything to upset her.

'Rowena isn't married,' Ceri announced triumphantly.

'Don't be daft. Of course she is. Terry—' Huw stopped.

What exactly was it that the vicar had said when he'd popped into the church the other Friday to give a donation? Huw was trying to remember when his train of thought was derailed as he caught sight of Rowena threading her way between the tables. She glanced across at him, and his stomach lurched. Her gaze raked into him, then she looked away and carried on walking. He tracked her until she reached the table she was sitting at, and as she resumed her seat, he became aware that one of the women sitting with her was studying him, and suddenly everything clicked into place.

The woman sitting next to Terry must be his wife. That made total sense: she was older than Rowena, possibly around the same age as the vicar himself.

He tore his gaze away as a server approached Rowena's table, holding a cake with a small sparkler on the top, and someone started singing 'Happy Birthday'. Then one voice became several, and more people joined in until the whole pub was singing, Huw included. He sang with so much gusto that Ceri pulled a face at him until he toned it down. But he was just so relieved to discover that he'd not been making eyes at the vicar's wife.

If he needed further confirmation that Rowena wasn't married to the vicar, he had it when the woman sitting next to Terry gave the man a smacker of a kiss on the lips.

Feeling a bit of an idiot, although it was an easy mistake to make considering Terry had told him that his wife had been out collecting signatures, and only a couple of hours earlier Huw had spoken to a woman with a clipboard doing precisely that, Huw also felt somewhat euphoric.

'Thanks, sis,' he said, keeping his eyes on the birthday boy's table.

'You're welcome. Aren't you glad you invited me this weekend?'

Huw tore his gaze away. 'If I remember rightly, you invited yourself.'

'Whatever. But you're glad I came, right? Can I be a bridesmaid?'

'What are you rabbiting on about?'

'When you two get married. I've never been a bridesmaid before.' Her expression was wistful.

'Give it a rest, Ceri! I haven't even asked her for a date yet.'

'But you're going to, aren't you?' she insisted.

'Probably.' Now that push came to shove, he was feeling quite shy. What if he'd imagined the spark of attraction? It might have been wishful thinking on his part.

'Do you want me to ask her for you?' Ceri smirked.

'Don't you dare!'

'Go on, let me. Remember when I told Vicky Llewellyn that you fancied her?'

Huw groaned. 'Vividly. I had the mick taken for months afterwards. And she never did go out with me.

So, no, I don't need your help, thank you. I wonder what she's doing now?'

'She married Connor Payne. They've got three kids and another on the way.'

'Blimey! Connor Payne? She started seeing him after she turned me down. I didn't realise she'd married him.'

Huw and his sister finished their dessert while reminiscing about past acquaintances, but all the while his gaze kept drifting towards Rowena. When she made her way to the door, Huw got to his feet. He had an apology to make.

'Wait there,' he said to Ceri, and hurried outside.

He caught up with Rowena as she was about to cross the green. 'Um, excuse me,' he called, feeling a bit of a prat. 'Can I have a word?'

Rowena turned around, and when she saw him, her eyes widened. The little girl holding her hand was also looking at him with large eyes, her expression solemn.

'Mammy, it's the funn—'

'Shush, Nia. Don't be rude.' Rowena's attention swung back to him. 'Hi,' she said, sounding uncertain.

'Hi.' Now that she was here in front of him, Huw was lost for words.

'Did you want something?' she asked.

Yeah, *you*, he thought. 'Um, I think I owe you an apology. For yesterday. I was rather abrupt.' She continued to stare at him, and he continued to babble. 'I left in a hurry. Sorry. It was a misunderstanding on my part.' He wasn't making much sense, but he didn't want to come right out and confess that he'd dashed off because he fancied her like mad and he'd thought she was married to the local vicar. He took a deep breath and ploughed on. 'Would you like to go out for a drink with me one evening?'

'Can I come?' a little voice piped up.

'Nia!' Rowena's silence was broken. 'Sorry, I haven't introduced you – this is Nia, my daughter.'

'I'm nearly five,' Nia said.

'That's good to know, because five is better than four,' Huw replied. 'Hello, Nia. I'm Huw.'

'You're funny.'

'I am?'

Nia nodded.

'Is that good?' he asked.

She shook her head, then nodded, then shook it again, a smile on her sweet little face. 'I've got a bike. It's pink.'

'I know. I saw you riding it yesterday.' He turned back to her mother. 'Will you have a drink with me?'

'I can do Friday?'

'Friday is great.' Huw almost did a fist pump. 'Here?' He gestured to The Jolly Fox. He would completely understand if she preferred to go somewhere else. He'd only had a tiny taste of life in the village, but he'd already realised how difficult it might be to keep anything private.

'The Jolly Fox is fine,' she said. 'Eight o'clock?'

'Fantastic. I'll see you there.' He hesitated for a moment, awkward and uncertain, knowing he should end the conversation, but not wanting to leave.

'Bye,' she said, making the decision for him.

With a last lingering look, she turned away, and as she began to walk across the green he heard her daughter say, 'Mammy, I want to have a drink with the funny man. Can I come?'

'No, Nia, this is for grown-ups.'

'But I like him.'

He thought Rowena replied that she liked him too, although he couldn't be certain. He really hoped she did.

Chapter 7

Rowena had been unable to contain herself this past week. So much had been happening that she didn't know whether she was coming or going. First, she'd discovered that Huw was single (woo-hoo!), then he'd asked her out for a drink (double woo-hoo!). Secondly, she was going to view a vacant shop on the green tomorrow (squee!) and last but not least, she had an appointment with one of the business managers in her bank in a few weeks' time (gulp).

Rowena was exhausted and her head was spinning by the end of the week, so it was with relief that she turned her attention away from where to purchase shampoo bars in bulk, to what she was going to wear for her date this evening.

Maybe it was a good thing she'd been so preoccupied, because she hadn't had a chance to dwell on Huw. However, now that the time was getting closer and her date with him was imminent, she had butterflies in her tummy and she kept wanting to giggle, which was most unlike her.

'You look pretty, Mammy,' Nia said, wandering into Rowena's bedroom as she was putting the finishing touches to her makeup. It had been so long since she'd worn more than a swipe of mascara that she worried she might be overdoing things. Foundation was followed by blusher, then eyeshadow and eyeliner (it took her three goes to get the flick at the end looking right). She'd decided not to wear lipstick because she didn't want to leave most of it smeared over a wine glass; anyway, she usually managed to lick it off after ten minutes.

She didn't do anything with her hair though, apart from washing it, and it tumbled down her back in a gleaming sheet, heavy and thick. It was her best feature, and she had no intention of pinning it up. Besides, she liked to pull strands of it forward to hang down over her face, so she could hide behind it a little if she felt the need. She was well aware that she had one of those faces that illuminated every thought and emotion she was feeling, so sometimes it was a good idea to use her hair to cover part of it.

'You look like a princess,' Nia added. 'Can you make me look like that?'

'You already look like a princess,' Rowena assured her. 'You don't need makeup to be beautiful, because you already are.'

'So are you, Mammy. What are you going to wear?'

Even at four (nearly five) Nia was a real girly-girl, loving anything pink and sparkly, and taking a keen interest in clothes. Rowena had no idea where this came from, because Rowena herself wasn't too bothered about fashion, and she most definitely didn't do pink. With her hair and colouring, if she wore pink she'd resemble a discount version of Barbie. Nia could get away with it, with her dark hair and creamy complexion like Finn, which Rowena guessed would tan to a light gold – unlike

Rowena, who tended to burn if she wasn't careful. Nia also had dark eyes, like Finn.

'I thought I'd wear this,' Rowena said, pushing thoughts of Nia's father out of her head and holding up a pair of jeans and a floral top.

'Yuck.' Nia wrinkled her nose.

'Thanks. That's your considered opinion, is it?' Rowena tried not to wince – there was no way she was taking fashion advice from a four-year-old.

'You have to wear a dress,' her daughter informed her.

'I do?'

The little girl nodded vigorously. 'Princesses have to wear dresses.'

'I'm not a princess.'

'You *are*.' Nia was emphatic. 'Princesses have long hair and pretty faces.'

Oh dear, Rowena thought, she'd have to make more of an effort with regards to her daughter's education – or stop her watching quite so much TV.

'All mammies are princesses,' Nia continued. 'Like the one in church.'

'Er... pardon?'

'At *Christmas*. Remember? Baby Jesus's mammy is a princess, and she wears a crown. You can't see it, but it glows so you know it's there.'

'Do you mean a halo? What about this?' Rowena had returned to her wardrobe and was now holding out a summer dress. It was plain, but she'd liven it up with a chunky necklace and matching earrings.

'Better. Yes, a halo. Mammy, saints are princesses, too, aren't they?'

'I don't think so, poppet.' Rowena wriggled into the dress and smoothed it down over her hips.

'But Miss Caldicott said that our mammies are saints to put up with us, and saints have crowns like Baby Jesus's mammy. But Eloise's mammy has really short hair, so how can she be a princess?' Nia's little face was creased in confusion, and Rowena let out a laugh.

Dear God, she loved this child so much that it made her heart ache.

'I'll explain it another time,' she said to her daughter. 'Right now I need to finish getting ready before Nanny arrives. You make sure you're a good girl and do what she tells you.'

'I'm always a good girl,' Nia announced confidently.

Hmm, Rowena begged to differ. Miss Caldicott was right – mothers had to be saints sometimes! And so did fathers, she thought to herself, to even things up.

What kind of a father would Huw be? was her next thought. Swiftly followed by the determination that no matter how much she liked him or how much she fancied him, Huw Morgan would have to be someone very special indeed if she was to invite him into her daughter's life. Nia deserved nothing less.

-

Although Huw had only lived in the village for three weeks, he was so conscious of the curious looks he and Rowena were getting from the locals that he was beginning to debate the wisdom of having their first date here, in The Jolly Fox, where they were very much in the public eye, so to speak, despite hiding away in the snug to avoid the quiz that was taking place in the main bar.

Rowena either hadn't noticed, was immune to it, or didn't care, because she studiously ignored every stare, nudge, and knowing smile. Her attention was on him, and her direct and open gaze made his insides fizz.

Gosh, she was gorgeous. If he'd thought so previously, he was doubly sure now. She was wearing makeup – although in his opinion she didn't need any – and her summer dress clung to her curves, outlining her lovely figure. Her long hair flowed over her shoulders down to her waist, and he had the urge to run his hands through the glorious tresses.

Hastily, Huw cleared his throat and picked up his pint. *Down boy*, he said to himself, taken aback at his visceral reaction to her. There was something about her that punched him low in the gut, stealing his breath and his wits, and he had to make a conscious effort to pull himself together.

'So,' he began, 'have you lived in Foxmore all your life?'

'More or less, apart from university and a year or so afterwards.'

'Which uni did you go to?'

'Cardiff.'

'So did I! What did you study?'

'Business management with logistics. You?'

He grimaced. 'Politics.'

'Are you a politician?' She had her tongue in her cheek.

'No, thank God.' He shuddered. 'I did have a rather naïve idea when I began the course that I could change the world, but…' He trailed off.

'What happened?'

'I came to the conclusion that there is little real difference between our political parties. Have you ever watched

91

that old TV series *Yes Minister*? It was followed a couple of years later by *Yes, Prime Minister*? It's meant to be a comedy, but from what I can gather it's quite close to the mark when it comes to how our country is run and what goes on in Parliament and Number 10. Anyway, let's not talk about politics. Or religion,' he added hastily, in case she asked about whether he went to church or not.

'That still leaves sex,' she said, giving him a wicked smile.

'Oh dear...' He shook his head. 'Best we don't talk about that, either,' he advised, feeling hot under the collar.

'Best not,' she agreed. 'What brought you to Foxmore?'

'Do you need to ask? It's stunning. I can't believe I used to drive straight past it on my way to Snowdon. But I'd hiked up that particular mountain several times, and it can get so busy at the top that I began looking for other peaks to climb. I found Aran Fawddwy, which led me to Foxmore. Do you like walking?'

'I used to. I don't do much since I had Nia.'

'She's cute.'

'She can be, but she also has her moments. She's the reason I'm wearing this dress. I was going to wear jeans and a blouse, but she insisted I dress up.' She sighed theatrically.

'I'm sure you'd look lovely whatever you were wearing,' Huw replied gallantly. 'But she's right – you look gorgeous in that dress.' He bit his lip, wondering if he was coming on too strong. It was unlike him to feel so awkward around a woman: he was usually much more laid back than this, but there was something about Rowena which made him clumsy and tongue-tied. He desperately wanted her to like him, but he got the feeling he was making a bit of a prat of himself.

Rowena lowered her eyes and he hoped he hadn't made her feel uncomfortable. But when she raised them again and said, 'Thank you,' he saw that she was flattered, even if slightly embarrassed, and he got the impression she wasn't used to receiving compliments.

'How are you finding Foxmore?' she asked, changing the subject.

'I love it. I can't believe I actually live here. My sister is so envious.'

'She seems nice.'

'She is, although she can be a pain in the backside sometimes.'

'Did you really think I was married to the vicar?'

'Did you really think I was married to Ceri?' he countered with a grin, thankful that his sister had been a pain on this occasion, because if she hadn't, it might have taken him a while to discover the truth.

Rowena grinned back. 'I like her.'

'So do I, but don't tell her – she'll be insufferable, and she's annoying enough already.'

'I wish I had a sister. Or a brother.'

'You can borrow mine; no doubt she'll pay me another visit soon. She's fallen in love with Foxmore, too.'

'Wait until the bad weather – you mightn't be so in love with it then,' Rowena warned, finishing her drink.

'Fancy another?' he asked.

'I'll get them.'

'No, let me. *I* asked *you* out, remember?'

'But—'

'Tell you what, you can buy the drinks next time. If there *is* a next time?' He crossed his fingers as he watched her face. 'I'd like it if there was,' he added, hoping he didn't sound too keen.

'I think there might well be,' she said, and handed him her glass.

Huw had a spring in his step as he headed for the bar. So far, his date with Rowena was going well, and although it was early days, he was delighted that she'd kind of agreed to go out with him again.

'Are you the bloke that's bought Rosehip Cottage?' a voice asked, as he was waiting to be served.

He looked around to see an elderly gent leaning on the bar next to him. He had a pint in one hand and an unlit pipe in the other. Huw recognised him as being one of the group of men who had been in the pub on his very first night in Foxmore. They'd been discussing sheep, if he remembered correctly.

'That's me,' he said.

'If you're buying, mine's a pint.' He waved his half-empty glass at him.

Huw took the hint. 'And a pint for this gentleman.'

'Kind of you. I'm Aled Harris.' The man shoved a hand at him.

Huw took it. 'Huw Morgan. Pleased to meet you.'

'Likewise. Ta,' he added, accepting a fresh pint of ale from Dai.

'Have one yourself,' Huw said to the landlord.

'I don't mind if I do,' Dai said, 'but don't let this old pisspot con you out of any more drinks. He's been boasting that he's about to come into a shedload of money. Next time, tell him he should be buying you a pint.'

'Nothing's been signed yet,' Aled said.

'Are you going to tell us what you're up to?' Dai asked, placing Rowena's wine on the bar and taking the money Huw was holding out.

'Not yet. Not until it's all done and dusted.' Aled wore a sly expression on his face, and Huw wondered what was going on. Deciding it was none of his business, he pocketed his change, picked up the drinks and headed back to Rowena.

'What was all that about?' she asked.

'I'm not sure, although I did buy Dai and Aled Harris a drink.'

'That was nice of you.'

'Dai didn't think so. He warned me not to buy Aled any more because he was about to come into some money and could afford to buy his own.'

'Maybe he's selling the farm? Dee hasn't said anything though, so if it is up for sale he's not going through Powell's Estate Agents.'

'It really is a case of everyone knowing everyone else's business here, isn't it?'

'You've no idea…' Rowena said. Her tone was grim but she was smiling as she said it. 'It's quite comforting really. Unless you are trying to keep something quiet, then it's not ideal.'

Briefly Huw wondered whether Rowena was speaking from experience, but he didn't think it was his place to pry, so he was relieved when the conversation moved on to less sensitive topics.

Over the course of the next couple of hours he discovered that he and Rowena had the same love of gritty dramas, and the same taste in food (although he disliked cheese, which Rowena adored).

He was thrilled to learn more about her, and when she got on to the subject of her job, she regaled him with stories about the children and their antics.

Which brought the conversation back to Nia.

'Who is looking after her this evening?' he asked.

'My mam. She usually has her on Saturdays, too. They adore each other – Nanny loves spoiling her and Nia loves being spoilt. When the two of them are together they get up to all sorts of mischief.'

Huw said, 'Does Nia see much of her dad?' He was trying to gauge whether Rowena's split from her child's father had been a recent one, and whether there was any chance they might get back together. The last thing he wanted was for him to start falling for her, only for Rowena and her ex to decide to make another go of it.

There was silence, and Huw prayed he hadn't put his foot in it.

'No,' she said slowly. 'She doesn't see her father at all.'

'Ah, I see. Sorry, I didn't mean to pry.'

She took a breath and looked him in the eye. 'She's never met her father, and I doubt if she ever will.'

'Right... Please don't think you had to tell me that. It's none of my business.'

Rowena shrugged. 'It's common knowledge, so it's hardly a secret. You might as well hear it from me as from someone else. Anyway,' she said with a sigh, 'it's all water under the bridge. Nia and I are perfectly happy as we are.'

'You seem it.'

'Although, I'm not averse to dating now and again,' she added, with a twinkle in her eye.

'Just now and again?'

'Let's see, shall we? So far, you're doing OK.'

'Glad to hear it.' His smile was wry.

'Last orders,' Dai called, then rang a bell, just in case anyone missed his shout.

'I hadn't realised it was so late,' Rowena said. 'Doesn't time fly when you're having fun!'

'Did you have fun?' Huw asked, picking up their glasses. 'Are you up for another?'

'I'd better get back,' she said. 'And yes, I did have fun this evening.'

On the way out, Huw popped their empty glasses on the bar, then held the door open for Rowena to go through ahead of him. 'I'm glad,' he said. 'So did I. Although I did feel a bit like a fish in a goldfish bowl.'

'You noticed, eh?'

'It was hard not to. Do you mind if we go somewhere else next time? Assuming you still want to see me again and I haven't said anything to put you off me.'

'I do want to see you again.' Her voice was low.

'I'm glad.' They strolled along the pavement and Huw wondered whether he should slip his hand into hers, but decided against it. 'Can I walk you to your door?' he asked instead.

'I'd like that, and yes, it might be a good idea to go further afield. Tongues will already be wagging.'

'Fancy a meal next time? We could always make it a daytime or early evening thing, so you could bring Nia.'

She stiffened. 'Maybe not. Let's just keep it to me and you for the time being.'

'Whatever you prefer,' he said.

He'd not dated a woman with children before, and he wasn't sure how to behave when it came to involving Rowena's daughter. He wanted Rowena to know that he was perfectly happy for Nia to come along, but on the other hand, he also realised that maybe Rowena wanted to get to know him a bit better first.

'When and where?' he asked. 'I'm easy when it comes to what day, and you know the area better than I, so can you suggest somewhere nice?'

'I know a nice place called The Falcon. It's about a fifteen-minute drive away, if that's OK? How about next Friday?'

Huw smiled at her. 'Perfect. It's a date!'

They'd been strolling along the main street in the opposite direction to the green, and had turned off onto a side road, when Rowena came to a halt.

'Home sweet home,' she said, looking up at the bedroom windows.

Huw followed her gaze. All was in darkness, although light seeped around the curtains of the downstairs window.

She turned to face him. 'I've enjoyed this evening,' she said. 'Thank you.'

'Me too. I'm already looking forward to next week. Here, let me give you my mobile number, in case something comes up.'

He took his phone out of his pocket and they swapped numbers. Then there was an awkward silence as he wondered whether he should kiss her. He wanted to, but he didn't know whether it was too soon. Or whether she was actually expecting to be kissed.

In the end, he settled for kissing her on the cheek.

Admittedly, he drew it out a bit, and it certainly wasn't a maiden-aunt peck. His lips lingered on the soft downy skin next to her mouth, and he breathed in the scent of her, the delicate perfume making his head spin.

Reluctantly, he drew away to find her eyes, large and luminous, gazing at him.

He gazed back, happy to lose himself in her for a moment or two.

Then movement over her shoulder caught his attention, and he realised someone was watching them through the window. 'I think we've got an audience,' he murmured. 'Your mam, I suspect.'

Rowena exhaled slowly and nodded, and Huw stepped back, giving her some space.

'I'm going to get the third degree when I get in,' she said.

'If it's any consolation, Ceri will demand an update on how the evening went. She thinks she's got a vested interest.' He took another step. 'You've got my number if you need to change our arrangements for whatever reason.' Then he added sincerely, 'I really hope you don't. I'm looking forward to seeing you again. Bye, Rowena.'

And with that, he turned on his heel and walked away, his heart thumping – because if he hadn't noticed they were being watched, he had a feeling that they might have shared their very first kiss.

It would have to wait until next time, and boy, was he looking forward to it!

Chapter 8

For someone who was about to go and look at a retail site for her potential new business, Rowena found herself not as excited as she had been when she'd made the appointment with Dee. For some reason, she wasn't as focused as she should have been.

For some reason, indeed! She knew precisely what the reason was, and it was to do with Huw and their date yesterday evening. She'd thoroughly enjoyed herself, and when he'd walked her home, she'd hoped he'd kiss her. He might have done, if it hadn't been for her nosey mother peering at them through the window. And when he'd stepped away, she'd been acutely disappointed. But at least he wanted to see her again, so that was something to look forward to.

She felt they'd really hit it off, and there had been only a couple of times when the conversation had stuttered, or she'd felt a little awkward – one of them being when he'd asked about Nia's father. Rowena supposed it was reasonable for him to have asked. If the shoe was on the other foot, she'd want to know. She'd told him that Nia's father wasn't on the scene and never had been, but she hadn't gone into details. There were very few people who even knew his name, and she intended to keep it that way. It wasn't anyone else's business. If she and Huw grew closer, she'd tell him about Finn, but not before.

'Well?' Betsan demanded, hurrying up to her. Rowena was outside the shop on the corner of the green, waiting for her best friend and Dee to arrive. 'How did it go?'

'Good,' Rowena said, not giving anything away.

'Is that all you've got to say for yourself – good? Huh!' Betsan snorted. 'Are you seeing him again?'

'I might be.'

'That's a yes, then. I've already been cornered by Bronwen Jones this morning – she couldn't wait to tell me that you were seen having a drink with the new man in town.'

'Good grief! I might have known. The number of odd looks and stares I got last night was unbelievable. In hindsight, we should have gone somewhere else, but I wanted to stay on home ground, so to speak, for our first date. Next time we're going to The Falcon. There was one thing, though – he asked if I wanted to bring Nia.'

Betsan said, 'That's good, isn't it?'

'Is it? I thought it might be too much, too soon.'

'Maybe he's trying to make a good impression?'

'Anyway, I said no, because until I'm sure this is going somewhere, I'm not going to bring Nia into it. There'll have to be a lot more dates before that happens.'

'I'll babysit one night for you, if you want to give him a trial run – at his place, of course.' Betsan waggled her eyebrows.

'Betsan Pritchard! Go wash your mouth out. And you a vicar's wife to boot! What would Terry's congregation say?'

'They'd probably cheer you on. Try before you buy, that's what I say.'

'Am I to infer that you took Terry out for a test run?'

'More than once! We had to keep it quiet, though – the bishop wouldn't have been too pleased if he'd found out. He was a bit old school. He's retired now, though. The new one is much more open-minded. Still, I doubt he'd take all that kindly to one of his reverends doing the walk of shame after a night of passion.' Betsan had lived in Foxmore all her life, but Terry was a newcomer, although he'd been in the village for twenty or so years now. 'When are you seeing Huw again?'

'Friday.'

'It's turning out to be a regular Friday thing.' Betsan winked at her.

'I hope so.' Secretly Rowena was hoping it would become more than a *Friday* thing. She'd dearly love to see him on Saturdays, Sundays, Mondays…

Giving herself a mental shake, she told herself to slow down and practise what she preached. Didn't she just tell Betsan that she intended to take it slow and be very sure of him and his intentions before getting in too deep? Yet here she was, wishing the week away so she could see him again.

Thankfully Dee arrived before Betsan could quiz her further, although her friend did manage to squeeze in a quick, 'Did you have a snog?' before Dee came within hearing distance.

'No, we did not!' Rowena exclaimed.

'Shame. He looks like he might be a good kisser.'

'Shush! Hi, Dee, how are you?'

'Good thanks. And you? I hear you had a date with Huw Morgan last night.' She fished the shop's keys out of her bag. 'Lucky you!'

'You'd better not let Vaughan hear you say that,' Rowena joked. Crikey, did everyone in Foxmore know already? That was quick!

'Go on, what's he like?' Dee asked, nudging her with an elbow.

'Nice,' Rowena said, knowing exactly what Dee was getting at but refusing to be drawn.

'Is that all you can say – nice?'

'He didn't kiss her, if that's what you want to know,' Betsan said.

'Why ever not?'

'Because he's a gentleman,' Rowena said, wishing Dee would hurry up and unlock the damned door so they could go inside and change the subject. She glared at Betsan, who smiled innocently back.

'Ooh, with looks like his, and he's a gentleman to boot? I'm so jealous,' Dee exclaimed, eventually pushing the door open and hurrying to silence the beeping alarm.

Rowena had been inside the building many times in the past, first when it was a shoe shop when she was a child – she vividly remembered having her feet measured for brand new shoes for school – and then when it became a toyshop she used to spend most of her pocket money in there. Its final reincarnation had been as a bookshop, but the owners had struggled to keep up with the discounts that supermarkets and the big chains offered, so they'd ceased trading just after Christmas and the premises had lain empty ever since, which was surprising considering it was in an ideal location.

What Rowena loved about it was that it had several rooms leading on from one another, but with a clear line of sight from the counter where the till used to sit, which was just near the door. Also, many of the shelves were still in situ, so she could utilise those without having to do a total refit.

Listen to her – refit! Anyone would think she knew what she was talking about.

Actually, she was starting to get to grips with retail terminology, and she felt rather proud of herself.

'What do you think?' Dee asked. 'Is it suitable?'

Rowena had felt obliged to tell Dee the reason she wanted to look at the inside of the corner shop on the green, and although she hoped the estate agent would keep it to herself, she wasn't going to hold her breath. So far, only Rowena and Betsan really knew what was going on, although Betsan had let Terry into the secret and also Terry's brother, who was an accountant, because he was helping Rowena formulate a business plan.

But after this little visit, Rowena had to accept the possibility that the story would leak, and she'd bet her last penny that it would be Dee who would do the leaking. She was hoping to keep the news under wraps until she'd had the meeting with the bank's business manager and knew she was definitely going ahead with her plans, but Foxmore was Foxmore and keeping a secret was almost impossible.

Details about Nia's father weren't common knowledge, thankfully, but that was only because Rowena had been living in Cardiff at the time of her daughter's conception, and never once had she introduced Finn to her family. She'd been planning on coming back to Foxmore for a visit and bringing him with her, but he'd ended their relationship before she'd had a chance to put the wheels in motion.

In some ways, she was pleased that he hadn't visited Foxmore, because for everyone to know the full details of their failed relationship and the subsequent outcome would have been hard to bear. Even without knowing the ins and outs, for months after Rowena had returned to Foxmore, she'd had to endure the pitying and curious looks of the villagers as her stomach swelled. And after she'd given birth, there had been questions about when the baby's father would be coming to see her. Rowena had kept her own counsel and eventually the questions and speculation had dried up.

Now, though, she was the subject of curious and speculative gazes once more.

She supposed she would have to get used to it if she intended to see Huw again – and she very much intended to. In fact, she couldn't wait for Friday to come around, and she was already fretting about what she was going to wear.

Maybe she'd ask her daughter for advice again…?

–

'How did it go?' Ceri demanded.

'Fine.' Huw jammed the phone between his shoulder and his ear as he tried to iron a shirt. Giving up for a moment, he switched the iron off at the mains and placed it carefully on the worktop. He'd have another go after he'd spoken to his sister.

'Are you still there? Huw!'

'I'm still here. You caught me doing the ironing.'

'I was hoping to catch you doing something else.'

'The vacuuming?'

'You know what I mean. Did you kiss her?'

'Not really.'

'Oh.' She sounded deflated. 'I really liked that one.'

'So did I. I still do.'

'You *do*? For a minute there I thought you'd kicked her into touch, like you always do.'

Ceri made it her business to try to vet his girlfriends. His sister hadn't liked the last one he'd had, for good reason. She hadn't treated him particularly well, and he'd smarted over it for a long time, to the point where he'd not risked his heart on having another serious relationship. Since that disaster, he'd only dated casually.

'You make me sound picky,' he said.

'You are.'

'You're just as bad,' Huw countered. 'What happened to your last boyfriend?'

'He slurped his soup. I can't be doing with a slurper. You ought to have heard the noise he made.'

'And you tell me *I'm* picky!'

'He also made eyes at another woman when we were at a party together.'

'Oh, that's different. In that case, I completely understand.'

'So, when are you seeing her again?'

'Friday.'

'That's nearly a whole week away. Talk about taking it slow. Do you think you can manage to kiss her next time?'

'I'm hanging up now,' he warned. His sister was the nosiest person on the planet, and he had no intention of going into details. It was enough for her to know that he had a second date.

'Don't go, I'm not finished,' Ceri protested. 'What was she wearing? What did you talk about? Is her daughter's father still on the scene?'

'A dress, all kinds of things, and no, he isn't.'

'That makes things less complicated if he's not around,' Ceri observed.

'For whom? I'm not sure Rowena sees it that way.' She'd had a strange expression on her face when she'd told him that Nia had never met her father, and he couldn't help wondering what had happened. He didn't intend to ask her though; no doubt she'd tell him when she was ready – if their relationship got that far.

After advising his sister to concentrate on her own love life and stop interfering in his, he ended the call. But instead of returning to the ironing, he gave his phone a speculative glance.

Would it hurt to send Rowena a quick message to say he'd enjoyed last night, or would that be a bit stalkerish? There was a fine line which he didn't want to cross…

Deciding it would probably be OK, he typed in a single sentence. *Thinking about you.*

Then he hastily deleted it, thinking it sounded a bit odd.

He tried another. *I enjoyed last night. Looking forward to seeing you again.*

Ah, that was better.

His thumb hovered over the send button.

He thought for a moment, was about to send it, had another think, decided he definitely would send it, then decided he wouldn't.

What was wrong with him? He was normally the most decisive person in the world. Look what happened when he'd visited Foxmore for the first time – within three months he'd bought a house. Yet now here he was, unable to send a simple message without dithering.

His thumb hovered again, but he deleted the words as an idea occurred to him. He'd book a table at The Falcon, then send her a message to tell her what time he'd pick her up. He could always add that he was looking forward to seeing her again to the end of that.

Decision made, he did a quick internet search for the restaurant's phone number, his heart thumping in anticipation.

As far as he was concerned, Friday couldn't come quick enough.

Chapter 9

Rowena loved her mam to bits and was usually happy to spend time in her company, but maybe not so much today. It had taken less than forty-eight hours for the gossip drums to reach her mother's ears.

'Did you hear what I said?' Tracey jabbed her with her index finger. 'Wakey, wakey. I asked you why you were poking around in that empty shop on the green? Dee said—'

'I can guess what Dee said,' Rowena interrupted with a sigh. 'She told you about the zero waste shop.'

'She most certainly did! I can't believe you'd tell her before me.'

'It wasn't like that. I had to tell her because I wanted to check out the inside of the premises, and I also needed to know how much the rent was, and so on. It was only natural for her to ask the reason.'

'Are you sure about opening a shop? It's a big commitment.'

They were sitting in her mam's garden after Rowena had dropped Nia off at school. She often called in for a cup of tea on her way home, and although she had so much to do that she didn't know where to begin, Rowena wanted to make time for her mam.

Right now, she was seriously regretting her decision. She could have gone home and put the finishing touches to the spreadsheet that Betsan's brother-in-law had emailed to her. She had almost finished working out the start-up costs, coming to the conclusion that she definitely would need a business loan – even if it was only a small one – otherwise all her savings would be eaten up before she'd opened the doors for the first day of trading. She wanted to ensure she had enough to live on for several months until the shop started paying for itself and she could draw a salary from it.

'No, Mam, I'm not sure. I'm still at the planning stage, but it's beginning to look more and more feasible. The rent and business rates aren't as high as I thought they'd be, so… yeah, maybe I am sure after all.'

There, she'd said it. Although she hadn't invested any money as yet, she'd invested a huge amount of time and a great deal of emotion into the project, and the more she learnt and the more she planned, the more committed she became. Apprehension had gradually been superseded by quiet excitement. This was something she could get her teeth into, something she was passionate about, and not only that, she'd also be providing for her and Nia's future, as well as setting a good example to her daughter.

Rowena was under no illusion that it would be easy. It would be hard work and would be a considerable commitment, but she was prepared for that. She'd still be able to take Nia to school and she might even be able to pick her up. Nia spent Saturdays with Nanny, so that was one less day Rowena had to worry about, and she was determined to set Sundays aside, no matter what, to be with her daughter. That was their day, their time together.

If Rowena had to do any work on that day, she'd wait until Nia was in bed and do it then.

'You're definitely going to go ahead with it?' her mam asked, adding, 'Owning a shop won't be easy.'

Rowena opened her mouth to retort that she knew it would be hard work, but before she could say anything there was a scuffling sound from next door and Mrs Moxley's head popped up over the fence. The shiplap fence panel was six feet high, so the old lady must be standing on a ladder to see over it, Rowena thought.

'Did I hear you say you were thinking of opening a shop? What sort of shop?' Mrs Moxley was peering at her intently, a seemingly disembodied head hovering on top of the fence. It was quite disconcerting. As was knowing that someone had been eavesdropping.

Rowena resisted the impulse to roll her eyes. Trust Mrs Moxley to overhear what was supposed to have been a private conversation. The news would be all over the village by teatime.

'An eco-friendly one,' she replied. 'It will be a refill shop.' She'd probably regret asking the question she was about to ask, as Mrs Moxley probably wasn't her ideal customer, but she asked it anyway. 'Would you buy from it?'

'It depends on what it sold.'

Fair point, Rowena thought. 'The focus would be on zero waste and zero packaging,' she explained. 'So fruit and veg would all be loose, and if you wanted half a kilo of rice you'd either bring your own container and I'd fill it up for you, or you'd purchase a reusable one from the shop.' Assuming she could get a good supply of vegetables, that is.

'Rice and veg?' the old lady sounded doubtful.

'Among other things.'

'Like what?'

'Flour, pasta, oats, dried fruit, nuts, lentils, dried peas – anything I can think of which I can buy in bulk. That includes cooking oils, cleaning products – all eco-friendly, of course – shampoo, conditioner, soap. None of it will have any packaging. I'll also sell bamboo loo roll—'

'Ouch!' Mrs Moxley shuddered theatrically.

'It's really soft, honest,' Rowena hastened to reassure her. She had ordered some herself online, to try it, and she could vouch for its softness. She carried on, 'The aim is not just zero waste when it comes to packaging, but also zero plastic, so I'll be stocking bamboo toothbrushes, reusable drinking straws... the list is endless.' She was exaggerating slightly, but the things she and Betsan had looked into were impressive.

The range might be impressive, but Mrs Moxley appeared to be underwhelmed. Her forehead was creased into a frown and she'd wrinkled her nose. Rowena felt discouraged. The face staring back at her over the fence wasn't filled with a great deal of enthusiasm, and neither was her own mother's. It looked like she was falling at the first hurdle. Maybe she should have canvassed opinions before she'd launched herself into it? Thankfully, she hadn't shelled out any money yet, so if she backed out now all she would have lost was her time.

And a dream of a better future for her and her child, a little voice in her head argued, but she tried to ignore it.

Mrs Moxley broke into her despondent thoughts.

'I, for one, think it's a marvellous idea,' she declared. 'When I was a girl, there was none of this plastic nonsense.

If you wanted leeks, you went to the greengrocer and you'd buy them loose with dirt still on them. None of this pre-washed nonsense. If you was lucky he'd put them in a paper bag. I can't believe supermarkets today wash 'em for you, chop most of the goodness off them, then wrap 'em in plastic. No wonder everything is going to the dogs.' She paused. 'I'm not sure about bamboo toilet paper though – I like the soft scented stuff. My piles are—'

'I'll give you a free roll to try!' Rowena announced recklessly – anything to deflect Mrs Moxley from talking about her piles.

'Now?' Mrs Moxley asked hopefully.

'Sorry, not now. I haven't bought any stock yet,' Rowena admitted. And neither would she until she was certain the venture would get off the ground.

Another voice from behind the fence piped up, and Rowena realised that Mrs Moxley's grown-up grand-daughter, Rachel, had also heard the whole conversation.

The woman was saying, 'I think it's ace. My kids are always on at me to put the right stuff in the right bin. They teach them all about recycling and whatnot at school. Mind you, the kids don't say anything when it's their birthday or Christmas and they want the latest fad. Some of those toys are wrapped in so much plastic that you need a crowbar to get at them. Same with meat from the supermarket. Have you tried to open a packet of shrink-wrapped lamb chops? I nearly took my finger off the last time I bought some.'

Someone else said, 'That's why I always go to the butcher's in the village.'

Good grief, how many people were in Mrs Moxley's garden, Rowena wondered? She must have a party going on over there. Rowena recognised the speaker as Janet, Mrs Moxley's daughter, who was about the same age as her own mam.

'He's more expensive,' Janet was saying, 'but at least you can unpack your steak when you get it home, and you know where the meat comes from, too. Only sells Welsh meat, he does. He even swears he knows the very cow it comes from.'

'By name?' Rachel laughed.

'Don't be silly,' Janet said. 'Budge over, Mam, and let me up.' Mrs Moxley's head moved a few inches to the right, and Janet's face popped up. 'That's better. I like to see who I'm speaking to.'

'Could have fooled me,' Rachel said to her mother. 'The amount of time you spend on the phone is ridiculous. And you lot accuse us younger generation of being glued to our mobiles.'

'I'm only on my bleedin' phone because you keep calling me,' Janet said over her shoulder. 'Can't wash a pair of socks without having to phone me and ask me about it. "Will the colour run? Can I put them in with the sheets? Where do the odd ones go?" When I was your age, I just had to get on with it.' Janet turned back to peer over the fence again. 'As I was saying before I was rudely interrupted, I think it's a good idea, as long as it's not too expensive. Will it be?'

This was a question Rowena had been dreading, because her little shop wouldn't be able to compete with the discounted prices the supermarkets were able to charge. 'A little,' she admitted. 'But you won't have to travel to Dolgellau if you run out of something.' She smiled ingratiatingly.

'Count me in, then,' Janet said. 'We've all got to do our bit, haven't we?'

'It's all right for you,' Rachel grumbled. Her face suddenly appeared next to her mother's. It was quite disconcerting to see three bodiless heads resting on top of a fence panel. Rachel continued, 'I've got to do my shopping where it's cheapest. The amount of food my kids can put away in a day would feed a small army for a week.'

'What about your job, love?' Rowena's mam asked her. 'Will you give that up?' From her tone, Tracey clearly hoped Rowena was going to say she wasn't.

'I'll have to. I can't do both.'

'Where will this shop of yours be?' Mrs Moxley wanted to know.

'I've been looking at the vacant shop on the green.'

'What are you going to call it?' This was from Janet.

'Sero.'

'Catchy. Does what it says on the tin,' Janet said. 'Zero... you don't need anything else, do you?'

Sero was Welsh for zero, so it was rather fitting. And with it being short, it should be easy to remember – 'zero waste shop' was a bit of a mouthful.

'I wish you all the luck in the world, lovely girl,' Mrs Moxley said. 'You deserve it.' She smiled sympathetically.

Tracey began to bristle and Rowena hastily said, 'I'd better get off – I've got a tonne of things to do before I go to work.' She got to her feet, and with a glare at her neighbour, Rowena's mother also stood up.

Rowena let out a small sigh of relief. Despite it being the twenty-first century and single motherhood being quite common, Mrs Moxley's outlook was somewhat archaic, and she'd been expressing exaggerated sympathy for Rowena's status ever since Rowena had returned to Foxmore with a baby on the way and no father on the horizon. It didn't bother Rowena in the slightest, but it often got her mam's back up.

Conflict averted, Rowena said goodbye to her mam, and hurried off home. She hadn't been lying when she'd said she had loads to do, and she was beginning to wonder how she'd managed to fill her time before this.

There was one good thing about her mam finding out about Rowena's plans for opening a shop – Tracey hadn't once mentioned her daughter having a drink with Foxmore's newest resident.

–

Huw adored bookshops – they were among some of his favourite places – and this one was particularly lovely. It was an indie shop, not part of a chain, and because of that it was able to stock all sorts of interesting books and not just those on the bestsellers list or marketed by the big publishing houses. The problem was, smaller bookshops like this one tended to find it difficult to compete, and all too often were either sold off or went under.

Hopefully, the plan which he was helping to put together would ensure this one stayed in business for many years to come. He'd found that if a community had a vested interest in a venture, then that venture was far more likely to thrive, and he had every faith this one would.

He stopped outside it for a moment and studied the window display. Someone was rather talented, and the window was full of beach reads, travel guides and various other tomes dedicated to summer. It was cheerful and inviting, and from the number of customers inside, it was doing its job of drawing people in. He was quietly optimistic that the shop would go from strength to strength.

He thought back to the day he'd started at the office in Dolgellau a few weeks ago – this was the first project he'd been involved in, and he prayed it would succeed. He'd met with a group of residents who wanted to save their local bookshop and had heard of Co-Op Cymru, and were interested in setting one up themselves. Huw had helped them with their crowdfunding campaign to buy the current owner out, and hopefully there would be enough funds left over to revamp the shop, which was in dire need of a makeover, despite the cheerful window display.

There was still some way to go yet, but this new co-operative was well on its way, and he was delighted with progress so far.

Although helping co-operatives with their initial start-up was his job, he always felt as though they were his babies, and he was as enthusiastic and as dedicated to their success as the shareholders themselves. It gave him immense pleasure and satisfaction to see a co-op succeed. He also found it quite emotional, and likened it to nursing a sick hedgehog or bird back to health, then releasing it into the wild. That might be fanciful, but it was the best analogy he could come up with.

After spending a couple of hours with some of the community shareholders, he made his way back to the office, and as he did so his mind turned to matters closer to home – namely Rowena.

He hadn't been able to stop thinking about her all day yesterday, and when he'd called into the pub for a Sunday roast, his eyes had kept straying to the table they'd sat at.

He'd thought about cooking his own roast dinner, but it hadn't seemed worth the effort when it was just him, plus he didn't want to eat his lunch alone, so he'd taken himself off to The Jolly Fox instead.

OK, he'd admitted as he'd sat with a lemonade in front of him, waiting for his meal, that maybe he'd been hoping Rowena would be there too.

His disappointment when she'd failed to appear was more acute than it had any right being considering they had only been on one date and they hadn't even kissed yet.

It didn't help that the pub had been full of tourists, some in hiking gear, but none of them on their own, so he had hurriedly finished his meal, headed home to change into his own walking boots, and had taken himself off on a nice long hike. But even as he huffed and panted up a particularly steep hill, his mind was on Rowena, and he wondered what she was doing right now.

It was probably silly to hope that she was thinking about him.

It wasn't so bad when he was occupied, as he'd been this morning, concentrating on the job he was employed to do, but when he had a spare five minutes – such as now, as he drove back to the office – his thoughts kept returning to her. She was in his head and he couldn't seem to get her out.

Right now, Huw wasn't sure if that was a good thing or a bad one – because he had a sneaking suspicion that he was starting to fall for her, despite having known her for less than a month. Huw Morgan, at thirty-two years old, had never fallen for anyone before, and he had no idea what he should do about it.

Chapter 10

Friday at last! Huw drove home from work on a cloud of nervous excitement. He'd been looking forward to seeing Rowena again all week. In fact, she had rarely been out of his thoughts. He'd been tempted to ask Ceri what was wrong with him, but he thought it best not to involve his sister at this stage. Anyway, he suspected the reason he couldn't get Rowena out of his mind was because he was falling for her, so he really didn't need Ceri's opinion. His sister had enough opinions of her own, without him asking for more.

It was also most unlike him to be in a tizzy about what to wear. He had a couple of suits, one of which was more of a funeral variety, and another which he wore to important meetings, and he had a selection of work clothes consisting of trousers and shirts, and a jacket or two that didn't necessarily match any of the trousers. He had hiking gear, none of which would be suitable to take a lady to a restaurant, and he also had an assortment of jeans, T-shirts and sweatshirts, plus a couple of pairs of chinos, and a few shirts that weren't work shirts but weren't too casual, either.

He took care getting ready, spending longer in the shower than usual, and making sure he was closely shaven. Rough stubble, which seemed to be quite on-trend, didn't suit him. He just looked scruffy. Anyway, he was hoping that this evening he might be able to kiss her properly and not just give her a peck on the cheek, so the last thing he wanted was to have a sandpapery chin. He didn't like the feel of it himself and he could only imagine how uncomfortable it might be for the woman he was kissing.

At the thought of kissing Rowena, his stomach did a slow roll and his heart skipped a beat. She had the most luscious lips—

Pulling himself together and determined not to think such lascivious thoughts so early in the evening, he hunted around for his nicest jeans, grabbed a pair of loafers from the bottom of the wardrobe, then stood there bare-chested, eyeing his shirt collection. Immediately he discarded the Hawaiian shirt that he'd been persuaded to buy for some idiotic evening or other that he couldn't now recall, and he debated between a crisp white button-down or a navy one with tiny white sprigs of flowers.

He went with the navy, for the simple reason that if he did have an unfortunate accident and happened to spill any of his dinner down him, it wouldn't show so much on a darker shirt. Not that he had any intention of spilling his food down himself, but he was so desperate to make a good impression that something was bound to go wrong. Sod's law, and all that.

With a quick squirt of some of the aftershave that his mum had bought him for Christmas, he gave himself one last look in the mirror and decided he was ready, so he grabbed his keys, shrugged a jacket over his shoulders and headed out of the door.

He was quite pleased that he'd managed not to give in to his temptation at the beginning of the week to text her, apart from to let her know that he had booked a table for eight o'clock and that he'd pick her up at seven-thirty. His heart had lifted when she'd sent a reply which had said, *That's great. Thanks for letting me know. Looking forward to seeing you x.*

It was the x at the end of the message that had caught his attention. However, knowing that some people added love and kisses quite liberally to any text or message they sent, he had to force himself not to read too much into it.

Huw pulled up outside her house at seven on the dot, to find her waiting for him on the step. Her daughter was peering out of the window and Rowena turned to wave to her. Then another face appeared, and he recognised Betsan. She waved too, and when he caught her eye she grinned at him and did a thumbs up.

He smiled back and gave a thumbs up in return. It was quite heartening to know that Betsan was on his side and appeared to be rooting for him, but he didn't want to get ahead of himself: it wasn't Betsan who he needed to impress, it was Rowena.

He hurriedly got out of the car, dashed around to the passenger side and opened the door for her.

'Thank you,' she said, slipping into the seat, and he closed the door with a gentle click, then went around to the driver's side and got in. As soon as he closed his own door, he smelled her perfume and he inhaled deeply. It was the same as she'd worn last Friday, and it made his head spin.

'You ready?' he asked, then wanted to kick himself. Of course she was ready, what a silly question. She wouldn't be sitting in his car if she wasn't.

'Definitely. I'm starving.'

'So am I,' he lied. He wasn't at all hungry – at least, not for food. He was hungry for *her*, and his gaze kept shifting sideways as he glanced away from the road to drink her in.

She looked as delicious as he remembered. More so. She had her hair down as usual, and this evening she wore a white strappy dress which accentuated her waist, and flowed down over her hips. It was simple and stylish, and suited her perfectly, and she looked elegant and unfussy. With a face as lovely as hers and with that gorgeous hair, she really didn't need anything to set off her beauty.

She seemed to be totally unaware of how lovely she was, and he found it incredibly attractive. Heck, *she* was incredibly attractive, and he was proud to have her on his arm this evening.

'Did you get fashion advice from your daughter this time?' he asked.

Rowena laughed. 'No! She wanted me to wear a tutu.'

'A what now?'

'It's a skirt that ballerinas wear, kind of all netting and sticky out. It wouldn't have been a good look, especially with the fairy wings she insisted had to be worn with it. Thankfully they didn't fit, so I had a perfect excuse not to wear them.'

He shot another glance at her out of the corner of his eye, speculating what she'd look like wearing a tutu, and he hastily looked away again as he imagined her long legs on display. 'Would you have worn them if they had fitted?'

'Maybe.' She smiled at him. 'It might have been worth it just to see your face.'

'I don't care what you wear,' he said. 'You're beautiful regardless.'

'Why, thank you, kind sir. You certainly know how to bolster a lady's spirit.'

'Just telling the truth,' he said, then he was lost for words, so he turned the music up a fraction.

'Ed Sheeran,' she said. 'I like his stuff.'

Huw could hear her humming softly under her breath, and he was more than happy to stay silent for the rest of the short journey and simply listen to her.

The Falcon was a square building constructed of grey Welsh stone, topped with a grey slate roof. It would have been imposing if it wasn't for the pretty seating area outside, and the large tubs of flowers dotted around. He'd looked it up on the internet, and it had a good reputation and an extensive menu.

He parked up and they went inside and were shown to a table near a window which looked out over rolling hills and the setting sun.

As they took their seats, the rays illuminated Rowena, making her skin glow more than usual and her hair shine like burnished gold. She looked ethereal and he smiled to himself, thinking that she didn't need Nia's wings because she already looked angelic.

After they had ordered their meals and once a drink had been placed in front of them, Huw said, 'What have you been getting up to this week? Anything to report from the school?'

'Not really, it's been quite quiet. Although there was an incident with some sponge pudding. But I don't think I'll go into detail just before we're about to eat.'

Huw shuddered. He wasn't squeamish, but neither did he feel the need for any gory details, not when he had stuffed mushrooms to look forward to. He picked up his glass and took a sip of orange juice, and said, 'Anything else?'

Rowena sighed. 'You've heard then?'

'Heard what?'

'About the shop.'

'What shop?'

'The zero waste shop that I intend to open. If everything goes to plan, that is.'

'No, I haven't heard a thing,' he said, intrigued. 'Tell me more.'

'It seems to be the talk of Foxmore,' she began, 'but you're still quite new.' She chuckled, adding, 'You will probably be quite new for at least ten years, but don't be offended by that.' She took a sip of her drink, then put the glass back down on the table, and continued. 'Before you say anything, just for the record, this is all Betsan's fault, so if it doesn't work out I'm going to blame her.'

'OK,' he replied slowly. 'Carry on.'

'A few weeks ago Betsan and I went to a rally in Cardiff. It was a march protesting against single-use plastic and excess packaging. It's a subject I feel quite strongly about. When we decided to have a break for a coffee and a quick bite to eat, we went into this cafe which had a zero waste shop attached to it.'

His eyes widened. 'I think I know it! The cafe part, I mean.'

'The shop gave us an idea. Foxmore has lots of lovely little shops, a cafe, and a gorgeous pub, as you well know. but not many of those shops sell food or other household items such as cleaning products. There is the butcher and he's really good, and the baker's, of course, but that's about it apart from the convenience store, which isn't as convenient as it could be. Have you been in there?'

'Once or twice, but I must admit I wasn't very impressed. I tend to do my shopping in the big supermarket just outside Dolgellau.'

'As do most people,' Rowena said. 'They only use the convenience store for emergencies, such as for the odd pint of milk or loaf of bread. Most of the stuff they sell is overpriced and overpackaged, and they have this really annoying habit of putting items that particularly appeal to children right by the checkout. I've lost count of the number of times that Nia has had a strop because I won't let her have a packet of brightly coloured something or another that really isn't any good for her.'

'Is that why you came up with the idea of opening a zero waste shop?'

'Yes. I was hoping to keep it quiet for a while longer until I had a meeting with the bank manager, but I went to have a look at an empty shop on the corner of the green on Saturday, and now the whole village knows about it.'

'That's probably not a bad thing,' Huw said. 'It'll generate some interest before you actually open. Have you got a date for that?'

'Not really. Nothing is set in stone as yet. A lot depends on what happens with the bank. I've got some savings but I don't want to plough them all into the business, so I need them to give me a loan.'

'Very sensible.' He looked up as a waitress appeared at their table, carrying two plates of delicious-looking food, and suddenly he discovered that he was rather hungry after all.

They stopped talking as they tucked into their starters, and when the conversation resumed it was on an altogether different subject.

Huw was so captivated by her that it was only in hindsight would he kick himself for not paying more attention to Rowena's plans.

—

'That was delicious,' Rowena said, dabbing her lips with a napkin and then placing it delicately on the table. She leant back in her chair and let out a sigh. 'Gosh, I'm full. I don't think I'll eat again for a week.' She'd managed to stop just short of being uncomfortably full, thank goodness, because she was hoping he would kiss her, and she wanted to savour every second of it and not worry about indigestion.

'It was rather good, wasn't it?' Huw agreed, patting his stomach.

'You haven't forgotten that we're going Dutch, have you?' Rowena had a feeling he would try to pay, and although she'd appreciate the gesture, she'd didn't think it fair that he should put his hand in his pocket for two dates on the trot. Splitting the bill was by far the easiest solution.

'No,' Huw said. 'But I was hoping you had.'

She raised her eyebrows and gazed at him.

He held up his hands in surrender. 'You win. We'll go halves.' He paused as a thought occurred to him. 'Is that why you only had soft drinks this evening?'

'Not at all,' she replied. It was because she didn't want to breathe alcohol fumes all over him if he did decide to kiss her. And that was also the reason why she'd chosen the same dishes as him. It was lucky that she liked what he'd picked, she thought with a giggle.

'What's so funny?' he asked.

'Nothing.' Her reply was innocent, but her thoughts weren't. She was imagining asking him in for coffee, knowing what it might lead to – and she might well have done if Nia wasn't at home. Anyway, it was far too early in their relationship for her to be having those kinds of thoughts. She wanted to get to know him much better before she invited him in for 'coffee'. And when she did feel ready for that, it would only happen if Nia wasn't around, because Rowena had no intention of her daughter waking up to find a strange man in the house.

It was tempting though… Rowena hadn't been intimate with anyone for such a long time. She vividly remembered when it was, and who the man was – Nia's father. That's how long ago it had been. Rowena hadn't looked at anyone since Finn had dumped her.

But she was looking now, all right, and very much liking what she saw.

Huw had been great fun and good company, so not only did she fancy him rotten, but she also really liked him as a person. He was funny, modest, sincere, and incredibly sexy. In fact, if she was asked to describe her ideal man, she'd probably describe Huw and not some film star, because Huw was here and was available, and from the expression on his face whenever their eyes met, he felt the same way about her.

If he didn't kiss her this evening, she'd be extremely disappointed.

She was quiet on the short drive back, all talked out and feeling somewhat anxious about how the evening would end. It wasn't an uncomfortable silence, though. Soft music filled the air, and she let it wash over her. He'd chosen a Julien Baker album this time, and as the car drifted to the kerb as Huw pulled up outside her house, the haunting melody of 'Favor' was playing.

He switched the engine off and turned in his seat. 'I'll walk you to your door,' he said, and she immediately knew the reason for his offer.

He could have kept the engine running, he could have stayed in his seat, he could easily have pecked her on the cheek again if he so wished.

But he was doing none of those things.

Instead, he was holding her door open so she could slide smoothly out, then he gently caught hold of her elbow and led her up the short path.

Rowena turned to face him. 'Thank you,' she said quietly. 'I've had a lovely time.'

'So have I. May I kiss you?'

She was surprised he'd asked. None of her other boyfriends had ever bothered.

'I'd like that,' she said, and lifted her face towards him, her invitation clear.

Huw moved closer until they were almost touching, and she could feel the heat of his body seeping through the thin material of her dress.

But he didn't gather her to him, as she assumed he would. Instead, he cupped her cheek with one hand. Her eyelids drifted shut and her lips parted. She could sense his mouth hovering over hers and she let out a soft slow breath, anticipation throbbing along her veins and making her heart pound.

His lips were feather-soft, a mere breath of a touch, and impatient for more she leant into him, deepening the kiss as her tongue found his and her arms wrapped around his neck to draw him closer.

He didn't let her, but pulled back slightly, and for a second she feared he was going to push her away and her heart sank at the imminent rejection. Then he whispered, 'We've got an audience,' and she realised they were being watched.

When Rowena opened her eyes, it was to find Huw gazing at her, his disappointment evident. She saw her own desire reflected in his face and she laughed softly.

'That's the problem with having kids,' she explained. 'They've got brilliant timing.'

'It's not your daughter, it's your friend,' he said, and she heard the frustrated amusement in his voice.

Rowena released him and stepped back. 'For goodness' sake,' she hissed. 'Can't a woman have a bit of privacy?'

'We are standing on your doorstep,' Huw pointed out. 'The whole street could take a gander if they wanted.'

She shook her head. 'They probably already have,' she groaned.

'Does it bother you?'

She studied him, noting his concern. 'Not in the slightest. Although I would prefer it if Nia didn't find out that I was kissing a man on the doorstep.'

'Do you think she will?'

'I hope not.' She let out a laugh. 'Oh, well, if she does, she does. It's not as though I do this every day of the week.'

'Glad to hear it.'

'You're the first,' she admitted.

'The first?'

'The first man I've kissed since I had Nia. If I'm honest, you're the first man I've actually been on a date with.'

'I am?' A delighted grin spread across his face.

'Don't get all uppity and think you're something special,' she warned.

'I won't,' he assured her, but he was still grinning. 'Does that mean you'll go out with me again?'

'I suppose I'd better – we've got unfinished business.' She caught her bottom lip between her teeth and raised her eyebrows suggestively. Then she burst out laughing as his smug grin disappeared and desire replaced it. 'You owe me a kiss,' she said. 'Nothing more. So don't get any ideas.'

'I'll settle for a kiss.' He began to walk away, then called, 'For now,' over his shoulder, and it was Rowena's turn to feel a spike of desire lance her in the stomach.

She was wondering whether she should ask him when their next date was to be, or whether the question would make her sound desperate, when he whirled sharply on his heel and in three strides he had scooped her into his arms and his mouth was on hers once more.

This time there was no tentative fluttering.

His lips were hungry and demanding, and he kissed her with a possessiveness that left her breathless.

Just as abruptly, he released her, and she was left giddy with longing and need.

'That's to be going on with,' he said, his eyes full of promise.

Then he was in his car, and with one final long lingering look he was gone, leaving Rowena wanting more. Much, much more.

Which had probably been his intention all along, damn him.

Chapter 11

'You didn't say much when you came home last night,' Betsan remonstrated as soon as Rowena opened the door to her the following morning.

Rowena pulled a face. 'I was tired and I wanted to go to bed. Thank you again for babysitting.' She gestured for Betsan to come inside, knowing there would be no getting rid of her until she got what she wanted, so she may as well put the kettle on and enjoy a cuppa with their natter. That wasn't to say Rowena wasn't going to make her friend work for it.

Betsan pulled out one of the kitchen chairs and dropped down into it. 'I saw you, you know. Kissing him. Come on, spill the beans.'

'If you saw, you'll know there were no beans to spill. It was a quick kiss, that's all.' Rowena deliberately didn't look at Betsan as she busied herself by getting some mugs out of the cupboard.

'More like two,' Betsan retorted. 'And they weren't that quick.'

'I can't believe you were spying on me.' Rowena pretended to be cross.

'I was just looking out for you,' Betsan argued.

'Being nosey, more like.'

Her friend grinned. 'Guilty as charged. Go on then, you can't leave it at that, you've got to tell me what happened.'

'Nothing happened,' Rowena insisted. 'You saw for yourself.'

Betsan waved a hand in the air. 'I mean what was the meal like, what did you talk about, are you seeing him again?'

'The meal was nice.' Rowena looked away, being deliberately awkward. This was fun!

'Grr, stop being so annoying!' Betsan growled with irritation.

Rowena poured boiling water into the teapot and put the lid on. She'd let it brew for a few minutes before she made the tea.

'All right,' she said, deciding to put her friend out of her misery. 'It was lovely,' she said, holding up her hands and seeing Betsan's annoyed face. 'The whole evening was lovely. I really like him,' she confessed.

Betsan smirked. 'I could tell. When are you seeing him again?'

'Now that I come to think of it, we didn't actually agree on a day.' She frowned and glanced at her mobile which was sitting on the worktop, wondering whether he'd messaged her.

'There's something else, isn't there?' Betsan probed.

'I really like him,' Rowena repeated, wrinkling her nose.

'Yeah, you said. Is that a problem?'

'Nia is the problem.'

'I don't understand. Why is she a problem?'

Rowena wasn't quite sure how to explain it, but she gave it a go. 'It's *because* I like him so much,' she began. 'I don't want to get in any deeper in case Nia doesn't like him, or he's no good around children. I can't have someone in my life who doesn't accept her. But on the other hand, I don't want Nia to get to know him until I'm sure how I feel about him. I refuse to be the type of mother who has boyfriends coming and going, and her children don't know where they stand.'

Betsan snorted. 'You haven't had a boyfriend or even gone on a date since you came back to Foxmore, so you're hardly "that kind" of mother.' She made quotation marks in the air with her fingers. 'If you are so worried about falling in love with him and then discovering that Nia doesn't like him, or that he's hopeless with children, hadn't you better get the introductions out of the way and see how he behaves with her? At least you'll know one way or the other,' she added.

'I'm not sure.' Rowena chewed at her lip. Her instinct, like any parent's, was to protect her child at all costs, and she didn't want Nia to become fond of Huw in case their relationship didn't go any further. Talk about being caught between a rock and a hard place. She felt as though she was damned if she did, and damned if she didn't.

She brightened. 'Nia *has* met him before – twice actually. The first time he was a bit odd, but that's when he thought I was Terry's wife.' Rowena sniggered. 'Nia referred to him as "the funny man". And the other time was when we were on our way home after Terry's birthday lunch, when he asked me to have a drink with him.' She narrowed her eyes as she recalled the conversation. 'He seemed OK with her. It's difficult to tell from just a couple of minutes.'

'It's a start,' Betsan acknowledged. 'How about you invite him to go for a walk and bring Nia along? If it bothers you that much, you could even pretend to meet him by accident instead, rather than make it a formal thing. Nia would never know. She'd just think he was a friend, the same as if you had met me while you were out for a stroll.'

'Hardly! You're not just a friend, are you? She regards you as a surrogate mother.'

'Aw, that's sweet – but you know what I mean. If you don't make a big thing out of it, neither will she. She'll base her reaction on how you behave, so if you appear casual, then she won't think anything of it.'

'That's an idea, and it might help break the ice and allow her to get to know Huw a little. What do you think he will make of it? Will he think I'm trying to become a bit more serious if I introduce him to my daughter?'

'Tell you what, how about if you come clean and explain?'

'*What?* Tell him I really fancy him and really like him and might be starting to fall for him, so perhaps it is time he met my daughter? You can't be serious?'

'I don't see why not. It's all well and good this pussy-footing around and second-guessing yourself, but will it help matters? Will it address the problem?'

'But what if I frighten him off?'

Betsan shrugged. 'You'll have your answer, won't you? And there's no harm done either to you – apart from hurt pride maybe – or to Nia. You'll be able to stop thinking about him and move on.'

'What if I don't *want* to move on?'

'You know the answer to that. If Nia doesn't get on with him, you'll *have* to.'

'I suppose.'

'Crikey, I've never seen you this het up over a fella before.'

'That's because there's not been a fella to get het up over,' Rowena shot back. She pursed her lips. 'You're right. Perhaps I could take a walk down by the river with Nia tomorrow, and arrange to meet him there.' She thought for a moment. 'I could make a picnic and invite him to eat with us. What do you think?'

'I think it's an excellent idea. If nothing else, Nia will enjoy the picnic, and at least you'll know one way or the other.'

'Right, I'll phone him,' she decided.

'Do it now,' Betsan urged. 'Before you chicken out.'

With her heart in her mouth, Rowena dialled Huw's number, and waited for him to answer with hands that shook a little. Gosh, she really did have it bad.

His voice was warm and soft when he answered. 'Hello, you.'

'Um, hi,' she replied, conscious that Betsan was listening to every word. 'Wait a sec.' She gave her friend a meaningful look and pointed to the garden, before slipping outside and closing the door behind her. 'I enjoyed last night,' she said, even though she'd told him that already. Her voice was as warm as his.

'So did I. When can I see you again?'

'Er, that's why I was calling. I wanted to… um… it's like this…' Tongue-tied and embarrassed, she ground to a halt.

'Ah, I see.' He sounded flat, and she suddenly realised what he must be thinking.

'It's not what you think,' she hurried to tell him, and rushed on. 'I want you to meet Nia. Properly. I know you've met her already, but—' Damn it. This was awkward. She took a deep breath. 'I'm just going to come right out and say it, and if you think I'm coming on too strong, or I'm scaring you off, then so be it. I like you and I want to see you again,' she said, 'but there won't be any point unless Nia likes you too. And you like her. So, I wondered if you'd meet us for a picnic tomorrow?'

Huw was silent.

'Are you still there?' She hoped he hadn't hung up on her.

'I'm still here. I like you, too, and I completely understand what you're saying. I'd love to meet you and Nia for a picnic.'

After arranging a time and a place, Rowena ended the call. Her heart was thumping and her cheeks felt hot. Blimey, that had been embarrassing, but he'd taken it in his stride and he had told her that he liked her.

It was a start.

And a damned promising one, at that!

–

When Rowena phoned him yesterday and had been so hesitant, Huw had immediately jumped to the conclusion that she was going to tell him that she didn't want to see him again, and in that moment between him thinking it and her telling him the reason for her call, the disappointment he'd felt had been acute.

His subsequent relief had been just as intense, and after he'd put the phone down he'd discovered that his hands were clammy and his heart was going nineteen to the dozen.

All yesterday and well into the evening until sleep claimed him, he'd mulled over the implications of Rowena wanting him to get to know her daughter, and vice versa. He guessed the decision must have been a hard one for her to come to, and his respect for her grew even more for her telling him how she felt. In his experience, not many women were as open and honest, and he could only guess what it must have cost her.

Rowena, he was coming to realise, didn't play games. Underneath what appeared to be a shy and retiring exterior, she was honest and forthright. He was also beginning to suspect she didn't take any prisoners: if she decided Nia didn't like him or he didn't meet Rowena's standards when it came to her daughter, he'd be toast. And he respected her for that, too. He mightn't have had much to do with children, but he could appreciate that Nia came first, and that was how it should be.

Although Rowena had mentioned they should pretend to bump into each other, he nevertheless wanted to contribute to the picnic, so yesterday he'd popped into the convenience store and had bought a couple of bottles of Shloer, which were now nicely chilled in his fridge. He'd also taken the bull by the horns and had knocked on the vicarage door.

To say that Betsan was surprised to see him was an understatement. But when he told her what he was after, she had beamed at him and had led him through the house and into the garden. In the shed, she had handed him a kid's fishing net on a bamboo pole, and a bucket.

'I had a hunch you might have one or two of these lying around,' he said to her.

'I take it you want to make a good impression?' was Betsan's reply.

He just hoped that Rowena wouldn't object to him paddling in the shallows with Nia, but he remembered how much fun he'd had as a kid when he'd dabbled for minnows and freshwater shrimp in the River Taff, and he hoped Nia would be just as enthused.

Besides, he'd also find it fun, he thought, as he packed the cold bottles of sparkling grape juice into a small backpack, hung the bucket from a strap at the side, picked up the net and set off.

He felt a little self-conscious carrying a child's fishing net, but he hoped it would be worth the odd looks he was receiving from dog walkers and anglers alike as he trotted down the rough path which ran alongside the river.

As rivers went, this one wasn't particularly wide, but it was incredibly picturesque, with mountains rising above it which sported a patchwork of fields and woodland on their lower slopes. Everywhere he looked was green and lush. Birds sang and the river gurgled, and once again he felt incredibly lucky to live in such a beautiful and tranquil place.

He was heading for the bend in the river where Rowena said she'd be waiting, and when he reached it, his heart soared at the sight of her. She was taking a throw out of a bag and spreading out on the grass. Her back was to him, and she didn't see him until he'd walked closer, but when Nia tugged on the hem of her T-shirt and said something, she turned around and a huge smile lit up her face.

'It's Huw, the funny man – only you're not supposed to call him that,' Rowena said, and Nia hid a giggle behind her hand. 'Hi, Huw.' She waved him over.

'Hello, what are you doing here?' he asked, slipping into the role she wanted him to play.

'We're just about to have a picnic. Would you like to join us?'

'What does Nia say?' he asked. 'Can I have one of your sandwiches? Can you spare one, or do you want to eat them all yourself?'

'We've got tuna and ham,' Nia said.

'In the same sandwich?' Huw pretended to look horrified.

Nia looked up at her mother. 'See, he is funny,' she insisted. 'No, silly—' this was said to him '—that would be nasty. Yuck!' She wrinkled her little nose.

'I tell you what – I'll swap you a sandwich for a glass of this.' He slipped his rucksack off his shoulder and brought out one of the bottles with a flourish.

Nia looked uncertain. 'Mammy... can I? Is it wine?' she asked him.

'It's better than wine,' he said to her. 'It's called Shloer and it's lovely and fizzy.'

'Yes, you can have some, but only if you let Huw have a sandwich,' her mother bartered. 'Deal?'

'Deal.' Nia nodded emphatically.

'Good, I'm starving.' Huw rubbed his stomach. 'I've not got any food in the house, so I was going to catch some fish for my tea.' He held up the net. 'I've got a bucket

141

to put them in when I catch them. See?' He showed her the bucket dangling from one of the straps.

'Mammy, can we let him have a piece of cake, too? Fish isn't nice.'

'I think she feels sorry for you,' Rowena said, as he handed her the Shloer. 'This puts my bottle of squash to shame.'

He leant closer and lowered his voice. 'I wanted to make a good impression. I also thought I might need some bargaining power. If you're OK with it, I thought Nia and I might have a paddle and see what we can catch. I used to love doing that when I was a kid. You're welcome to paddle, too,' he added. 'I promise we won't go in above our ankles.'

'I've got to warn you, she'll talk your ear off.'

'Isn't that why I'm here – so she can get to know me?'

'And for you to get to know her,' Rowena pointed out. 'This is a two-way thing.'

He nodded to show that he understood and was taking it seriously. Then he felt a tug on his sleeve. 'I think she wants me to sit down,' he said, as Nia tugged at him again.

'Mammy made fairy cakes,' she announced. 'Want one?'

'After my sandwich,' he said, earning himself an approving look from her mother.

So far, so good, he said to himself. He'd been nervous about spending time with the child, not sure how he should behave or what he should say, but as the picnic progressed he started to relax. Nia was a delightful little girl, talkative and precocious, and several times some of the things she said had him laughing out loud.

'She's a credit to you,' he said, when Nia finished eating and had wandered into the meadow behind to gather daisies to make a chain. She was going to teach Huw how to make one, and he looked forward to learning a new skill, even if it was one he might never have call to use again.

'She's a good kid,' Rowena said. 'She does have her moments, though.'

'Don't we all!'

'Pray tell?'

'Erm, maybe another time. You don't need to hear that I hung up on my sister the other day because she was being annoying. I don't do childish things like that.' He gave her a sideways look, a smile playing about his mouth.

'Glad to hear it – one child in my family is enough,' she retorted, then she turned scarlet as she realised what she'd said. Could she possibly be allowing herself to think that one day he might become part of her family? It was an interesting thought.

Thankfully Nia distracted them by dumping a squashed handful of sorry-looking daisies into his lap, then plonking herself down beside him and announcing that she was going to make him a daisy crown.

Huw caught Rowena's eye and smiled softly at her. Her blush deepened when he continued to gaze into her face, but she didn't look away and it was Huw who broke the connection first. He had to, because he didn't have any choice: Nia was waving a hand in front of his face to get his attention!

Rowena propped her bag on the ground behind her and leant against it, the throw under her backside and the sun on her face.

It was a perfect early summer afternoon. The air was filled with the smell of freshly mown grass and growing things, the scent of the river, and the lingering aroma of red grape fizz and Huw's aftershave. The sun was hot, but not unpleasantly so, and there was a faint breeze channelling itself across the surface of the water to waft across her pink cheeks. She was still blushing from the comment she'd made earlier, and she cringed. What on earth must Huw think of her, implying that he was family when they hardly knew each other.

He hadn't appeared to be too perturbed, and she hoped he'd taken it as a slip of the tongue.

However, the three of them did make a nice family unit, and if anyone had happened to walk past they could be forgiven for thinking that was what they were. She had to admit that Huw and Nia did look like they could be father and daughter, as she watched him help her take her socks and trainers off, then held her hand as Nia tottered unsteadily over the coarse shingle which had formed a small beach dotted with pebbles and rocks.

Nia's squeal was ear-piercing when her warm toes touched the cold water, but she was laughing too, and she laughed even harder when Huw yelled and hopped around, pretending to be appalled that the water was so cold.

It was very shallow on this bank, and Rowena remembered paddling here when she was younger. As a teenager, she and her friends used to dare each other to swim out of their depth, heading for the opposite side where the river ran deep and still, and the overhanging trees shaded the surface of the water, making it appear dark and mysterious.

She watched her daughter settle down as her feet became used to the chill, and soon she was happily dipping her net into the little pools between the rocks where fish liked to hide. Now and again Huw would turn a rock over to see if there were any freshwater snails underneath, and every so often their two heads would come together as they peered at something.

Rowena couldn't decide whether she was relieved that they got on so well, or concerned about it. Because with that hurdle out of the way, it meant she didn't have any excuse not to allow herself to fall in love with him.

After seeing the way he behaved with her daughter, Rowena was halfway there already. He was a natural with her, no forced jollity or false enthusiasm, and although she knew that neither he nor his sister had children, he behaved as though he'd been around kids all his life.

Or maybe he was just re-enacting his own childhood, she mused with a fond smile. Nia had a habit of bringing people down to her level, in more ways than one, Rowena thought, as she saw Huw crouch down beside the child to examine the contents of the bucket.

Nia glanced around and, seeing she had her mother's attention, she gave her a wave and a big smile. It made Rowena's heart sing to see her daughter having such a good time. This was the kind of thing Terry used to do with his kids, and often still did with Nia now that his own had almost flown the nest.

That was it! Watching Nia and Huw together reminded her of Nia and Terry. Huw interacted with her child in the same way as Terry did, giving her his full attention, his expression alive with interest. Huw hadn't once seemed bored or appeared to wish he was sitting on the blanket with her instead of playing with Nia.

And it was then that she knew she could easily fall in love with this man. Heck, she was a bit in love with him already, and for once the thought of having a man in her and her daughter's life didn't scare her. If the truth be told, she was looking forward to it.

–

'Huw said it was a herrin, Mammy.'

'A herrin?' Huw had walked Rowena and Nia home, gallantly carrying her large bag when she had been forced to pick up a tired but happy Nia. And now Rowena was attempting to persuade her daughter that she needed to have a bath and get ready for bed. They'd been home a couple of hours, Huw having deposited them at their house with a ruffle to Nia's head and a smile for Rowena, and Nia hadn't stopped talking about him or her riverside adventure since.

Huw hadn't made any attempt to kiss her, and Rowena, although she'd desperately wanted to feel his lips on hers again, had appreciated his restraint and perception – he must have guessed that she wouldn't welcome any physical show of affection between them in front of Nia. Instead, he'd walked off with a promise to be in touch soon, and she'd watched him stroll away, the now-empty bucket swinging from a strap on his backpack, the net in his hand, and a circlet of drooping and slightly crushed daisies in his hair.

It was the daisies that did it – he'd kept them in and that had meant the world to Nia, because the child was as proud as Punch that she'd managed to make a daisy chain and he'd agreed to wear it.

'Yes, a herrin,' Nia repeated.

'Do you mean a heron? Big bird, tall, long neck, long legs, standing in the water like this?' Rowena tried to do a heron impression as she stalked around the bedroom, which had Nia in fits of laughter.

'You're silly!'

Rowena pouted. 'Are you making fun of my heron impression?'

'Huw did it better.'

'He did?' Rowena pulled the pyjama top over Nia's head, and her daughter's voice was muffled until she popped out of the neck.

'He did a duck and a swan. We didn't see any swans, though. But there were lots of ducks.'

'How many?'

Nia held up her hands, showing all ten fingers. 'Twenty-three.'

'That many, eh?'

'Uh huh. And a moorhen. But I liked the stickybacks best.'

'Sticklebacks,' Rowena corrected. 'I think you had a good time today.'

'Can Huw take me fishing again?'

'We'll see.'

'Awww.' Nia pulled a face. 'You always say we'll see, when you mean no.'

Rowena kissed her on the nose. 'Huw might be too busy to take you fishing,' she said.

'Can you ask him? I want to catch an eel.'

'Ugh. They're all long, and wriggly, and slimy,' she cried, tickling her daughter, who screeched with laughter and began to squirm.

Finally, after Nia had eaten her supper and brushed her teeth, she was ready for bed, but before Rowena read her a story, Nia stood on the bed, caught Rowena's face in her hands and announced, 'Mammy, I like Huw. He's nice. If you want to marry him, I don't mind.'

Rowena blinked. 'Marry *Huw*?'

'Uh huh.' Nia released her, and dropped down onto her backside, the mattress bouncing.

'What if I don't want to get married?'

'Princesses have to marry.' Nia was quite firm.

'Princesses don't have to marry at all. In fact, princesses can do whatever they like.'

'Can I be a bridesmaid?'

Rowena narrowed her eyes. 'Is that the reason you want me to get married, so you can be a bridesmaid?'

'Sioned is going to be a bridesmaid.' Nia looked away, and Rowena burst out laughing.

'I'm not going to get married just because you want to be a bridesmaid like Sioned,' she said. 'If I get married, it will be because I love someone and want to be with them.'

'That's OK, then,' Nia said, scooting down under the duvet. 'When you and Huw get married, can I wear a pink dress and a tiara?'

Rowena was thunderstruck. Nia was getting a little ahead of herself.

But even as she tucked her in and kissed her goodnight, her daughter's conviction lingered in her mind, and as she turned the possibility over, a smile curved her lips – because marrying Huw wasn't as outrageous as it seemed.

The thought was quickly followed by the realisation that she hadn't been as good at hiding her growing feelings for him as she'd thought.

Chapter 12

Rowena couldn't resist taking a peep through the grimy windows of the corner shop as she walked Nia home from school on Tuesday. Cupping her hands around her face, she peered inside, then laughed as Nia did the same.

'What's in there, Mammy?'

'Nothing at the moment. It's empty. See?'

'Why is it empty?'

'Because the people who used to own it decided they didn't want to sell anything anymore.'

'Why—?' Nia was distracted from asking another question by someone calling Rowena's name.

Rowena tore her gaze away to find Dee hurrying towards her. 'I was hoping to catch you,' she said. 'Have you made a decision yet?' She glanced meaningfully at the shop.

'Yes, and no. I really want to rent it and the price is good, but it all depends on my friendly business manager at the bank. I hope he *is* friendly,' she added quickly. 'I've not met him yet. I've got an appointment on Monday, so I can't commit to anything until I've met with him first. It's all so up in the air at the moment.'

'I'll keep my fingers crossed for you,' Dee said.

'I'm hopeful,' Rowena replied. 'But you never know,' she cautioned, not wanting to sound too confident in case she came a cropper.

Dee pulled a face. 'By the way, I think the cat is out of the bag. Everyone knows about your plans to open a zero waste shop.'

'My mam found out that I'd gone to have a look at it and asked me why, so I had to tell her, then Mrs Moxley overheard, and so did Janet and Rachel,' Rowena explained.

'I think it's a fabulous idea. I, for one, will shop there.'

'If it gets off the ground,' Rowena reminded her.

'I can name all the colours of the rainbow,' Nia announced, and began to reel them off. 'Red, orange, yellow, pink—'

'I don't think pink is one of them,' Rowena said, smiling down at her.

'It is,' Nia insisted. 'I painted a rainbow and it's got pink in it.'

Rowena bit her lip, holding back a laugh. However, her mirth was soon replaced by exasperation when Dee said, 'I've heard you've been seeing Huw Morgan.'

'It's no secret.' Even if she wanted it to be, it was almost impossible to keep one if you lived in Foxmore.

'You went for a drink, and a meal,' Dee said, raising her brows knowingly.

Nia said, 'We had a picnic and Huw taught me to tickle stickybacks. And we saw a herrin – I mean a heron. He's funny.'

Dee gazed at Nia. 'The heron?'

'No, Huw. He pretended to be a heron. He had a net and a bucket.' She said that as though a net and a bucket were the most important things in the world. Which, Rowena thought, was probably the case if you were four and you wanted to catch small fish.

'I'm going to wear a pink dress,' she said, but before her daughter could say anything further Rowena leapt in with, 'How about fish fingers for tea?'

'Yay!' Nia hopped up and down.

'And a corn on the cob?'

'With butter?'

'Of course, with butter.' At this precise moment Rowena would have given in to any request her daughter made as long as it took Nia's mind off wearing a pink dress and the occasion on which she hoped to wear it. She could do without a rumour such as that circulating, thank you very much!

'Come on,' Rowena said. 'Let's get you fed and watered. Bye, Dee...' Rowena ground to a halt as something caught her attention.

A car was pulling out of a side road, indicating to turn right. For a fraction of a second, before it made the turn, Rowena had a clear view of the driver.

Her heart stopped, there was a rushing noise in her ears, and she suddenly felt clammy, because she could have sworn that someone she had never expected to see again was behind the wheel – *Finn Bowen*.

–

Some days it was possible to finish work early and some days it wasn't. Today was an early finish day. Huw had achieved everything he'd set out to achieve, and had even wrapped up some of those annoying things that were so bitty that he tended to put them off.

It was with a feeling of bunking off school early that he left the office and headed back to Foxmore and the walk he intended to go on. It was a lovely afternoon and he wasn't going to waste this unexpected free time by lazing in front of the telly or doing chores.

Briefly, he debated messaging Rowena to ask if she would like to join him, then realised she'd be picking Nia up from school and would probably want to spend some time with her daughter after not having seen her all day – apart from during her stint as a dinner lady, of course, but he guessed that didn't count as she would have had goodness knows how many other charges to keep an eye on.

He'd speak to her later, after Nia had gone to bed, and they could firm up their next date. He suspected it would be the weekend again, and he wondered where he could take her. If she was able to find a babysitter, they could brave The Jolly Fox for a second time, or try another restaurant, although he was conscious that eating out was expensive and with Rowena insisting that they go Dutch, she mightn't have the funds to spare.

If she couldn't get a babysitter in the evening, maybe they could do something during the day instead. She'd told him that her mum usually had Nia for a good chunk of most Saturdays, so perhaps they could go on a hike, or pay a visit to a castle, or maybe they could head into Dolgellau and see a matinee? There was bound to be a film showing that they both liked.

He was still none the wiser by the time he got home, had changed into more suitable gear, and was heading back out again, so he decided to shelve the problem for the time being and enjoy his walk.

Setting off from the cottage, he passed behind the church and made his way to the footpath running through some fields adjacent to the main road. He'd follow that path for a while, then take a right and head up the hill towards Aled Harris's farm, but before he reached it, he'd veer off, his target being the impressive tump rising directly beyond it. From there, he'd have a great view of Foxmore and, if the conditions were right and it wasn't too hazy, he might even be able to make out the coast in the distance.

The weather wasn't quite as nice as he'd hoped, but he didn't mind, he was just glad to be out in the fresh air. And anyway, if it was too hot, it would make stomping up a ruddy great hill rather uncomfortable.

He was just getting into his stride, his arms swinging, his legs in a rhythm that would carry him for miles, when he noticed two men in the distance. They were standing to one side of the field and gazing out over the hedge and into the road beyond. It wasn't a particularly busy lane but there was enough traffic to make walking along it rather dicey, hence his decision to use the footpath which crossed the fields, even if it did take him out of his way a little. Anyway, it was much more pleasant having earth and grass underfoot than dusty tarmac, so he didn't mind the extra half a mile or so, and the additional exercise would also do him good.

As he grew closer, the breeze brought snippets of the men's conversation to his ears.

'…always has been a beacon for walkers. And families. There are two caravan parks nearby, and…'

Huw clambered over a stile and dropped lightly to the ground on the other side, and once again the men's voices drifted towards him. He recognised one of them as being Aled Harris. He didn't know the other, but the guy looked out of place standing in an overgrown field while wearing a suit. Even from this distance, he looked a sharp dresser, and Huw thought regretfully of his own considerably scruffier formal attire languishing in his wardrobe at home.

'Yes, you mentioned that in your email,' the man was saying. 'Which is one of the reasons I'm here. That, and the fact that the nearest decent-sized supermarket is ten miles and a twenty-minute drive away.'

'Aye, but only if the holiday traffic is light and there aren't any road works, otherwise it's more like thirty. I'm telling you, this place is ripe for it.'

Huw wondered what exactly it was ripe for. Neither man had noticed him yet, but he kept on walking, hoping to get past before they did. The last thing he wanted this afternoon was to be drawn into a conversation with Aled.

'And don't let the size of the village fool you,' Aled said, his voice growing louder as Huw approached. 'You've got to take all the outlying farms and hamlets into consideration, and when you factor in that these fields are only a mile from the A470, less as the crow flies, there's bound to be more people who'd want to come here, rather than drive all that way.'

'One point three, to be exact. And I'm well aware that Foxmore's resident population was only 1800 at the last census, but is larger when the surrounding hamlets are included. We've calculated the catchment area to be within acceptable limits. Add campers, caravaners, cottage renters and second-home owners to the equation, and the site appears profitable in a footfall sense. On paper, at least. But I must inform you that Foxmore isn't the only location we're interested in, and it's my job to do due diligence on any locations deemed ripe for development.'

The guy sounded pompous, but Aled seemed to be lapping it up and was hanging on his every word.

'All right, Aled,' Huw said as he passed, and he noticed with amusement that Aled jumped in surprise.

'What are you doing here?' he demanded.

'Just out for a walk,' Huw replied mildly, wondering what had rattled Aled's cage, before it occurred to him that the man in the suit might be behind the cryptic comments the farmer had been making.

Aled scowled, and Huw imagined he could feel the man's stare drilling a hole in his back as he carried on walking. He did manage to have a quick gander at the other man's suit though, and his first impression from a distance was confirmed as he scanned it on the way past. If Huw wasn't mistaken it was hand-made and his shirt was crisp and white, the tie possibly silk.

As he strode on, Huw wondered what development Foxmore might be ripe for. Housing, possibly? A new holiday complex? He hoped it wasn't the latter – it would change the vibe of the village. But he was also aware that rural places such as the one that he had moved to might benefit from additional opportunities for employment. He'd been lucky in that he'd been able to negotiate a transfer – otherwise he would never have been able to contemplate purchasing his lovely cottage.

Oh well, no doubt he'd find out in due course. From what Rowena had told him nothing stayed a secret in Foxmore for long.

Putting Aled and his mysterious visitor out of his head, Huw carried on with his hike, letting the peace of the

Welsh countryside wash over him as he left the fields in the valley floor behind, and began to climb up the hillside. Soon he was on the mountain proper with its steep slopes and windswept blanket of heather and bracken. Now and again a solitary tree, bent and shaped by the wind, valiantly poked its head above the waist-high ferns, but even those thinned out as he reached the top of the mountain.

Breathing deeply, his heart pounding from the exertion, Huw scanned the valley below, picking out Foxmore, and even the road on which his house sat. Then his eyes tracked left; he thought he could see Rowena's, but it was difficult to tell because there was a stand of trees in the way. All he could see was the chimney pot and a sliver of grey slate roof.

Sitting down to enjoy the view, he took out his water bottle and drank deeply.

He still had difficulty believing that all this beauty was on his doorstep. Unlike when he lived in Cardiff, where there had always been a car journey involved, even if it was only a short one, he didn't need to drive anywhere to enjoy this.

There was no need to hurry home, so he decided to stay a while longer and enjoy the serenity. He would have liked to have watched the sun go down, but he hadn't brought a head torch and he didn't want to risk wandering off the track and the very real possibility of falling and twisting an ankle, so he left it as late as he dared and until his tummy began to rumble, then he got to his feet to begin the far easier descent.

By the time he'd reached the village he'd finished all his water and was feeling thirsty. Hungry, too, but food could wait, as he fancied popping into the pub for a pint to round off his walk. He considered ordering a meal but he had plenty of food at home that needed using up, so after buying a pint of Potter's Clay ale, he took himself off to the snug. Food wasn't served in there, so he'd be out of temptation's way, so to speak. It was also quieter, and he wasn't in the mood for lots of noise and bustle.

There was only one other person in there, he saw, when he pushed the door open with his shoulder and went inside – and it was someone he recognised.

Sitting at a table with a laptop in front of him was the snappy-suited man from earlier. He'd shed his jacket and had removed his tie, and looked considerably more casual, but it was definitely the same guy. Curling dark hair sat above a chiselled jaw and sharp cheekbones, and dark brown, almost black eyes met his as Huw went to the other side of the small room and took a seat. He was a good-looking fella, Huw thought.

The man nodded at him, and Huw nodded back. The man returned to studying his laptop and Huw took out his phone. There were a couple of messages from friends back in Cardiff, a funny video or two, a photo from Ceri of her eating an enormous cake and getting cream on her nose, but not much else. He still hadn't decided where to go or what to do on his next date with Rowena, and he was carrying out an inventory in his head, aided by a casual trawl of local attractions on the internet, when the door opened again and Aled Harris stuck his head around it.

The farmer scowled when he spied Huw, but his attention was mostly on the other guy in the room. 'I thought you'd left, but Dai mentioned you were in here.'

The man looked up from his laptop. 'I decided to stay the night. Get a bit more of a feel for the place.'

'I'm gonna have to tell them something. They've been asking questions.' Aled jerked a thumb towards the bar and scowled at Huw again.

Huw looked blankly at him, wondering what he was being accused of.

'Who are "they"?' the guy asked.

'Them, in there. Someone saw me talking to you.' Aled shot Huw a venomous look, and Huw shook his head.

'Not me, mate,' he said, mildly irritated.

'Yeah, well… Anyway, what do I tell them?'

The man rose and walked towards Aled. He took hold of the farmer's elbow and turned him away, so their backs were to Huw.

Normally Huw wouldn't have bothered to listen, but for one, Aled had got his back up by accusing him of something he hadn't done, and two, he was intrigued. There was clearly something going on and he wanted to know what.

Straining to listen to the hushed conversation, he heard the guy in the suit say, 'You tell them nothing, not until everything has been signed and sealed. We've already—' He stopped abruptly and glanced over his shoulder.

Hastily, Huw dipped his head and stared at his phone, but from the way the guy lowered his voice even further he guessed his eavesdropping had been noticed. Now all that he could hear was a whispered rumble, mainly coming from the guy in the suit, and when he risked looking up again Huw saw Aled nodding.

He turned his attention back to his phone, and only looked up again when he heard the door open and close. The guy returned to his seat.

For some reason, Huw felt a little uncomfortable, as though he'd witnessed something he shouldn't, but he had no idea what – unless he'd guessed correctly and there *were* plans to build new houses in the area.

Although he was in two minds about Foxmore expanding, he was aware of the need for more affordable housing in this part of Wales, so maybe it would be a good thing. At least it would bring more people into the village, and that would mean more customers for Rowena, if she went ahead with opening her shop.

With a sigh, he finished his pint and left, his head now filled with thoughts of Rowena and what he was going to do to wow her on their next date.

Chapter 13

Date number four. This was getting to be a regular Friday night habit, and one which Rowena didn't want to break. If anything, she would like to see Huw more often, but it was difficult when she had Nia to consider. She was reluctant to deviate from their weekday routine during term time when Nia had to get up for school the following morning; and Saturday evening was out because Nia was usually with her Nanny and Rowena wanted to spend it with her daughter because she wouldn't have seen her for the biggest part of the day.

It didn't give her much scope for love and romance, but she was determined to get the most out of whatever time she did manage to spend with Huw.

This evening they were going out for another meal, preferably somewhere not quite as expensive as The Falcon, because even though she'd only paid half of the resulting bill, the amount had made her eyes water. She had hung on to the money left to her by her grandmother for far too long to simply fritter it away on dining out. Anyway, she didn't know how much of it she'd need to use in order to get the shop up and running. She prayed she wouldn't have to use all of it, and that the bank would dip into its vastly deeper pockets.

As she was getting ready (casual and warm, Huw had told her), the house was quiet without Nia, who was currently at Betsan's house helping to make cakes for a church event tomorrow. Helping was a loose term, because Rowena knew from experience that Nia's help needed a great deal of help of its own. But the child loved baking, and enjoyed licking the bowl out even more, so Rowena was sure she'd have a good time. Betsan would then bring her home, bathe her and put her to bed, for which Rowena was immensely grateful. Which made her feel awful that she was keeping something from her friend, because Rowena had nearly fainted when she'd seen that all too familiar face in Foxmore on Tuesday. Thankfully either Dee hadn't noticed her reaction or Rowena had been better at hiding it than she'd realised, because she wanted to keep it to herself. Mainly because it was no one else's business, but also because, in hindsight, she was fairly sure she must have imagined it.

She'd only caught a fleeting glimpse and for a second she'd been utterly certain it had been Finn, before common sense had kicked in. Finn Bowen wouldn't be seen dead in a small rural village like Foxmore. He was a bright lights kind of man – unless he'd changed beyond recognition, and she didn't believe many leopards could change their spots so dramatically. Finn hadn't liked the outdoors: he hadn't liked rural places or small towns, or grass, or sheep, or anything to do with the countryside. He liked wine bars and theatres, fine dining, and sleek minimalist living.

It was his sophistication which had attracted her to him in the first place. Having come from a little village like Foxmore and then spending the next three years immersed in student life before getting her first proper job, she hadn't met anyone like Finn before. He had been assured, confident and worldly-wise, despite being only seven years older than her. Looking back, she supposed she had been ripe for his suave seduction, and she'd truly believed him when he had told her that he loved her.

But for a man like Finn, love must come easily and go just as easily, because he'd had no qualms about dumping her when a better prospect came along. Her only consolation at the time was that he'd left her for a job, and not another woman.

If he'd have asked her, she'd have happily moved to the Midlands with him.

But he hadn't asked, and she had refused to beg.

Maybe she would have been more insistent if she'd known she was pregnant, but by the time she'd realised that her lethargy and fatigue weren't due to a broken heart, he was long gone and had ended all contact with her weeks ago.

Then she'd discovered she was expecting.

Depressed, distraught and scared, she'd fled back to the safety of Foxmore and her mam, and she'd been there ever since.

Once the shock of thinking she had seen Finn behind the wheel of that car had worn off and she'd been able to think logically, Rowena arrived at the conclusion that she must have imagined him. Beginning her first proper relationship since Finn must have sent her subconscious into overdrive. By dating Huw, she was finally letting another man into her life, and into her daughter's, and she had to consider the possibility that if their relationship progressed Huw might one day be Nia's stepdad.

It was a scary thought, but one she had to face if she had any intention of falling in love again. She could hardly keep Nia at arm's length from him, hiding her daughter away, which was why she'd asked him to join them for a picnic last weekend.

Rowena hugged herself; it had gone so much better than she had anticipated. Huw had behaved perfectly, and Nia was already demanding to know when he'd take her fishing again. It warmed Rowena's heart to remember how kind and gentle Huw had been, how he'd not talked down to the child, or had been impatient with her. He may very well have acted like that to impress Rowena, but if he had, it had worked. She *was* impressed. Time would tell if Huw was genuine or whether it was an act. But even as she thought it, she knew deep down that he hadn't been acting. He'd hit it off with Nia and she with him.

Huw had arranged to pick Rowena up at six thirty, hence the reason Nia was at the vicarage, and Rowena wondered what he had in store for her. They were definitely eating out, but she didn't know where, and asking her to wear comfy warm clothing had puzzled her. The day had been a glorious one, the sun warm, and not a cloud in the sky. The temperature would drop when the sun went down because there was no cloud cover, but she didn't expect it to get too cold. Anyway, most pubs and restaurants with outside tables usually had heaters these days – although that was another thing she didn't agree with because of the amount of energy they wasted. But heigh-ho, it wasn't as though she did something like this every weekend, and the temperature might remain pleasant enough to warrant not turning the heater on.

Her heart flipped when she heard a knock on the door, and she rushed to grab her bag and her padded jacket. She wished she knew where they were going because she'd feel a little underdressed if they were going to a nice pub and she was wearing jeans and trainers, but when she saw that Huw was wearing roughly the same, she relaxed.

'Snap,' she said, spotting a puffer jacket on the back seat of his car, and she tossed hers on top of it; it was far too warm at the moment to have a thick coat on. 'Are you going to tell me where we're going?' she demanded as he started the engine.

'Barmouth,' he said.

'And? Are we going to a pub? A bar? Having fish and chips on the front? *What?*'

'The last one is closest to the mark, but not quite,' he grinned.

'Ooh!' she cried in frustration.

'You're not good with surprises, are you?'

'Not when I'm on the receiving end,' she said. She almost added that she'd had enough surprises to last her a lifetime – that she'd had the biggest surprise of all when she'd realised she was pregnant – but she kept quiet. It was too much information for so early in their relationship. When she got to know Huw better, she'd share some more. But she'd have to be very certain of his commitment and his love for her before she told him the name of Nia's father, and there was no guarantee they'd get that far, despite how attracted she was to him and how she was already developing feelings for him. They had a long way to go yet.

'OK, I'll put you out of your misery,' he said, his face wreathed in a smile, his eyes crinkling at the corners. 'We're going to a beach party.'

'Crumbs – I wasn't expecting that.'

'It should be good fun. There'll be bands, and stalls selling food, and beer tents, and a bonfire.' He glanced at her. 'Is that OK? I mean, we can go somewhere else, if you like.'

'No, it's perfect. What could be better than dancing on the beach?'

'Do you have to hurry home? I'm only asking because it doesn't really get started until the sun goes down.'

'Betsan is babysitting, so... Hang on a sec.' Rowena took her phone out and quickly thumbed a message off.

Within seconds she had a reply, and when she read it her face lit up. 'Betsan is going to keep Nia at her house for the night, so we can stay out as long as we like.' She felt like a kid playing truant. She also felt self-conscious, excited and slightly nervous. If Nia wasn't going to be at home, should Rowena invite Huw in when he dropped her off? And what would his expectations be, if she did? How far was she prepared to take things?

That consideration was for later, though. For the moment, she intended to enjoy herself.

Excitedly she leapt out of the car as soon as Huw pulled into a parking space, and gazed around. Barmouth was one of her favourite seaside destinations. Only a forty-or-so minute drive from Foxmore, the town was easy to get to and incredibly picturesque with its wide sandy beach, tufty sand dunes, pretty harbour and the river after which it was named flowing to the south of the town and emptying into the sea. Mountains provided a stunning backdrop, and the town itself had lots of lovely old stone houses and steep steps.

But it was the smell of woodsmoke, onions and candy-floss, overlying the salty scent of the sea, that caught Rowena's attention, and her stomach gurgled.

'Shall we have something to eat first?' Huw suggested.

'Yes, please!' But there were so many stalls dotted across the sand that she didn't know which to head for first, or what she fancied to eat, because she wanted to taste all of it. Except for the cockles and whelks – she wasn't too keen on those.

Eventually she decided on a bowl of Thai red curry, and Huw had the green, so they could share. After they'd sat on a dune, Rowena shared the meals out so both of them had a portion, and then she fell on the food with enthusiasm. There was something about eating in the open air that seemed to make her extra hungry and the food taste extra nice, and before she knew it, she'd scoffed the lot and was seriously thinking of going back for more.

'Would you think I was being greedy if I told you I'm still hungry?' she asked.

'Not at all! I'm relieved if I'm honest, because that curry didn't touch the sides. Shall we have a wander and see what else we fancy? I quite like sharing because I get to taste more than is on my plate.'

After he'd disposed of their rubbish, he held out his hand to pull her to her feet, and when she took it and he hauled her upright, he didn't let go, but kept hold of it, his skin warm against her palm, his fingers curled around hers. It seemed the most natural thing in the world to dawdle along the beach, hand in hand. She felt like a teenager again, young, carefree, and with nothing else on her mind except for the here and now. It was a novel experience for her. This evening she wasn't someone's mother – she was herself. Without having Nia to look after and worry about, she allowed herself to simply be, and although a little part of her wished her daughter was here because Nia would have loved this, Rowena didn't feel guilty for stealing a few hours for herself, for her own pleasure.

And pleasure it most definitely was, because after they'd shared a slice of pizza (her choice) and a hot dog (his), had eaten an enormous ice cream each, and had swigged ice-cold ginger beer, they were ready to dance.

A makeshift stage had been set up on the dry sand above the high-tide mark, and music blared from huge speakers on either side. The band was good, the beat intoxicating, and soon Rowena was swaying to the music, her arms in the air, her face raised to the sky, losing herself to the simple joy of dancing.

Huw seemed to be enjoying himself too, and every now and again he'd grab her around the waist and pull her to him. It felt natural that their lips would meet before the beat caught them again and spun them apart.

Whenever she caught his eye, she beamed at him, and once she yelled, 'I haven't had this much fun in years!'

She missed dancing, she realised, closing her eyes and letting the music fill her. She hadn't danced in nearly six years, not properly, not like this, with almost complete abandon. At the rare wedding that she'd been invited to she'd been restrained, self-conscious, and aware that she had responsibilities beyond her own enjoyment, and one eye had always been on Nia, making sure her daughter was behaving herself, making sure she was safe.

Rowena spun and whirled, twisted and dipped, without caring what other people thought. The only person whose opinion she cared about was having as much fun as she was. At some point their jackets had come off and so had their trainers, and on and on they danced, barefoot and happy, until eventually Rowena was so desperate for a drink she simply had to stop.

'Thirsty,' she gasped, leaning against Huw for support, holding his arm in a fierce grip in case she fell over. She could still feel the beat thudding through her chest, and she wanted to dance again, but not until she'd drunk at least a gallon of water.

Huw bent to pick up their jackets and shoes, and they made their way over to a stall selling plastic glasses of soda and fizzy water.

After downing two in rapid succession, Rowena developed hiccups.

'Don't lau-hic-ugh,' she protested.

'Boo!' he yelled at her. 'There, that should do the trick.'

'Hic. Didn't work. Hic.'

'Come on, let's go for a walk and enjoy what's left of the sunset,' he suggested, wrapping his hand around hers. 'The band, or another one like it, will be here for a few hours yet. I don't know about you, but I can do with a break – my ears are ringing and I can still feel the bass thudding in my chest.'

Rowena could feel it too, but she didn't think it was the music causing it. It was *Huw*. Now that they'd stopped to take a breath, she was acutely aware of him, and his nearness was making her pulse trip and her senses whirl.

He led her along the beach, and the further they walked the quieter it became as the crowds and the noise was left behind. The sun had disappeared beneath the sea, but the sky held on to the last of its light, glowing pink and orange. Behind the mountains above the town, inky night crept and stars began to emerge, twinkling in the velvet darkness.

It was so romantic, with the waves breaking on the sand and the distant music, that she didn't want the evening to end.

'How far do you want to go?' she asked, feeling as though she could walk along this beach forever.

'As far as you want,' he said. His voice was husky and low, and she swallowed nervously; she was pretty sure he wasn't referring to the distance their feet could take them.

She stopped and turned to face him. 'Let's take it slow,' she murmured as he moved closer.

'As slow as you want.' His promise was double-edged, and desire cascaded through her. The thought of making long, slow love with this man was sending her into a tailspin, and she didn't know how long she could hold out before she crashed and burned.

When his head bent towards her, she hitched in a breath, then let it out in a long sigh of pleasure as his mouth sought hers. Tangling his fingers in her hair, he deepened the kiss and she pressed herself against him, passion igniting into a burning flame inside her.

It was a long time before they broke apart, leaving Rowena breathless and shaken. Her lips felt bruised and tender, and never had she been so thoroughly kissed, or wanted a man as much as she wanted Huw.

In silence, they made their way back to the noise and lights of the beach party, arms around each other's waists, and every now and again they'd stop to kiss.

She had asked him how far he wanted to go...

Rowena wanted to go all the way. Physically and emotionally. Because she could so easily fall in love with this man, heart, body and soul.

She only hoped he felt the same way.

—

As Huw negotiated the bends on the road, trying to focus on his driving, his concentration was hijacked by the woman sitting in the passenger seat. Rowena was making it difficult to focus on anything other than her.

He could still taste her on his lips, the intoxicating scent of her lingered in his nose, and he could still feel the silken tresses of her hair in his hand, and the soft skin of her back under her T-shirt as he had caressed her spine.

God, how he wanted her, and it had taken every bit of self-control he'd possessed not to lower her onto the warm sand and make love to her right there.

Being in a public place notwithstanding, there was another reason he'd not given in to his desire. In the stark and unforgiving light of day and after their initial lust was satiated, he didn't want her to regret making love with him.

And that was why, when he dropped her at her door at the end of the evening, he got out of the car to kiss her goodnight, but left the engine running. It was a clear message to her that he didn't expect her to invite him in, that although he was aware Nia wasn't there and they'd have the house to themselves, he wasn't going to try to take advantage.

After he'd kissed Rowena soundly, stroked her cheek, then released her and walked back up the path to the car, he hadn't been able to tell whether she was relieved or disappointed. He hoped she didn't think he didn't want her, because he very much did: he wanted her more than he'd wanted any other woman he'd ever met. But that didn't mean he should make love to her at the first opportunity. He'd meant it when he'd said he would take it slow. There was no rush – although he did wonder how long he was going to be able to keep his hands off her.

'What are you doing tomorrow?' she called after him.

He stopped and turned around. 'Nothing.'

'Fancy coming for lunch? Nia will be at her Nanny's house.'

She looked nervous standing there, her tousled hair cascading over her shoulders, her face flushed, her eyes luminous in the glow of the street lamps.

'Would you prefer to come to mine?' he offered. 'I'm a decent enough cook when I put my mind to it.' He had a gut feeling that she'd be more relaxed without the worry of Nia and her Nanny turning up unexpectedly. Not that he and Rowena would have anything to hide, but he assumed she wouldn't want her mother or her daughter to catch her snogging the new man in town.

'If you don't mind, that would be lovely,' she said. 'Can I bring anything?'

'Just yourself. Will you be happy with steak and chips? I can do a mushroom sauce.'

'It sounds wonderful. I've got some strawberries that could do with using up – we could have those for dessert.'

What Huw wanted for dessert wasn't strawberries.

Telling himself off for having such lustful thoughts when he'd promised to take it slow, he said, 'Great. Strawberries, it is. Would one o'clock be OK?'

'I'm looking forward to it.'

As was he. Very, very much indeed.

Chapter 14

Huw scanned the cottage for a final time, his eyes darting here and there, seeking anything that was out of place or needed a clean. He'd been through every room with a fine-toothed comb, but the odds were that the very minute he thought he'd finished cleaning he would see something that needed addressing. Although by nature he was neat and tidy and never allowed things to get in a mess, he was nevertheless going out of his way to make a good impression today.

To his shame, he'd even put fresh sheets on the bed, even though he had no intention of luring Rowena into it – to justify what he'd done, he told himself it would be pointless having a spick and span house and not changing the bed linen. He was just being thorough, that was all. Besides, the bed could probably do with a fresh set; although rushing out to the nick-nack shop on the high street to buy a scented candle and placing it on the bedside table might have been overdoing it.

He'd also bought two pieces of steak while he was out, plus some tomatoes and mushrooms from the convenience store, and another bottle of Shloer, considering the first one had been such a success. He didn't think she'd appreciate wine on a Saturday lunchtime when she'd have to pick up Nia later, but neither did he want to serve her cola. And he debated whether to purchase cream to go with the strawberries, before eventually deciding he would. He'd find some use for it if it didn't get eaten today.

Finally, he was ready. The house was spotless, the meal was prepared as much as it could be without actually cooking it, and he was showered and shaved and wearing his nicest aftershave.

He had just pulled on a clean but old pair of jeans, and a clean but old T-shirt (he didn't want to risk ruining decent clothes by splashing something on them while he was cooking – which was usually what happened) when there was a knock on the door. He padded, barefoot, down the stairs to let her in.

'Hi,' he said, feeling suddenly shy.

She looked stunning – her hair was gathered on top of her head in some kind of messy arrangement, she wore shorts, a T-shirt and sandals, and it was all topped with a beaming smile.

'Hi to you, too. Here.' She thrust a cloth-wrapped glass bowl at him. 'I'll have the beeswax cloth back when you've finished with it,' she told him, and he gave the material a closer look.

'Is this the kind of thing you'll be selling?'

'Absolutely! You can wrap lots of stuff up in it and it saves on foil or cling film. Didn't you notice last Sunday that the sandwiches were wrapped in it?'

Huw hadn't noticed anything except Rowena and Nia. He'd been more intent on making friends with Nia than checking out the food. In fact, he couldn't remember what had passed his lips, and he'd only known he'd drunk the Shloer because he'd brought the empty bottles home with him to put in the recycling bin.

'Er, no. I didn't,' he confessed. 'This is a good idea though. What is it, exactly?'

'A wax wrap. It's made from cloth and beeswax, and lasts for ages. If you want to wrap something in it, you use the heat from your hands to seal it, and it stays in position until you peel it off. Then all you need to do is give it a wipe and it's ready to use again.'

'You're really enthusiastic about this, aren't you?'

She narrowed her eyes. 'Shouldn't I be?'

'You most definitely should. It helps to be passionate about what you're selling or making. In fact, I'd say it was a necessary requirement in order to run a business effectively. And there's nothing worse than doing something you don't love – especially when you own it and it's your livelihood.'

He could see her relax as she listened to him, and he briefly considered asking her more about her venture in the hope that he could share his expertise with her, but he decided against it. This was her business, her baby, and he shouldn't get involved. Not only was he in danger of coming across as a know-it-all or interfering, he didn't want to spoil today with talk of work. If she ever asked for his advice he'd give it freely, but until then, he didn't want to even think about work. Not his, anyway – although he was more than happy if she wanted to talk about her new shop. It was bound to be on her mind a lot, so if she wanted to chat, he'd listen.

Huw took the strawberries into the kitchen and switched on the oven. Placing a tray of chips inside, he turned his attention to the steaks. 'How do you like yours?'

'Medium, please.'

'While I'm making the mushroom sauce, would you like to open Nia's fake wine?'

'Pardon?'

'Look in the fridge.'

When Rowena saw what was in there, she laughed. 'Perfect. I'm not in the mood for alcohol.'

He wondered what she *was* in the mood for, then gave himself a mental slap on the wrist for having such lewd thoughts. She was here for lunch for goodness' sake – nothing else.

As she pottered around in his kitchen, fetching the bottle of grape juice out of the fridge and reaching for some glasses, he thought how nice it was to have her there. He quite liked living on his own (he'd not shared a house with anyone since his student days) but he had a sudden vision of how it could be if this was a permanent thing, and he discovered that the idea very much appealed to him. He wouldn't say he was lonely as such, but his sister was right – he *was* starting to feel the lack of having someone to share his life with. It had been far too long since he'd been in a serious relationship – although that hadn't ended well, because the woman in question had gone back to her ex just when Huw at been on the point of proposing to her. He had avoided getting too involved with anyone after that, not wanting to be hurt again, but now he thought he might be ready to take the risk. Since meeting Rowena and getting to know her, he was beginning to hope she might be that special someone.

He flipped the steaks over and checked on the chips, then he turned his attention back to the sauce.

'Can I do anything to help?' she asked, running a finger around the top of her wine glass.

Huw found the gesture incredibly sexy, and he swallowed down a surge of lust. 'It's all in hand,' he said. 'Just relax and enjoy yourself.'

He saw her catch her bottom lip with her teeth, and realised she was as nervous as he. He found that gesture incredibly sexy as well, and his stomach clenched at the memory of kissing that same mouth. He wanted to do more than kiss her lips – he wanted to kiss her all over.

Thankfully, his desire took a back seat while he dished up the food, and only made a tentative reappearance as they ate. It was a low-grade tingling that he could cope with if he didn't think about it too much, but every now and again he had a vision of her in his bed, her hair spread over his freshly laundered pillowcase, and he had to stifle the urge to sweep her into his arms and carry her off upstairs.

Occasionally he'd catch her looking at him with quiet intensity, and he'd feel a tremble shoot through him.

Huw managed to control himself until the meal was done and the dishes were washed. He even managed to rein in his growing desire while they finished the last of the Shloer, sitting side by side on the sofa.

But his good intentions flew out of the window as she removed his empty glass from his hand and placed it on the floor. When she leant towards him, her eyes full of promise, and rested her hand on his thigh, it took every ounce of willpower that he possessed not to push her down onto the cushions and show her how much he wanted her. He had to take this at her pace, take his cues from her; she would let him know when she was ready. *If* she was ready – because he wasn't going to take anything for granted.

Her lips were gentle, hesitant, a light flutter teasing his mouth, then they parted and her tongue slipped inside to tantalise him further. He moaned softly, his arms snaking around her, to draw her into him.

She sank into his embrace and deepened the kiss and for long, long minutes they explored each other's mouths, until he was unable to resist sliding his hands underneath her top and stroking the bare skin of her back. She arched her spine, pulling her lips away from his, and for a split second he thought he'd scared her off with his enthusiasm. But to his intense delight, she tugged his T-shirt up and ran her hand across his chest.

His reaction was immediate, intense and unmistakable, and when he lay back against the cushions, she followed him down with a soft sigh, her body against his. Once again he claimed her mouth, his kisses more urgent.

Her fingers roved over his chest, stroking the fine hairs that grew there, trailing over his stomach, down, down—

She pulled away so abruptly that it made him gasp. Flushed and flustered, her eyes brimming, her cheeks pink, she sat up. 'I can't do this,' she whispered. 'Not yet. Sorry.'

He tugged his T-shirt down and shuffled into a sitting position, his ardour cooling rapidly. 'Hey, there's no need to be sorry.'

'But I… we…' She looked as though she was about to cry. 'Sorry,' she repeated.

'I don't know what you think you need to be sorry for,' he said. 'That was lovely.'

'I can't give you what you want.'

'Kissing you is enough. There doesn't have to be more.'

'Really?' She seemed unsure, as though she didn't believe him.

Of course he would have loved to have taken her to bed and made love to her. But he meant it when he said that kissing her was enough. He felt honoured she'd allowed him to do that, and thrilled she had seemed to enjoy it as much as he.

'Fancy more Shloer? There's another bottle in the fridge. Or are you all grape-juiced out?' He sat up properly.

'Tea?' she suggested.

'Normal or herbal?'

'Er, normal, please.' Although he could tell she was still uncomfortable, some of her embarrassment was easing.

'We can drink it outside, if you like? And you can give me your opinion on my garden. Ceri is the green-fingered one in our family and she's promised to give it a makeover. It's functional but hardly inspiring.'

'You ought to see mine,' Rowena said, following him into the kitchen. 'It's tiny, but I do have lots of shrubs and flowers.'

She was still wearing that just-kissed look, and he tried not to think about what they could have been doing right now. It was enough that she hadn't rushed off. She was still here and still talking to him, and that meant more to him than anything. The rest could wait.

'It's just that I haven't dated anyone since Nia's father and I split up,' she said, abruptly.

He filled the kettle and switched it on. 'You don't have to explain.'

'Oh, but I do. It's not fair of me to lead you on, then pull the plug.' Her cheeks burned a brighter pink, and his heart went out to her.

'I assume you have your reasons,' he replied mildly.

'I do.' Her eyes on the kettle, she said, 'I was twenty-three and in love for the first – and only – time. I was living in Cardiff, sharing a house with a friend that I'd met at uni, and had just landed a new job. His name was Finn and he was seven years older than me. He had his own place – a plush apartment in the Bay – a good job, and a fast car. He was sophisticated, charming, good looking and I idolised him.'

The kettle came to the boil and Huw poured water into a couple of mugs. His movements were slow, his attention on the story Rowena was sharing with him.

'We broke up when he told me he was moving to Birmingham,' she said. 'He had a job offer he couldn't refuse.'

'Didn't you want to go with him?'

'He didn't ask me to.'

Huw heard the pain in her voice, and it occurred to him that maybe she wasn't over her ex.

'He'd been gone nearly two months before I realised I was pregnant.' She swallowed and raised her eyes to the ceiling, her pupils bright with unshed tears. 'I've never told him about the baby.'

'Ah, I see.' He fished the teabags out of the mugs with a spoon and put them on the draining board. 'Is that why Nia has never met her father?'

'Do you hate me?'

'Good grief, no! Why would I hate you?'

'My parents, Mam especially, think I should have told him. So does Betsan.'

'Once again, I assume you had your reasons,' he repeated.

'I did, but I might have been wrong. Finn has a right to know he has a child, but it's too late now. It will be awful if he suddenly discovers he has a daughter he knows nothing about, and I've also got Nia to consider. I don't want to upset her.'

'I'm sure you did what was best for you and her, and you'll continue to do that.'

'Do you still want to go out with me?'

'Why wouldn't I? I don't care about your past – I care about our future.' He emphasised *our*. 'Yours, mine and Nia's.'

'I'm sorry I couldn't… that we didn't…' She ground to a halt. 'It's been a long time, that's all, and I need to be certain about us first. That there *will be* an us. Because I care about you, and I don't want to risk being hurt again.'

Huw opened his arms, and after a tiny hesitation she stepped into his embrace.

He held her tight, his face buried in her hair, and said, 'I care for you, too. Very much. The last thing I want to do is hurt you, or see you be hurt. We've got all the time in the world. For Nia's sake and for yours, you have to make sure that this is what you want. Take your time – I'm not going anywhere. *I promise.*'

Chapter 15

Rowena felt incredibly nervous. Glad that she'd brought Betsan along, she shot her friend a terrified glance. They were sitting in the bank's foyer waiting for Mr Grimes, the business manager, and even Betsan was feeling the tension.

'I've never done anything like this before,' Rowena whispered, and Betsan gave her hand a squeeze.

'It'll be fine,' Betsan whispered back. 'You've done your homework. I'm sure they'll see what a good idea it is.'

'They very well might,' Rowena replied in a low voice, 'but they might not think it's profitable. Why did I let myself get so carried away? This is a daft idea.'

'It isn't! I just said so – it's a great idea.'

'Not the zero waste shop – Foxmore needs one of those – but me owning it. What do I know about running a shop? I should have got a job in one first so I could learn the ropes, but oh no, I thought I'd do it the hard way and dive straight in with no experience whatsoever.'

'You'll be fine,' Betsan insisted. 'You're intelligent, you've got bags of enthusiasm, you're passionate about reducing plastic – that's got to count for something.'

'Let's hope the bank thinks so, because I can't afford to set this up without their help. I wouldn't be so worried if I didn't have Nia to think about.'

'You'll be fine,' Betsan reiterated.

Rowena prayed she was right. There was so much riding on this meeting, and if the bank didn't loan her the money she needed, she didn't know what she was going to do. Or rather, she *did* – she'd have to knock the shop on the head. It would be such a shame: she'd put her heart and soul into the idea, and Foxmore could sorely do with an alternative to the convenience store.

She dearly wished that her plan to open a shop hadn't become common knowledge, because if it all fell through, she'd have egg on her face, which would make her feel doubly bad.

'Ms Lloyd? Would you like to follow me?' An assistant hovered in front of her with a professional smile on her face.

Rowena tried to smile back, but she suspected she looked like she was suffering from wind instead. With a deep breath, she gathered her file together and got to her feet. The bank already had copies of the paperwork she was holding, but she'd brought them along anyway, in case she needed to refer to them, even though she knew every decimal point intimately.

Betsan followed closely on her heels, and once again Rowena was grateful to have such a friend in her life. Betsan was her rock, her sounding board, her muse. She was level headed, loyal, and ever so slightly bonkers. But Rowena knew she could depend on her. Betsan would always have her back.

They were shown into a small room where a besuited man in his forties was sitting in front of a computer. As soon as they entered, he got to his feet. Rowena heard the door close gently behind them, and she swallowed nervously. This was it, this was crunch time.

'Hello, I'm Samuel Grimes.' He held out his hand, first to Rowena, then to Betsan, who was standing behind her. 'Please, take a seat.'

His smile of greeting was swiftly replaced by a more sombre expression, and Rowena had a feeling that this meeting wasn't going to go as well as she hoped, and her heart plummeted to her shoes.

–

'I knew it!' Rowena hissed to Betsan after they left Mr Grimes's office. Tears pricked but she was determined not to let them fall until she was at home. Her weeping would be done in private, not on the streets of Dolgellau.

'I'm so sorry,' her friend said. She linked her arm through Rowena's as they walked across the foyer towards the doors. 'I honestly thought the bank would loan you the money.'

Too big a risk... larger input of capital from the client... not enough experience in the sector... Hope we can do business with you in the future... Mr Grimes's words had washed over her, leaving her feeling sick and extremely deflated. She hadn't realised quite how much she had wanted this opportunity until it had been denied her. She'd set her heart on opening her shop, but now it wasn't to be, and she felt heartbroken.

'Ms Lloyd? Ms Lloyd!'

Rowena turned to see Mr Grimes hurrying after her.

'Have you got a minute?' he asked.

For a second, her heart leapt, until she realised it was unlikely he had changed his mind. She guessed the decision hadn't been his alone, and that there was probably a panel who discussed this kind of thing. He'd merely drawn the short straw in having to pass the bad news on.

'Why?' she asked.

He glanced around and lowered his voice. 'I've got an idea. The bank won't take kindly to me sharing this with you, so can we go outside and have a chat?'

'What have you got to lose?' Betsan asked, seeing her dithering. 'You may as well hear him out – he might have something useful to say. Anyway, I, for one, could do with a coffee before we go back. What do you say, Mr Grimes. Do you have time for a coffee?'

'I do. Just let me tell Maire that I'm popping out. There's a nice little coffee shop three doors down. I'll meet you there.'

'This is a waste of time,' Rowena protested as Betsan hustled her out of the bank and down the street. 'They're not prepared to lend me the money, so that's the end of it.'

'It might not be. Let's hear what he's got to say for himself, eh? Sit over there, and I'll get us a couple of coffees. Mr Grimes can get his own.'

When he entered the cafe, he spotted them immediately, came over to their table and sat down. 'I can't stay long, I'm afraid. I shouldn't really be here at all.'

'So why are you?' Rowena asked.

'Because I think I have a solution to your problem. Hear me out, before you dismiss it?'

Rowena shrugged and nodded. Betsan sat forward, her attention on the bank manager.

'Have either of you heard of co-operatives?' he began.

'Yeah, they are a chain of supermarkets and funeral directors.' Rowena pulled a face. What did this have to do with her little shop?

'Isn't it a bank, too?' Betsan asked.

'Yes, but that's not what I meant.'

Rowena snorted. 'For a minute there, I thought you were going to tell me to try to get a loan from them.'

'That would be more than my job's worth. Of course, it's up to you if you want to try another financial institution.'

'Get down off your high horse,' Betsan said, 'and tell us what you want to tell us.'

He nodded to a member of staff behind the counter and held up one finger, then he turned his attention back to Rowena. 'Co-operatives are businesses or organisations that are owned and operated by their members. An example would be a pub which a brewery was about to close, being bought out by its clientele. Everyone who puts money in to buy it would each own a share and everyone has an equal say in how it is run. Or it could be a bookshop – a co-operative-run one has recently opened up just around the corner from here. Or it could be a group of farmers coming together to form a co-operative. The possibilities and the types of businesses and organisations are endless.' He paused.

Rowena and Betsan stared at him.

'It was just a suggestion,' he said. 'You might want to look into it.'

'How on earth am I going to form a co-operative when your bank doesn't think I have the experience to even run a shop?' Rowena's blood began to boil. What a ridiculous suggestion.

'There is help out there to get you started,' Mr Grimes said. 'In fact, there's a branch of Co-Op Cymru right here in Dolgellau. It wouldn't do any harm to have a chat with them.'

'Sam? Your coffee is ready,' the woman behind the counter called.

'That's my cue to leave,' he said. 'Think about it. What have you got to lose? And it might just get your business off the ground.'

Rowena was silent, her mind whirling, so it was Betsan who thanked him for his time. As soon as he was out of earshot Betsan said, 'That was nice of him – he didn't have to do that.'

'Nice or not, I'm done. I can't go through this again.' Rowena was adamant.

'Go through what?' Betsan scoffed. 'A bank has turned you down for a loan. So what? It's a setback, not a death in the family.' She crossed herself, then touched the wooden tabletop. 'You could at least look into it. That's if you really want to run your own business. Or was all this just playing shop?' Betsan arched an eyebrow at her. 'It's not like you to give up at the first hurdle.'

'Being refused a loan is hardly a hurdle. It's a ruddy great big brick wall.'

'Nonsense. Make an appointment and go see these people. If nothing comes of it, so be it. But if you don't, somewhere down the line you'll wish you had. Even if it's only to satisfy your curiosity.'

Rowena blew out her cheeks and leant back in her chair. Betsan was right – she probably would regret it if she didn't. And what possible harm could it do? They'd either agree to help, or they wouldn't.

But there was one thing she was sure of – if she left things as they were currently, her little zero waste shop would never open its doors.

–

Huw tapped out a rhythm on the desk with his pen. It wasn't a beat as such, more of a background noise to help him think, and it was probably irritating his colleagues no end. There were usually five of them in the open-plan office, but two were out on visits, so it left only the remaining two to glare at him over their screens.

'Sorry,' he said, putting his pen down. 'It helps me think.' He should have been concentrating on the proposal that he'd been allocated, with a view to setting up a meeting, but his mind was on Rowena, so whatever thinking he was doing wasn't work related in the slightest.

How could he focus on work when he could still feel her in his arms? And if he closed his eyes, he could still smell her on his skin, despite having showered several times since Saturday afternoon.

'Late night, was it?'

'Eh?' Huw snapped his eyes open. 'No, just… thinking.'

'You could have fooled me.' Emrys was in his fifties, overweight and with a florid complexion. He rubbed his chest. 'I love bacon,' he said with a burp, 'but it doesn't love me. Got any indigestion tablets on you?'

'Sorry, no. I never get indigestion.'

'Lucky you. It's a bugger.' He burped again, and Huw winced. 'What has got you thinking so deeply that you need to close your eyes?' Emrys asked. 'Not work, I warrant.'

Huw felt guilty and hoped it didn't show on his face. 'Er...'

'That's OK – I bet you think of work when you're at home. I know I do, so it kind of evens itself out, I suppose.'

Emrys wasn't his immediate superior, but held the same job as Huw, so Huw wasn't worried about being reprimanded; however, he did pride himself on being professional and conscientious, so slacking off went against his principles. Right now, he couldn't help himself. Rowena had set up camp in his head and she wouldn't budge. He didn't *want* her to budge: he liked having her there, but she was having a detrimental effect on his job, so he'd have to make more of an effort to set thoughts of her aside while he was at work.

But not until he'd worked out a little conundrum that their next date was causing him. Once he'd done that, he promised himself that he'd concentrate on the proposal in front of him.

His problem was that he wanted to take her somewhere nice, somewhere that Nia would like too. If he was going to be a part of Rowena's life, he had to make an effort to include her daughter. Not on every date, because he wanted to spend some time alone with Rowena, but some of them at least. He wanted to surprise them both (his first attempt when he'd taken Rowena to the beach party had been a roaring success) but he didn't want to come across as a flash git and take her somewhere expensive, because he knew that would make her feel uncomfortable.

A meal was out of the question, because although Rowena would enjoy it, Nia probably wouldn't, and he wouldn't blame her. When he was a kid, he wouldn't have wanted to sit at a stuffy table in a stuffy restaurant: he'd wanted to do fun things, like going to an adventure park, or visiting a castle and pretending to be a knight. If he was lucky, his mam and dad might have bought him a sword from the gift shop.

Maybe not a castle for *their* next date, though… Somehow he couldn't see Nia wielding a sword.

The problem was, he only really knew about adult attractions and activities. Walking was a possibility, but he had the feeling Nia's little legs would soon get tired.

Giving up, Huw resorted to the internet for inspiration.

And after a bit of searching, he found exactly what he was looking for.

–

'Would it hurt to speak to them?' her mother asked when Rowena called around to give her the news.

Rowena had dropped Betsan off at the vicarage, then had gone straight round to her mam's house for a second opinion. Tracey Lloyd could be depended upon to be honest and not sugar-coat things.

Rowena had fully expected her mam to tell her to knock it on the head, but she hadn't. She'd listened with an open mind, then told her to look into it.

'I didn't think you approved of me opening a shop,' Rowena argued.

'It's not that I don't approve – I just want you to be sure you know what you are doing. Look at it from my point of view. The first I heard of it was when Bronwen Jones told me you'd been scouting out that empty shop on the corner. Then Dee Powell said you were thinking of renting the place. Imagine how *I* felt? My own daughter hadn't mentioned a word. I had to hear it from someone else.'

'No one knew except Betsan – but she was with me when we got the idea. Oh, she did tell Terry. And Terry's brother. But she only told his brother because he helped formulate a business plan.'

'That's my point. Everyone knew except me. Anyway, are you sure this is what you want? Running a shop is hard work. I'll help out where I can, of course, but there's only so much I can do – I do have my own job to go to.'

'I know, Mam. I'm not asking you to help.' Sometimes her mother could be downright annoying.

'So you don't want my help?'

'That's not what I'm saying. What I mean is, I don't *expect* you to help, but if you want to and you've got time, that would be great.'

'I'll do what I can, but I can't promise anything.'

'Good, glad that's sorted. Back to the co-operative thing – you think it's worth looking into?'

'I just said so, didn't I? Until you know more about it, you won't know whether it's a good idea. Why don't you look it up now? You don't have to leave for work just yet.'

Rowena checked the time. She could spare a few minutes: she'd deliberately made the appointment with the bank for as early as possible, anticipating that it might take a couple of hours.

It had taken about ten minutes. Plus the impromptu meeting in the coffee shop.

Rowena picked up her phone and typed Co-Op Cymru into the search bar and clicked on their website.

'Well? What does it say?' her mam demanded.

Rowena began to read out loud. 'They say that they help co-operatives to start and thrive by providing advice and training. Hang on.' She scrolled down the page. 'They provide support in areas such as HR, finance, marketing, membership and governance.' She looked up. 'What do you think they mean by governance? How it's run, maybe?'

'Probably. Can you make an appointment or give them a call?'

She read some more. 'Blah, blah... Yes, you can.' She glanced up from the screen. 'Do you think I should?'

'Do you believe in zero waste shops?'

'I do.' Rowena's reply was emphatic.

'Do you believe that Foxmore needs one?'

'Yes.'

'Do you believe in yourself?'

Rowena hesitated.

'*I* believe in you,' her mother said.

'Thanks, Mam.' She lifted her chin. 'Yes, I do believe in myself.'

'Make an appointment, then. What have you got to lose?'

Betsan had said the exact same thing, so with renewed hope, Rowena decided that was what she was going to do. If nothing came of it, then at least she would have tried.

Chapter 16

When Huw told her that for their next date he was taking her and Nia to Lake Vyrnwy on Saturday and that they were hiring bikes, Rowena had been rather apprehensive. For one thing, she'd not ridden a bike since she was a kid, and for another she didn't think Nia would be able to keep up. Her bike was only small and so was she. But after Huw had explained that she could hire a tandem for her and Nia, Rowena found herself looking forward to it.

By the time Sunday rolled around, both Rowena and Nia were in a state of high excitement – Nia because she was going to go on an adventure, and Rowena because she was seeing Huw again.

It had been a long week, and she'd spent most of it alternating between worrying about her appointment next week with Co-Op Cymru and looking forward to the weekend when she'd see Huw again.

They hadn't gone out on Friday because Rowena didn't have a babysitter, and she'd found herself unable to settle once Nia had gone to bed. She had almost given in to the urge to call Huw and invite him over. She might have done if she hadn't been seeing him today. Her mam was off out with friends, so she'd swapped her day to have Nia from Saturday to Sunday, which meant that Rowena could also spend all day with Huw tomorrow. Alone.

Her skin tingled with anticipation…

Telling herself to behave, she helped Nia out of her car seat, and the three of them strolled over to the bike hire place. As they walked, Rowena took in the scenery. The lake was actually a man-made reservoir, but that didn't detract from its beauty. In fact, the massive dam holding back the water was breathtaking, although the drop on the one side was rather scary.

Nia almost hopped out of her little trainers when she spotted a fairy-tale turret on the far side of the lake. 'Mammy! Look! A princess lives there,' she declared, her face glowing with excitement. 'Can we visit her?'

Rowena looked to where Nia was pointing. The pumping house did indeed resemble a castle, with its turret and spires, and slim arched windows. The building projected into the water and was connected to the bank via a stone bridge with arches underneath. It was a magnificent piece of architecture. Rowena had to take her hat off to the Victorians – they built for beauty as well as function.

'Aw, I wish we could, but she's not in today,' Huw said. 'She's doing princess stuff, like granting wishes.'

Nia gave him a scornful look. 'Princesses don't grant wishes. Fairy godmothers do. Don't you know *anything*?' She frowned at him, her brow wrinkling.

'Clearly not,' he replied with a laugh.

'She's obsessed with princesses and all things pink,' Rowena told him, biting her lip so she didn't laugh too. Nia took her princess obsession very seriously.

'I'm going to be a princess when I grow up,' Nia declared.

'You can't,' Huw told her, and when the little girl pulled a face and opened her mouth to object, he added, 'You're already a princess.'

Nia thought about it for a moment, her face screwed up in concentration, before saying, 'My mammy says I'm a princess, but I thought she was fibbing. I thought she was just being nice.'

'She's telling the truth. You *are* a princess. Every little girl is a princess.'

'No, they're not. I don't want Sian Edwards to be a princess. She's mean.'

'OK, not Sian Edwards.'

'Good.' Satisfied with Huw's response, she turned to Rowena, whose sides were aching from trying to hold in her mirth. 'Can I have an ice cream?'

'Maybe later. We've got a bike ride to go on first.'

'But Mammy, we didn't bring my bike!' Nia's face fell and her chin wobbled, and Rowena was constantly amazed at how swiftly her daughter could go from happy to distraught.

'We didn't need to. Look.' Rowena pointed to a row of bikes parked on stands next to the visitor's centre.

Nia looked. 'But they're all big bikes,' she said. 'There aren't any bikes for little people like me.'

Huw caught Rowena's eye and she nodded. This was his idea, so it was only fair he took the credit. Plus, Rowena wanted Nia to associate Huw with fun things.

Stop it! She was getting ahead of herself. They'd only known each other for six weeks, and they'd been dating for less than that. For her to start thinking that things could become more permanent this early on was madness.

They hadn't even slept together yet, so she was definitely jumping the gun.

And whose fault is that? she asked herself. She'd had the opportunity last weekend, but she'd bottled it. He'd been so nice about it, too. And he hadn't judged her when she'd told him about Finn.

But the time hadn't been quite right. She hadn't felt ready and Huw had respected that.

She'd had a week to think it over though. A week of remembering how it had felt to be held by him, how his kisses had melted her, turning her insides to liquid longing, and she found she couldn't wait for the two of them to be alone...

She tuned back into the conversation in time to hear Huw explain that Nia would sit on the smaller seat at the front of the tandem and her mum would sit on the back, so she could help Nia steer. Little did Nia realise that Rowena would be doing *all* the steering. And all the pedalling, too. It was going to be hard work, but at least it would be on the flat.

'It's twelve miles around the lake,' Huw said to her, once they'd sorted the bikes out and were fully kitted up with helmets. Rowena had made sure to bring Nia's, but she herself hadn't owned one since she was a child, and neither had Huw, so they'd had to rent theirs.

'Can we knock on the castle door and see if the princess is in?' Nia asked. 'She might be home now.'

'I'm pretty sure she won't be,' Huw said. 'She's had to go and slay a dragon, and you know how long that can take.'

Nia nodded sagely. 'Dragons are fierce and they sound like this.' She made a roaring noise, then puffed out her cheeks. 'I can't blow fire, but they can. She won't get hurt, will she?'

'Not a chance! She can beat a dragon any day.'

'Can we look inside her house?'

'I expect it will be all locked up,' he said, and Rowena's heart melted just that little bit more at the way he played along with her daughter's imagination. Huw was a natural with her – nothing was forced, and he seemed to enjoy the child's company.

They set off, Rowena and Nia in front, Huw bringing up the rear.

She felt a little self-conscious at first, hoping that her bum didn't squidge over the saddle, and her thighs didn't bulge as she pedalled, but before long she realised that she was enjoying herself far too much to worry about whether Huw was looking at her backside. And Nia was having the time of her life, resting her feet on the pedals, her legs going up and down as she pretended to do her share, and turning the handlebars on her part of the bike from side to side. Thankfully it was Rowena's handlebars that controlled the direction the tandem took, otherwise the pair of them would have ended up in the lake by now.

It took a couple of hours, but they eventually made it all the way around the lake, and by the time they arrived back at the dam Rowena's legs were aching, her rump was sore, and she was dying for a cup of coffee.

They handed the helmets and bikes back, Rowena feeling as though she was walking like a cowboy who'd lost his horse, and popped into the cafe for some refreshments.

'I'm tired,' Nia said. 'I worked hard, didn't I, Mammy?'

'You certainly did, cariad.' Rowena sat down gingerly and stretched out her legs. It had been hard work cycling for two, but she'd had a good time and so had Nia, so it had been worth it. The child hadn't had so much fun in ages, and Nia was even happier when she managed to wheedle a fairy cake and an ice cream out of Huw.

'You're spoiling her,' Rowena said, watching her daughter get ice cream on her nose. God, she looked so blimmin' cute!

'Sorry, I should have asked you if it was OK first.' He looked so contrite that Rowena burst out laughing.

'It's fine. I trust you not to fill her full of treats just before a meal, but tea won't be for a while yet, and all this fresh air and excitement has made her hungry.'

'You will tell me if I do something you don't approve of?' he asked.

'Definitely. But you're doing OK for a newbie. Are you sure you haven't had much to do with kids?'

'Cross my heart and hope to die,' he said. 'The last time I had anything to do with children, I *was* one. I just remember it well.' He leant in and whispered, 'Mentally I'm probably only a year or two older than Nia, so...' He shrugged and grinned at her. 'I'm just a big kid at heart. You're the only grown-up around here.'

Nia was occupied with her ice cream and wasn't taking the slightest bit of notice of the adults' conversation, so Rowena felt able to lower her voice and murmur, 'You look pretty grown up to me.' She knew she was flirting but she didn't think he'd mind.

His grin told her that he didn't. 'Later,' he whispered back, and the huskiness in his voice sent a shiver right through her.

'Would you like to come to mine for supper?' she asked, hastily adding, 'Just supper,' in case he thought something else might be on offer.

'I'd love to, thanks. What are we having?'

'Fish fingers, potato wedges, sweetcorn and broccoli.'

'Mmm, fish fingers… my favourite. I haven't had those since I was a student.'

'Maybe if you eat all your broccoli, it might convince Nia to eat hers. She hates vegetables, especially anything green.'

Huw bared his teeth. 'Can I let you in on a secret – I hate broccoli, too. But I'll eat it for Nia's sake.' Then he added, 'Maybe I'll mash it up and pretend it's dragon food? It might taste better then.'

'For goodness' sake…' Rowena rolled her eyes, but she was smiling as she did so, because she was falling for Huw Morgan more and more. Soon she will have fallen for him completely, and for some reason it didn't worry her in the slightest.

–

'I forgot to ask, how did your meeting with the bank go?' Huw asked as they sat down at the dinner table later.

Rowena tapped Nia's plate to remind her to eat, as the child was currently busily staring at the dollop of green next to her fish fingers. True to his word, Huw had mashed his broccoli and had added a tiny amount of butter and some salt and pepper.

Nia eyed hers with suspicion. 'What is it?'

Rowena gave Huw a meaningful look. This was his idea, so she'd leave it to him to explain.

'Dragon food,' he said earnestly. 'That's what makes them fly.'

'It's green.'

'What colour did you expect dragon food to be?'

Nia pulled a face. 'Not green. Are you *sure* it's dragon food?'

'I'm sure.' As though to prove his point, he scooped some up with his fork and popped it in his mouth. To be fair to him, he didn't grimace once.

'OK.' Nia ate some with a frown, but when her daughter attempted a second mouthful Rowena hoped she might eat it all. She hadn't given her much, but it was a start.

'Dragon food?' Rowena mouthed at Huw.

Huw grinned, pleased with himself.

With Nia occupied for a moment, Rowena answered his question about her meeting with the bank. 'Um, not too well. They didn't approve the loan, but they provided me with some alternative avenues to pursue.' Her reply was deliberately brief. She'd done nothing but think about it all week and she didn't want to spoil a lovely day by talking shop, so to speak.

Before Huw could ask Rowena anything further, Nia pushed her plate away. 'Can I fly now?'

Rowena raised her eyebrows and sent Huw another one of her looks; she was interested to see how he was going to get out of this one.

'How much did you eat?' he asked Nia.

'All of it.'

'That's good. It's a start. But it's not enough to make you fly. Dragons have to eat lorryfuls of the stuff.'

'I can't eat a lorry.'

'No, but you can eat more dragon food the next time your mammy gives you some.'

Nia thought. 'Can I have some for breakfast?'

'No, you cannot.' Rowena narrowed her eyes at Huw and glowered. 'Dragons don't eat bro— that for breakfast.'

'What do they eat?'

'Worms,' Huw said.

'Do worms make them fly?'

'No, worms make their tails grow.' Huw was clearly on a roll. 'See, they've only got a certain amount of fire to use, so they don't want to waste it if they can flatten people by knocking them over with their tails instead.'

'I don't like worms.'

'Neither do I, and neither do I want to grow a tail. Would you like to have a tail?' he asked, seriously.

Nia shook her head. 'It would be in the way when I sit down.'

'Exactly. But do you know what else dragons like to eat? Sweetcorn.'

Nia hadn't touched hers. 'Why, what does that make them do?'

'Nothing. But they think it's gold, so they eat it.'

'Dragons are silly.'

'They must be silly to think it's gold,' he agreed, 'but you're not silly. You know that sweetcorn makes your hair grow. Your mam has eaten all hers and her hair is really long.'

Nia eyed him with suspicion, but she picked up her little fork and jabbed at a kernel.

'Crumbs, you can come to supper every evening, if you can get her to eat her you-know-what,' Rowena said in admiration.

'If you're offering to cook for me every night, I'd probably agree,' Huw replied, chuckling to show that he hadn't taken her seriously.

'How about you come to mine to lunch tomorrow?' she asked. 'As you know, Nia will be at my mother's, so it'll be just the two of us.'

'I'd like that,' he said, looking deep into her eyes, and she blushed, hoping he didn't think she was offering anything other than food.

Although… she might be…

After he'd helped with the dishes, it was time for Nia to have a bath and get ready for bed. The child was exhausted after such a busy and exciting day, and although she vigorously protested that she wanted to stay up, she could hardly keep her eyes open.

'Say goodnight to Huw,' Rowena told her, and Nia rushed over to him and threw herself into his arms.

'Oof!' Huw was sitting on the sofa in the living room, a glass of wine on the lamp table next to him, and Nia's enthusiasm drove him deeper into the cushions. 'Wow, Nia, I thought you nearly flew then. That dragon food must be starting to work already.'

Nia wrapped her arms around his neck. 'Can you read me a story?'

'Not tonight, little one. I'm too tired after all that pedalling. You're lucky, you had your mum to help you. I was all on my own on my bike.'

'I'll ride on yours next time,' she said. 'Then Mammy will be tired, and you can read me a story.'

Huw closed his eyes and pretended to snore, earning himself a poke in the ribs. 'Sorry, did you say something? I didn't hear you because I was asleep.'

'You'd better go to bed,' Nia replied solemnly. 'Mammy will tuck you in.'

His eyes flew to Rowena's and she saw a sudden spark of desire in their depths. She had to look away when her daughter followed it with, 'You could sleep in my bed with me, but it's only little and Mammy says I wriggle. Mammy's got a big bed – you can share hers. She won't mind. I used to sleep in her bed a lot when I was a baby, but I'm a big girl now.'

'So you are,' Huw said to her, his voice sounding strangled.

Rowena's didn't sound any better as she said, 'Time for bed, Nia. You've said goodnight to Huw.' Without waiting to check that her daughter was following, she hurried out of the room and into the hall.

Dear God… She fanned her hot face with her hands and leant against the wall for a second until Nia appeared.

'Can I play with the bubbles?' Nia asked as Rowena took her hand and towed her upstairs.

'Another time. A quick bath, and a story. A short one, mind: we don't want poor Huw to sit there on his own for ages, do we?'

'He'll fall asleep,' Nia giggled. 'Then you'll have to wake him up and put him to bed.'

Rowena swallowed and cleared her throat, pushing the image that her daughter's words had evoked firmly out of her mind.

Oh dear, maybe it had been a mistake to invite him back for supper…

Eventually she got Nia settled and made her way downstairs, feeling slightly apprehensive.

During the drive back from Lake Vyrnwy and all throughout the meal she had been longing to get him on her own, but now that she was about to do precisely that, she was nervous. Her tummy was doing somersaults, her mouth was dry and her palms were damp – what an awful combination! If Huw was aware of the state she was in, he'd no doubt run a mile, and she wouldn't blame him.

She looked a fright too, and she wished she hadn't had the brilliant idea of putting a mirror in the tiny hall, because seeing her reflection right now wasn't doing her confidence any good. She looked like she'd been dragged through a hedge backwards and sideways. Her hair was a mess, her face had caught the sun and her eyes looked wild.

How could any man possibly resist!?

At least it solved her immediate problem of worrying whether Huw would want to make love to her. He'd probably take one look, make his excuses and leave.

When she stepped into the living room, closing the door softly behind her, she noticed that he had poured her a glass of wine. He handed it to her and she gulped it gratefully, then sat next to him on the sofa. She'd considered sitting in the chair, but he'd scooted over to give her room.

'If you want to get going, I understand,' she said. 'I'm sure you've got lots to do.'

'Do you want me to go?'

'Er… not if you don't want to.' Blimey, this was awkward.

Huw gently took the glass out of her hand and put it back on the table. 'Good. I'd like to stay for a while, if that's OK?'

'It's fine.' Her reply came out as a squeak.

He inched closer until she could feel his soft breath on her face and the heat of him through her T-shirt.

Then all rational thought fled as his mouth claimed hers, and her heart leapt with excitement.

She gave herself up to his kiss as he pulled her close, his arms caging her, solid and unyielding, and she melted back into the cushions, taking him with her. Her urgent hands roamed up and down his back, and she uttered a little whimper as he deepened the kiss. His tongue found hers, teasing, tasting, and his answering groan made her pulse soar.

Liquid with desire, she tugged at the waistband of his jeans, desperate for more of him. *All* of him. But without warning, he dragged his mouth away from hers and lifted himself off her, to sit back, breathless and trembling, and she wondered what she'd done wrong – until she saw the naked hunger in his eyes and knew he wanted this as much as she.

He had more restraint than her, more self-control, and he was already reaching for his wine and taking a steadying gulp.

Rowena slowly sat up, pulling her top down where it had ridden up, and said, 'Thank you.'

'You're welcome,' he rumbled, his voice hoarse. This near-miss had affected him as much as it had her. If it hadn't been for him pulling away, she'd have made love to him on the sofa without a second thought.

It made her feel slightly sick to think that Nia could have trotted downstairs at any point and caught them at it.

'I'd better go,' he announced. 'With you looking like that, I don't think I'll be able to control myself much longer if I stay.'

'How *do* I look?'

'Delectable. Beautiful. Sexy. I want you so much it hurts.'

Rowena laughed jerkily. 'Do you still want to come for lunch tomorrow?' she asked.

'Hell, yes.'

His growled reply took her breath away, and shakily she saw him to the door. On the step, where anyone could see, their kiss was chaste and restrained. But there was enough of a promise in it to keep her awake long into the night.

Chapter 17

Hoping Huw liked salmon, Rowena checked that the fish had thawed, relieved to find that it had. Leaving it in the fridge, she prepared the new potatoes. They were only small and it took her an age to scrape their soft, thin skins off, but she knew they'd be tasty so the effort was worth it. It also helped to keep her hands busy, because she hadn't slept too well last night for thinking about him. And from the second she got up this morning, he had completely occupied her thoughts, and the reason was that they would finally be alone in the house. She didn't need to be psychic to know what the outcome would be.

After nearly getting carried away yesterday evening, she didn't think either of them would be so restrained today. Also, there was no possibility of her mam bringing Nia back early because her parents were taking her to Machynlleth to buy her a new pair of shoes, although Rowena suspected the real reason was that Nanny might also purchase some for herself, and Rowena knew that her mother wouldn't stop at shoe shopping. She'd probably want to have a good nose around, and she'd already informed Rowena that they were intending to have lunch out, which meant that it would be late afternoon before there was any chance of Nia arriving home.

A lot could happen between then and now, and Rowena suspected that a lot would.

Something had shifted inside her yesterday. It had begun last weekend after she'd told him about Finn. Huw's reaction had been everything she had hoped it would be. And after yesterday and the way he'd been with Nia, and then last night when he'd held back, respecting her wishes to take it slow, she'd fallen for him a little bit more. If she was honest, she was halfway to being in love with him, and it wouldn't take much to tip her over the edge.

As soon as she finished preparing lunch, she rushed upstairs for a quick shower, before carefully applying some makeup. Not wanting to look as though she'd made too much of an effort, she slipped into a pair of jeans and a sweatshirt and shoved her feet into some pumps, then she brushed her long hair until it shone and flicked it over her shoulder.

She'd just finished making herself presentable when there was a knock at the door and her heart stood still.

This was it. If she let him in, the inevitable would happen and there would be no going back.

Was she ready for this? She'd not so much looked at a man since Finn, let alone contemplated going to bed with one. What if she had forgotten what to do?

But it wasn't the physicality which worried her, it was the emotional commitment. She'd had a few boyfriends in the past, and had slept with a couple of them, but each one had meant something. She hadn't just hopped into bed, no matter how much she happened to fancy the guy she was dating. She'd had an emotional commitment, and in the case of Finn had even secretly been contemplating marriage.

That she fancied Huw was a given. That she found him incredibly sexy was also true. If that was all she'd felt, she would never have opened the door to him, but open the door she did, knowing full well what his entry into her house today would undoubtedly lead to.

Rowena fully expected to take Huw to bed.

She hoped her nerves didn't show, but she was trembling as she gestured for him to come inside and followed him into the living room, where he stopped and turned to her. He was holding a bunch of flowers, not the store-bought kind or a professional bouquet from a florist. These were flowers he'd picked himself, and he had tied their stems together with string.

'For you,' he said. 'From my garden. I've no idea what most of them are, and I apologise if they are weeds, but I thought they looked pretty.'

Rowena gulped and took them from him. She wasn't used to receiving flowers. The last man to have bought her any was Finn. She remembered them vividly. She'd been at work when a lovely bouquet had been delivered, and she'd thought she was the luckiest and most special woman in the world. What a fool she had been.

This simple rustic bunch of flowers meant much more to the man who was giving them to her than that magnificent bouquet had meant to Finn. Huw had chosen them himself; he had picked each bloom with his own hands and had tied them with string himself. Finn had clicked a button and had presented his credit card. The two gifts were worlds apart.

Rowena buried her face in the delicate petals and inhaled deeply, the sweet scent filling her nose. 'Thank you. They're beautiful.'

She walked into the kitchen to find a vase, very aware that Huw was right behind her. As she dug one out of the cupboard and filled it with water, he seemed to infuse her small kitchen with his masculinity, and fill her senses with raw need.

Taking a deep breath, she willed her hands to stop shaking and her knees to stop trembling as she snipped the bottom of each stem at a forty-five-degree angle and put them in the vase, working in silence.

Every so often she would glance at Huw from behind her hair to find him studying her, and the hunger in his eyes made her go weak and her head spin.

Finally done with the flower arranging, she put the vase on the kitchen windowsill and turned to face him.

He didn't move and he didn't speak – he didn't need to.

Wordlessly, she stepped into his embrace and let his passion sweep her away.

–

'We'd better eat,' Rowena said, wriggling out of Huw's arms and sitting up in bed.

Huw gazed at her, trying to capture this moment. Satiated (for now), he let his eyes wander over the curve of her hip, the bones of her spine, the narrowness of her waist. A soft, delicate nipple peeped out from between the strands of her hair, and he remembered how she'd moaned when—

'Are you listening to me?' She sounded as though she was speaking to a child, and he grinned.

'No. I'm thinking about making love to you again,' he said.

'*Again?* I'm not sure I can manage a third time.'

'I want to take it slow, very, very slow...'

Her sharp intake of breath and the way the blush spread across her skin had an instant and undeniable effect on him.

'Oh, my,' she whispered. 'Slow sounds good...'

It *felt* good, too.

–

'*Now* are you ready for lunch?' Rowena asked, a long while later.

Huw had a feeling lunchtime had come and gone several hours ago. 'I think calling it lunch may be a bit optimistic.'

Rowena checked the time and paled. 'Oh, God, we'd better get dressed – Nia could be back any second.' She leapt out of bed, her expression panicked.

Huw was disappointed – he would have loved to have stayed in bed for the rest of the afternoon. Next to making love to her, cuddling Rowena was his second-favourite thing to do, he'd discovered. He just wished the last three and a half hours hadn't sped by so fast. Or that he could turn the clock back and relive them all over again.

He pushed the sheet back without complaint and rooted around for his clothes. Most of them were scattered up the stairs and across the landing. Hers, too, and he chuckled as he gathered them up. For them to have actually made it as far as the bedroom that first time had been a miracle – so eager had they been for each other.

He kept catching her eye as he dressed, and the lingering looks they shared made him want to throw her onto the bed and have his wicked way with her all over again.

It hadn't been wicked at all, though: it had been magical, and their lovemaking had touched his very soul. He was more than halfway to being in love with her – if he wasn't actually there already – and he simply couldn't imagine not having her in his life.

Very aware that a couple of romps under the covers didn't make a relationship, he was certain that their connection went deeper than the mere physical. It was as though he'd known her forever. As he'd explored her body, it was at once gloriously and excitingly new, and at the same time familiar and comfortable. He'd seemed to instinctively know what she liked, what would bring her to the peak of passion, then leave her limp and sated. And he'd done it again, and again, until she'd begged him to—

'I think I'd better get going,' he said as he reached the bottom of the stairs, but when her expression closed in, he hastily added, 'I'd love to stay and cook with you, but… Take a look in the mirror.'

She looked. He came to stand behind her, wrapped his arms around her waist, and she leant back into him.

'I see what you mean,' she said. 'We both look like we've been doing what we've been doing.'

'At least if you're on your own when your mum drops Nia off, you can say you were tired and went back to bed for an hour. If she sees me here…' He let the rest of the sentence hang.

Her lips were pinker and fuller than usual from his kisses, her face glowed, her hair was tangled, and her whole demeanour was one of a woman who'd been well and truly made love to.

When he caught sight of his own reflection, he looked much the same – minus the pink lips, the glowing skin and the tangled hair, although his hair was ruffled and sticking up at all angles. He was wearing a cat that got the cream expression, without the smugness. In fact, he felt honoured and privileged, and incredibly lucky to have found her.

After giving Rowena what was meant to have been a quick kiss but which turned into a five-minute affair involving roaming hands and breathless sighs, she pushed him away.

'Sorry, I can't seem to help myself when it comes to you,' he said. 'I'm definitely going now. Stay there. Don't move, because if you try to kiss me again I won't be responsible for my actions.'

Rowena pouted at him, and he groaned.

'Stop it. If you don't, I might just take you right here in the hall,' he warned, and had the satisfaction of seeing her expression change to one of alarm.

'Shoo!' She flapped her hands at him. 'Unless you want to risk running into my mother and her twenty questions, because she *will* grill you, you know. Especially if she guesses what we've been up to.'

'Er, no thanks. Although I would like to meet your parents at some point.'

'You will. Foxmore's a small place, remember? In fact, you might have already met them and just not realised they were related to me.' She paused, and the sass bled from her face. 'Are we at the meeting-the-parents stage, then?'

'Almost. I want to keep you to myself for a while longer before I let my family loose on you. You've already met Ceri – if she knew what was going on, it would be like

throwing you to the wolves. When can I see you again?'
His sister was threatening to pay him a visit next weekend, but he would try to put her off. He wanted to spend every available minute with Rowena.

'I'll have to check on the babysitter situation,' she said.

'You don't have to. I'm happy for Nia to come along.'

Rowena's eyes bored into his. 'I'm not. I want more...' She blinked slowly, leaving him in no doubt what she wanted more of.

Dear me, it was best he made a move, back to his own house and a cold shower. 'I'll phone you later,' he promised. 'When Nia has gone to bed.'

He walked home on a high, his heart full, a spring in his step, and thanked whatever fairy godmother was looking down on him that Rowena had come into his life.

If he wasn't in love yet, he was damned close to it, and although it was still early days he'd never felt as happy as he did right now. Everything was coming together to make his life perfect.

He was one lucky guy.

Chapter 18

'I can't believe I'm having to do this all over again,' Rowena complained crossly, as she steered her car into a space outside the offices of Co-Op Cymru. 'I'm not actually sure I want to.'

'Look, lovely, if you don't feel this is right, we can leave.' Betsan made no move to get out of her seat. 'You haven't lost anything, so you can walk away from it right now, no harm done.'

Rowena gnawed at her lip and hitched in a breath. 'I'm just worried I'll make a mistake. Or make a fool of myself. Or both. What if everyone thinks this is a bad idea? What if they think it's a good idea, but they don't want to put their money where their mouths are? Or they say they'll join the co-operative and then don't?'

'What if you walk away now and never know whether it would have worked or not?' Betsan retorted.

Rowena's laugh was more of a bark than a tinkle. 'There is always that,' she agreed. She rested her head on the back of the seat and stared into space. 'What have I got to lose?'

'Right this very minute? Nothing.'

'Exactly! But I'm scared, Betsan.'

'I expect you are. But look at it this way – if you do decide that forming a co-operative is the way forward, and

Co-Op Cymru agrees, and people do actually join, then Foxmore will have a zero waste shop and you'll be running it, but the burden, both financially and in terms of time commitment, will be reduced. The onus won't all be on you. Or are you scared of losing control?' Betsan arched an eyebrow. 'This is your baby after all, your vision. But if you go ahead with the co-operative, you won't own it – it'll be owned by whoever joins.'

'I know,' Rowena sighed. She'd spent the last week looking into every aspect she could, weighing up the pros and cons, and trying to decide whether Foxmore needed a zero waste shop more than she needed to be the one who owned it. 'I'd still have a say, I suppose.' She unclipped her seat belt. 'Come on let's do this. The worst that can happen is that they'll tell me it's a bad idea, or that it doesn't meet the requirements. And at least I'll know one way or another.'

She reached towards the back seat and hooked her bag with a finger, feeling an odd sense of déjà vu. It was only last week that she'd done the exact same thing, and look how that had turned out. She was no more confident that she'd obtain any better result from Co-Op Cymru, but even as she thought it, she knew she'd still be incredibly disappointed if her dream ended in the next hour or so. She'd put such a lot of work into it, so much time, so much effort, and so much hope… All she could do now was to cross her fingers and pray that nothing went wrong.

–

Huw pushed his chair away from his desk and stretched out his legs. It was only ten o'clock but he felt as though he'd been at work for hours. *And* it was only Monday!

How he was going to get through the rest of the week was beyond him. The way he was going, he'd be lucky to make it to the end of the day.

To say that he was tired was an understatement. After leaving Rowena's house yesterday afternoon (and narrowly missing Nia's return – he'd just rounded the corner at the end of Rowena's street when he'd spotted a familiar little face in the back seat of a silver hatchback), he'd been too full of the day's events to settle in front of the TV. So he'd gone for another early evening walk. This time he'd not bumped into Aled or a slick guy in a suit: he'd seen no one apart from a couple walking a dog in the distance, and more sheep than he could shake a stick at.

The walk hadn't helped as much as he'd hoped it would, because he still hadn't been able to relax when he'd got back – his head had been too full of Rowena and how they had spent the afternoon, to be able to concentrate on anything. Rather than let all that excess energy go to waste, he'd gone out for a jog – something he hadn't done for a good five or six years. And this morning he was regretting it, not only because his leg muscles ached, but because he'd *still* been unable to relax, and he'd lain in bed, tossing and turning, wondering how soon he could see Rowena again. It didn't help that they'd exchanged several messages, and some of them had been quite raunchy, which meant that he had been doubly unable to drift off.

Eventually he'd managed about three and a half hours, and had typically been in a deep sleep when his alarm had jerked him awake.

He felt a little sluggish even after several cups of coffee and a bacon roll, and it hadn't helped that the first thing he'd faced as soon as he walked into Co-Op Cymru's reception area was the news that Emrys had suffered a heart attack. The poor man! Thankfully he was being treated in hospital, had had a stent put in, and was expected to make a full recovery, although he would be off work for some considerable time.

Huw thought back to last week when Emrys had been complaining of heartburn, and he wondered if that had been an indicator. Huw had signed a get-well card and had donated to the whip-round, but maybe he'd visit him in hospital when Emrys was feeling a little better. He hadn't known the guy long, but he liked him and he hoped they'd continue to work together for a good long while yet.

Huw was contemplating another cup of coffee and some matchsticks to keep his eyes open when the receptionist popped her head around the office door. He was the only person in it right now, as one of the team was on annual leave, one was on a course and the other, Karen, was still in a meeting. His heart sank as he had a feeling he knew what she was going to say.

'Can you take Emrys's next appointment? Karen said she would, but her meeting is running on, and she's got too much on her plate already.'

'No problem, I'll do it,' he said, trying to hide his weariness. 'Do you have any details? I'll need to get up to speed before I speak to them.'

'As far as I can tell, it's an initial chat – there's nothing on the database. Emrys just wrote "query info gathering" in his diary. Thanks, Huw, you're a star!' The receptionist made to leave.

'Do we at least have a name?' he called after her.

'Lloyd,' she shouted back. 'I've put them in meeting room two.'

Huw disconnected his laptop from the server to take in with him, and found a pen and a notepad, wishing he'd taken the opportunity to grab another shot of caffeine while he'd had the chance. Never mind, if this meeting looked like it would go on for a while, he'd offer to make the clients one.

Slipping on his jacket, he straightened his tie, rubbed a hand across his face to wake it up, and then made his way to the meeting room, a familiar rush of anticipation hijacking him before he got there.

It was always a thrill to be involved in a co-op right from the very beginning. There was nothing better than watching an idea blossom into a healthy and thriving organisation, or seeing people who were passionate about it inject new life into an ailing company.

He opened the door, a smile of welcome and Mr Lloyd's name on his lips, and froze.

Two women were sitting at the round desk, and he recognised both of them. One of them he knew intimately.

For a minute he thought his mind was playing tricks on him, then his brain kicked into gear and he realised that the Lloyd that Karen had referred to was *Rowena* Lloyd – the woman whose bed he'd shared yesterday, the woman who he had made love to, the woman he thought he might have fallen in love with. Because that was what had kept him awake for most of last night – the realisation that he was in love with her. He'd felt exhilarated and terrified at the same time.

The penny dropped with an almighty clatter. *This* was what Rowena had meant when she'd said 'alternative avenues to pursue'. Co-Op Cymru was an alternative avenue, to be sure. He berated himself for not taking more notice, but then again, she hadn't seemed to want to talk about it and he hadn't wanted to pry. He'd operated under the premise that if, or when, she wanted to share anything with him, she would.

It suddenly occurred to Huw that the two of them had never gone into great detail about their work lives, and he'd not talked about his place of work or job role at any point during their dates, the two of them having found their conversations flowing naturally off onto unrelated tangents.

He closed his eyes briefly and when he opened them again, it was to see Rowena and Betsan staring at him.

'You work *here*?' Rowena glanced at Betsan, who shrugged. Both women seemed surprised to see him, but neither of them was unduly bothered.

He was, though. 'Um, could you excuse me for a minute?' he said, and was out of the door and closing it firmly behind him before she had a chance to reply.

In the corridor, he leant against the wall and thought hard. Could he do this – sleep with Rowena, then give her advice about starting a co-operative? Would it be a conflict of interest? Would Co-Op Cymru frown on one of its employees being in a relationship with a client, even if it had begun before the Co-Op became involved? He'd only just started working at this branch and he didn't want to blot his copybook already. He didn't want to blot his copybook at all. Maybe it would be prudent to ask Rowena to make another appointment and come back a different day.

His hand was on the door handle, and he was just about to go inside and explain to Rowena that she'd have to come back, when he heard Betsan say, 'It's up to you, of course, but I think you'll regret it if you walk out now.'

Knowing that nothing good ever came of eavesdropping, Huw nevertheless paused to listen.

Rowena's voice was quieter, but he managed to hear her say, 'Did you see the look on his face? He clearly wasn't happy to see me.'

'It was a bit of a shock, admittedly. Didn't he tell you where he worked?'

'Not really. He did mention his job, but I'm pretty sure he didn't tell me who he worked for. He did say he worked for a development agency and that his job was mainly admin, but I honestly didn't put two and two together. We should leave. I'd hate for him to feel uncomfortable.'

'You'll hate giving up on your dream even more,' Betsan retorted. 'Maybe not tomorrow, or next week, but it'll eat away at you... what if, what if. And it's not as though you're asking him to authorise a loan, because Co-Op Cymru don't issue loans.'

'No,' Rowena agreed.

'There you go then.'

Huw was torn, and he stood there, undecided. If he wanted to continue seeing her (and he did, very much) it might be best to tell her he couldn't be her advisor. But if he tried to persuade her to rearrange and see someone else, there was a possibility she might chicken out completely, and he knew how much this meant to her.

On the other hand, he felt a deep sense of satisfaction at the thought of being able to help her achieve her dream, and he knew that with his advice she'd give this her best shot. Excitement flowed through him at the thought of working with her, of having a professional relationship with her as well as a personal one. He'd never wanted any business to succeed as much as he wanted hers to, and he vowed to put his heart and soul into making her dream come true.

'Shh,' Betsan hissed, loud enough for him to hear as he opened the door. 'He's coming back.'

'Sorry about that. You caught me on the hop. I think I already know what this is about,' he began, 'but in case I've got it wrong, why don't you explain?' His attention was on Rowena, who hesitated before speaking.

'I told you that the bank turned me down for a loan,' she began, and carried on explaining her vision.

When she'd finished, he asked what she knew about Co-Op Cymru and what she hoped to achieve, and it was at this point that she began to flounder, and he assumed that this was so new to her she hadn't had a chance to look into co-operatives fully. Guessing she might benefit from seeing one in action, he asked if she could spare another hour or so. On being told that she could, he left to make a phone call. She was going to love this, he simply knew it!

—

Rowena stood in the centre of the bookshop and gazed around. '*This* is a co-operative? It looks just like any other shop.'

Huw chuckled. 'What did you expect it to look like?'

'I don't know.' She had assumed there would be clues as to the structure and organisation behind it, but what those were she had yet to determine.

After she had recovered from the initial shock of seeing him, she had been concerned to discover that it would be

Huw who would be helping her set up the co-operative. But he'd been totally professional throughout the meeting and she'd gradually relaxed. It wasn't ideal to have the man she was in love with to be so involved in her new business, but he was only there to give advice and guidance, and she had total faith that he'd do his best for her in that regard.

In love with… Rowena's thoughts flitted to what she and Huw had got up to yesterday, and she had to bite back a smile and force herself to concentrate on the matter at hand. After having a good look at the shop, she had a quick chat with Martin, the guy who ran it, who told her that he was the only paid employee and the rest of the staff in the shop were volunteers.

Thinking this set-up would suit her perfectly, she continued to ask questions.

Martin said, 'When I heard that the bookshop was going to close, it seemed such a shame. It's been here since I was a kid. Some of the shop's regular customers were also upset, so we got together and decided to do something about it. We needed money to buy the lease and it was also in dire need of a makeover, so we offered shares for sale to members of the local community, and that's how the co-operative was formed.'

It was a lot to take in, and Rowena knew she'd be digesting the information for a while yet.

'One thing you will need to do,' Martin advised, 'is to have a public meeting to gauge the level of interest, because if no one wants to buy shares your plan is dead in the water.'

Rowena looked to Huw, who nodded. 'I can help with that,' he said. 'Co-Op Cymru, if you decide to go ahead with this, can offer a raft of advice and guidance.

We'll work together on what you need, and what you don't need. But I reiterate what Martin said – you will have to set up a meeting with the community to garner interest. Then if there are sufficient pledges, you can take the project to the next stage.'

Rowena quailed at the thought of standing in front of the residents of Foxmore, trying to convince them that a zero waste shop was such a good idea that they should buy shares in it, but she knew she had to do it.

Huw continued, 'In the meantime, let me have copies of all your paperwork and I'll make sure your proposal is watertight, then we can work on the share offer together as soon as you make the decision to go ahead.'

Gosh, this really was all down to her, wasn't it? Not that she wanted or expected Huw to take charge (the bank wouldn't have either – it would have just given her the money and she would have had to get on with it), but for some reason she'd expected more hand-holding. Or was that because she had slept with the guy whose hand she expected to hold?

As though sensing her panic, Huw said, 'Don't worry, Co-Op Cymru will be with you every step of the way, and even after your co-operative is established we'll still be here to offer advice and support. *I'll* be here, I promise. I'm not going anywhere.'

I can do this, Rowena suddenly realised. With Huw by her side giving her love and support, she could do *anything*.

Chapter 19

Rowena had returned from her meeting with Co-Op Cymru and Huw, fired up and raring to go. She'd loved what the bookshop had done and chatting to Martin had inspired her. The more she thought about it, the better the concept of a co-operative seemed. The only obstacle in her way was Foxmore itself, as the idea might go down like a lead balloon.

A little voice in her head was whispering to her that Huw might also be a problem. Was it such a good idea to be romantically involved with him now that she'd discovered he was to be her mentor in helping her to get the co-op off the ground? What if it soured their relationship? However, she wasn't the best at judging people (look how badly she'd got it wrong with Finn), and she was aware she might be overthinking things.

Betsan said as much to her after Rowena had taken Nia to school, and Rowena confided how she felt. They were sitting in the office at the vicarage with a mug of tea in their hands, and were about to get stuck into designing some flyers inviting people to the meeting. Or, rather, *finalising* the flyers, because Betsan had already done most of the work. She was almost as invested in the shop as Rowena, now that she had an opportunity to be a shareholder.

'Men don't think like us,' her friend said. 'Often, they don't think at all.'

'That's a bit harsh,' Rowena replied.

'It's true, they don't. Remember that saying, "men are from Mars and women are from Venus"? We're like two different species. He'll probably be at home tonight sitting in front of the telly, engrossed in the footie, thinking everything is hunky-dory, while you'll be sitting at home in the dark, worrying your socks off.'

Rowena had to laugh. 'I won't be in the dark.'

'I'm still right, though: you will be fretting.'

'Maybe.'

'Stop it! Everything's fine. Anyway, why are you getting so wound up, considering you've only just got to the kissing stage?' Betsan's eyes widened when Rowena didn't answer. 'You haven't? You didn't? *You did!* When? Where? I want all the gory details!'

'It wasn't gory – it was wonderful.' Rowena knew she was wearing a dreamy expression, but she didn't care. It *had* been wonderful.

'When?' Betsan demanded again.

Rowena dropped her gaze. 'Sunday.'

'Where?'

'My house.'

Betsan's eyes widened even further. '*And you didn't think to tell me?*' she shrieked.

'I don't tell you everything,' Rowena said, primly.

'You sneaky so-and-so. No wonder you were all het up this morning.' She sobered. 'Stop looking for problems that aren't there. It's not going to affect your relationship. If anything, it'll strengthen it, and I suspect he'll do his utmost to make the co-op work anyway, regardless of whether he's sleeping with you or not, because he's that type of chap.' Betsan jabbed a finger at the computer screen. 'We'd better get to work – you can fill me in on the details of your *wonderful* tryst later. Right, I've booked the church hall for Thursday evening, and if we put the flyers up this afternoon that should give people enough notice. The sooner we hold this meeting the better, because if we leave it until Friday, half of the villagers will be in the pub and the other half will be glued to that new series on the telly, about a serial killer. It's the fourth episode,' she added as Rowena looked at her blankly. 'You must have seen it,' Betsan continued. 'Oh, silly me, you were out with your boyfriend when the first episode was on, and the second. You'll have to watch it on catch-up.'

Rowena's mind was spinning – when Betsan got the bit between her teeth she turned into a whirlwind of enthusiasm and gung-ho get-it-done determination. Rowena decided to sit back and let her get on with it. Betsan was better at this kind of thing than she was – probably due to all the church fetes she'd organised. Being a vicar's wife meant she often had several irons in the fire at once, so she was particularly good at getting on with things.

Finally the flyers were done and while they were chuntering out of the incredibly slow printer, Rowena dashed off to work. She'd be back later to put them up.

It was all go, and she hadn't had much of a chance to think about Huw for the last couple of hours, but as she hurried to the little school, her thoughts inevitably turned to him once more, and she felt a delicious glow in her chest. She still couldn't get over the fact that he worked for Co-Op Cymru and that he'd be helping her get her own co-op up and running. It was fate. Everything was starting to come together and she had such a good feeling about it.

Rowena had a skip in her step and a song in her heart for the rest of the day.

–

Good lord, she was tired. Rowena caught hold of Nia's hand to wearily cross the road, keeping hold of it long after they'd reached the other side. Although Foxmore's main street wasn't particularly busy, there were enough people on the pavement to warrant it.

Reflexively, she glanced at the corner shop as she passed, hoping no one else was thinking of renting it, and making a note to ask Dee whether there had been any interest from anyone else. Although she was no closer to opening her zero waste shop than she had been when Dee had taken her to view it, she nevertheless thought of it as hers and she was becoming quite proprietary.

Dawdling as she walked past, Rowena turned her head to peer in through the window yet again. She was still staring at it as Nia tugged at her hand, the child wanting to get home to have the snack and drink she'd been promised. Rowena resumed walking, then let out a squeak as she narrowly missed stepping right into someone's path.

'Sor—' she began, glancing at the man who she'd almost bumped into, but when she saw who it was the word turned to ash in her mouth. '*Finn?*' It came out as a whisper, but it was loud enough for him to hear.

He did a double-take, blinked, and then realised who she was. 'Rowena! Fancy seeing you here. How the devil are you?'

Rowena was frozen, her brain turned to mush, her only movement a small tick under her right eye.

'You're looking well,' he continued. 'How long has it been? Four years? Five?' He was staring at her, curiosity in his eyes, a confident smile on his lips.

He looked much the same; better dressed maybe, with a shorter haircut, but essentially the same.

Rowena took in his every detail, her eyes trained on his face.

Still as good looking, still as suave and smooth.

Her heart missed a beat, before giving an extra big one to catch up. It made her cough, and she cleared her throat. 'Finn,' she repeated.

'That's me! You're looking good.'

So was he, but she'd never tell him that. He appeared not to need any more confidence – he had bucket loads of the stuff already; he always had.

'What are you doing here?' she croaked, and cleared her throat again. Without conscious thought, she tightened her grip on her daughter's hand.

'A spot of business,' he replied airily. 'How about you? On holiday, are you?'

'I live here.'

He blinked again. 'You do?' The face he pulled told her just what he thought of Foxmore.

'I grew up here,' she reminded him.

He paused, then said, 'Ah, so you did. I wondered where I'd heard the name before, but I get about such a lot. You didn't stay in Cardiff?'

'Clearly not.' Rowena's initial shock was wearing off and anger was bubbling to the surface. To think she'd slept with this man, told him her innermost secrets, shared her dreams and her fears with him, and had given him her heart, and he couldn't even remember that Foxmore was where she was from?

'I'm going to be here for a couple of days – business, you know – so do you fancy a drink and a catch-up?' he was saying. 'For old times' sake? We had some fun, didn't we?' His gaze dropped to her chest, before returning to her face, leaving her in no doubt what he hoped the catch-up might entail.

He certainly had. Rowena not so much, not in the end. 'I don't think so,' she said.

'Mammy, I'm thirsty.' Nia stared up at her hopefully, and Rowena felt such a rush of protectiveness that she let out a gasp.

Shit! *Nia!* Oh, hell…

'Ow, Mammy, not so hard,' Nia complained, and Rowena realised she was crushing her daughter's hand. She hastily loosened her grip.

She wasn't concentrating on her daughter, however – her attention was on Finn, because *his* attention was on Nia. The confident smile that didn't quite reach his eyes had gone. In its place was a frown.

Rowena wanted to drag Nia away and run home as fast as she could, and lock and bolt her front door, because she could see what was going through Finn's mind. With father and daughter standing barely three feet apart, the resemblance was clear. Nia had the same curly dark hair as her father, and she also had Finn's eyes and mouth.

His gaze left Nia, rising to look Rowena in the eye. 'Is she yours?'

Rowena nodded, not trusting herself to speak. She guessed that her face was probably doing more talking than she wanted it to.

'How old is she?'

Rowena found her voice. 'Four,' she croaked. 'She's four.'

'Mammy! I'm nearly five,' Nia protested. 'It's my birthday in three weeks.'

Rowena wanted to curl up in a ball and wait until this hideous situation had passed, as she saw Finn working it out and arriving at the realisation that the child standing in front of him was his.

He looked as though he'd been punched in the gut. His face lost its tan, and his mouth was open in an 'O' of shock. He kept staring from Rowena to Nia, and back again, as though he couldn't believe it.

Rowena thought he was going to walk away, that he might turn his back on his daughter and disappear to where he'd come from, and part of her hoped he would do exactly that. They didn't need him in their lives – they could do without the complication. Nia had never known him, and what she didn't know she couldn't miss. Finn could leave and no one need be any the wiser, apart from him. They could pretend this brief encounter had never taken place.

But another part of her was relieved that he finally knew. Nia deserved to have her father in her life, and Finn deserved to get to know his daughter. No matter how difficult things might become for Rowena – arranging visits, sharing Nia's affections – she knew it was only right and proper that he played a part in his child's life.

Finn swallowed. 'I think we'd better talk.' He hadn't taken his eyes off Nia; he seemed to be devouring her with his gaze, as though he couldn't get enough of her, disbelief written across his handsome features.

God, she had some explaining to do. Guilt churned in her stomach and she felt sick. What had she done? She had denied him the chance of being a father. How could she have been so selfish? But here was a chance to put things right, to make up for her mistake.

Her daughter knew something was up: Nia was staring at this strange man with a solemn expression, her eyes boring into him as though there was something she should be seeing but she didn't know what. She wore the same expression when she was reading and trying to work out a word that she'd seen before but couldn't quite grasp what it was.

Thank God she was too young to join the dots. If this encounter had taken place in another four or five years, Nia might have jumped to the correct conclusion, and this was not how Rowena would have wanted her to find out.

'We do need to talk, but not right now,' she said. Rowena knew she was going to have to answer his questions, to face him sooner or later, but she had Nia to think of. How could she have such a delicate and emotional conversation when their daughter was in earshot?

'When?' he demanded. His mouth was a thin line, and his eyes were hooded. He was angry with her and it was justly deserved. She would be furious if she was in his shoes.

She took a shuddering breath. 'Later. Come to my house,' she said, giving him her address. 'Eight o'clock?'

Nia would have been in bed for an hour and should be sound asleep by then.

He nodded curtly and pushed past her, striding off up the street.

Rowena watched him go, dismay filling her. Her little girl's world was about to be turned upside down by a man she'd never met, and it was all Rowena's fault.

–

Huw cricked his head from side to side, feeling the crunch of the vertebrae in his neck as they realigned themselves. He'd been poring over a spreadsheet for what seemed like hours, until he was convinced his spine was going to stay in that position.

Ow, that hurt, but it felt nice too, so he rotated each shoulder in turn for good measure.

He was going to head off home in a minute but he wanted to finish a few things first. Then after a quick bite to eat and a shower, he'd pop around to see Rowena. She had sent him a message earlier to let him know that she and Betsan were going to put up flyers around the village this afternoon and that the meeting was going to be tomorrow evening, so he wanted to have a brief catch-up with her about it.

He'd leave it until Nia had gone to bed, because he didn't want to interrupt the child's night-time routine. That's what he told himself, but the real reason was that he was hoping to cadge a kiss or two. Nothing more than a kiss, because he didn't want Rowena to think he'd popped in for a booty call, and although he would dearly love to take her to bed again, he knew it wasn't going to happen. Not tonight anyway. Maybe on the weekend, if she could get a babysitter. Or if Rowena's mum had Nia on Saturday.

Despite knowing that this evening would just be a quick chat, and a kiss if he was lucky, he found himself looking forward to seeing her very much indeed.

Chapter 20

'You'd better come in.' Rowena stood to the side to let Finn in. As she did so, the scent of his aftershave wafted up her nose, and she grimaced. Although he wasn't wearing a cologne she recognised or associated with him, his familiar smell lay underneath, bringing with it unwanted memories. She tried her best to hide her reaction. If he was going to be a part of Nia's life, Rowena would have to get used to him being around and the memories he invoked.

He stepped past her, and she poked her head outside to scour the street in both directions.

No one appeared to have noticed Finn's arrival, so she hastily closed the door and followed him into the living room. She didn't want anyone to know about him until she'd introduced him properly to Nia and they'd sorted out the details of him being involved in her daughter's life. *Their* daughter, she amended.

Typically for Finn, he wasn't just standing there minding his own business – he was staring at the photos on the wall. They were of Nia, taken every year from when she was a baby until her last birthday, a visual record of how she'd changed and grown. Rowena intended to put one on the wall every year on her birthday until she was eighteen.

Slowly, he turned to face her. 'The child is definitely mine?'

'Yes.' Her voice was small, and she felt a tiny bit resentful that he'd asked at all, but she supposed he had to be sure.

'When did you find out you were pregnant?'

'Not until after you'd left.' She hung her head. She had a lot of apologising to do, and she had to make it up to him and Nia, but it wasn't too late to make amends. The logistics of visiting rights was going to be difficult, but she was sure that between them they could make it work.

'I see.' He walked over to an armchair and sank into it. 'Why didn't you tell me?'

'I didn't realise straight away. I was nearly four months before I guessed I was pregnant. You'd been gone for two of those. I was in shock.'

'And you think I'm not?'

'I'm sorry.' Rowena wanted to cry. Of course he was in shock. It must be awful to learn you have a child you knew nothing about.

'So you should be!' His voice rose and she heard the distress in it.

'Keep your voice down,' she said. 'My daughter's asleep.'

'*Our* daughter. She's mine, too.'

'She is,' Rowena agreed, feeling the prick of tears behind her eyes, and blinking them away. She had absolutely no defence for what she had done. 'I did try phoning, before I realised I was expecting, but your number was out of service.'

'Ah, yes...' Finn lowered his gaze. 'I wish you had made more of an effort once you did find out you were pregnant.' He sighed and pulled a face.

Rowena's heart lurched. She wished she had made more of an effort too, tried harder to track him down. If she had, she would have saved herself a great deal of heartache. They could have been together all this time, as a family. Instead, she'd fallen apart, sinking into a depression that had taken her months to claw her way out of.

But there was something in his expression that made her pause.

'Would you have taken me to Birmingham with you?' she asked, but even as she said the words, she knew what his answer would be, and her heart broke all over again. She might not love him anymore, but she was hurt that even with a baby on the way, he still wouldn't have wanted her. But at least Nia would have had a father.

He continued to avoid looking at her. 'I could have...' He trailed off.

'Been a part of *her* life, if not mine,' she finished for him.

'Not exactly.'

'What do you mean?'

'I would have supported you if you didn't want to keep it.'

Rowena was stunned. Had she heard him correctly?

His expression told her that she had, and disbelief was swiftly followed by burning hot anger.

'*It?*' she cried, incredulously. How could he call his gorgeous daughter *it*? And after seeing her, how the hell could he even think about ending Nia's life before it had begun? 'Look at her!' she hissed, venom dripping from every word as she flung an arm out to point at the photos he had just been looking at. 'You would have asked me to—' She couldn't even bring herself to say it.

'It wouldn't have been... she wasn't... oh f—' He stopped short of swearing and blew out his cheeks.

'Get out.' Her voice was flat, and she slowly dropped her arm so it hung by her side. She was done with this. She was done with Finn. If there had been the slightest smidgeon of love left for him in her heart, he had successfully poisoned it. The only emotion she felt was deep, dark bitterness. She would have wished *he'd* never been born, if it wasn't that in wishing for such a thing Nia wouldn't exist. And Nia was the most precious thing in the world. If Finn couldn't see that, he was a fool.

'We need to decide what we're going to do about her,' Finn said, making no move to shift his sorry behind out of her armchair.

'*We're* not going to decide anything,' she said. 'You might have a biological connection to Nia, but after what you just said, you are never, ever going to see her again.'

He looked so shocked that Rowena immediately relented, and her anger subsided. What he might have thought or might have wanted her to do back then, when the baby would have been an abstract concept for him, didn't have any relevance now. Nia was here, a real little girl, with a personality and a character of her own. And it was what Nia needed that was important. Plus, Finn had rights, too. She couldn't, in all conscience, keep his child from him.

She was about to tell him that she didn't mean what she'd just said, when he spoke.

'That's good, because I don't want to,' he said.

'Don't want to what?'

'See her.'

'I don't understand.'

'I'm married.'

Rowena was dumbfounded. Speechless, all she could do was shake her head.

When they had met earlier today and before he'd noticed Nia, he'd said he wanted her to have a drink with him, to catch up. The way he'd said it, and the way he'd looked at her, had left Rowena in no doubt as to the kind of catching up he had been hoping for. Yet he was *married*? Her gaze dropped to his left hand. It was ringless, and she pitied his poor wife. Although Rowena might have been distraught when he'd dumped her, it looked like she'd had a lucky escape, else it might have been her that he was hoping to cheat on.

'If my wife finds out about her...' he said, bringing Rowena's thoughts back to Nia and Finn's fatherhood, and she didn't understand how him being married made any difference to him being a father to his child.

Then a bulb lit up in her head – did he think she wanted *money*? 'I don't want any money from you,' she said. 'We're managing fine, without you having to put your hand in your pocket. But you can still see Nia whenever you want.'

Finn looked shocked. 'You aren't listening. I don't want anything to do with the child. I'm not going to pay maintenance, and under no circumstances do I want my wife to know about her.'

'Why shouldn't she know? It's not like you had an affair. You and I happened a long time ago. I'm sure she'll understand.'

'Whether she will or won't, is a moot point. I'm not interested in being a father. Is that clear?'

No, it wasn't. How could he not want any contact with Nia? Anger returned, welling into her chest to spill out of her mouth. 'Don't worry, if your wife ever finds out you've got a daughter, it won't be from me. Now, get out. I never want to see you again.'

'That might be difficult. I'm in Foxmore on business.' Hurriedly he held up his hands when she glared at him. 'Not for long, but I will be back and forth for a while, so I'm sorry, but we might bump into each other.' He looked as unhappy about the situation as she.

'Can't you do your business somewhere else?' she demanded, thinking that the other side of the world wouldn't be far enough after his rejection of the most precious child in the world.

'Not really. It's complicated.'

'I bet.' Everything had always been complicated when it came to Finn.

Despite herself, she was curious – what business was he in that had brought him to Foxmore? The last she had heard, and the reason he had left Cardiff, was that he'd landed a job with a big supermarket chain.

Finn suddenly looked very pleased with himself. 'It's a bit hush-hush, but everything will be revealed in due course.'

'Whatever.' If he wanted to be coy about it, she honestly didn't care. She just wanted him to leave. 'I think we're done,' she said, jerking her head towards the hall.

She followed him to the door. She was going to lock and bolt it after him, then try to forget he existed. All she needed to do was to keep him and Nia apart for the duration of his stay in Foxmore. It was unlikely that anyone *would* guess their relationship, but she didn't want to take any chances. Someone might spot the resemblance if they got a good look at Finn and Nia together, but that was never going to happen. Rowena didn't expect Finn to pay her another visit, and she was damned sure she would do everything in her power not to bump into him again, even if it meant she had to live like a hermit for the next few days.

'Where are you staying?' she asked, reaching the door.

'At The Jolly Fox. Why? Are you thinking of paying me a visit?'

He gave her a smile that made her feel sick. Did he honestly think she would want any kind of relationship with him knowing he was married, and knowing that he'd rejected his daughter? The man was unbelievable!

Rowena rolled her eyes in disgust but didn't say anything. He simply wasn't worth the effort. She opened the door, catching his scent once more as she stepped to the side to let him pass. It made her stomach churn.

'We were good together once. *Very* good,' he added, then leant close and she had a horrible suspicion that he was about to kiss her.

Rowena froze, then she shoved him away as she realised two things simultaneously.

The first was that Huw was standing on her doorstep, one hand raised as though to knock.

And the second was that she could hear a child's sleepy voice. 'Mammy, I need a wee.' Nia was at the foot of the stairs, rubbing her eyes.

Time slowed.

Huw's expectant expression turned to one of confusion, followed by realisation as he looked at the man standing in her hallway, then looked at the child at the other end of it.

Rowena's heart plummeted and she understood that the cat was well and truly out of the bag.

—

Huw stood frozen to the spot, his gaze flitting from the man in Rowena's hall to the child at the foot of the stairs. He recognised the chap as being the slick-suited guy who he'd seen twice before, both times with Aled.

What was he doing in Rowena's house?

And why did Rowena look sick, as though she'd just been given bad news, or something awful had happened. But what could be so awful that—?

Was she seeing this guy as well as him? Huw could have sworn he'd heard the guy say something about them being good together. It hadn't just been the words themselves, but the way he'd said them, and Huw had a feeling that if he hadn't been standing on her step about to knock on her door when it had opened, the guy would have kissed her.

And there was something else, something he couldn't put his finger on...

'Rowena?' Huw scanned her face and frowned, trying to read the emotions flashing across it, hoping she'd explain.

'It's not what you think,' she told him, her voice hitching, which made him think that might be exactly what it was, otherwise why would she say it? The stranger didn't say anything, and neither did he make any move to leave.

'Mammy, I need a wee,' Nia insisted. 'Huw? Have you come to tuck me in?' The little girl was still half asleep, but was waking up fast.

'No, I—' he began.

Rowena gave the man a push. 'Finn, please leave.'

Suddenly the answer to the stranger's identity hit Huw like a hammer to the chest, and he took a step back.

This man was Nia's father.

–

'Huw, come in if you want, I've got to see to Nia.' The poor child was squirming around with her legs crossed. Rowena had to see to her daughter first, before she did anything else, so she left the two men standing there, one on her step, the other in her hall, and took her daughter back to bed via the bathroom.

'Why was that man here, Mammy?' Nia asked as Rowena tucked her in.

'No reason.' Her heart was hammering so loudly, she was convinced Nia could hear it. She didn't want to lie to her, but what choice did she have?

Finn's accusations that she should have told him were true – but that he'd only wanted to know about his baby in order to get rid of it made her feel sick. If he'd have wanted to be a father to Nia now, she could have forgiven him, but the fact that he'd turned his back on his daughter was something she could never forgive. And to top it all off, he'd had the brass cheek to think she might be up for sleeping with him.

What an absolute creep!

But Finn and his particularly nasty brand of slime wasn't the thing that was causing her the most distress. It was Huw.

The look on his face when she'd opened the door and he had realised who Finn was, would stay with her forever. He had looked appalled and disbelieving, and totally horrified.

'Will Huw come and kiss me goodnight?' Nia snuggled into her duvet and Rowena tucked it under her chin.

'We'll see.'

'Aww...' Nia pouted. 'You always say that when you mean no.'

'Do I?' Rowena gave her daughter a cuddle, followed by a kiss on the forehead.

She was anxious to get back downstairs and find out what was going on. Although she'd been listening hard, she hadn't heard raised voices, and neither had she heard the door close.

'Night, night,' she said, and was just about to leave the bedroom when Nia said, 'I don't like that man. He's mean.'

Rowena froze.

Nia didn't like her father.

She waved her fingers at her sleepy daughter and left the door open a couple of inches to allow the dim glow from the night light on the landing to seep into the room, then she went downstairs to face the music.

But when she got there, both Huw and Finn had gone.

—

Reeling, Huw staggered back to his little cottage, his heart breaking, his thoughts a jumbled mess. He distinctly remembered Rowena telling him that Nia had never met her father and that she probably never would.

Nia had met him now, all right, and Rowena and her ex seemed to be playing happy families.

Huw didn't think he'd been mistaken – Finn *had* been about to kiss Rowena. And he'd definitely heard the guy say that they'd been good together once. They must have been, to have produced a poppet like Nia.

He couldn't believe this was happening to him for a second time. He'd been there, done that, and had had a broken heart to show for it. History was repeating itself, and pain tore through him as he realised that Rowena and her child's father were back together.

How long had it been going on? Why hadn't Rowena told him?

He fell into a chair, and rubbed his palms across his face. He felt like crying, but he held back the tears. What good would they do? Refusing to give in to his wretchedness, he blew out his cheeks and closed his eyes, letting his arms dangle limply by his side.

Rowena had told Finn to go. She'd told Huw to come in. But he hadn't. He had guessed what was coming and he didn't want to hear her say that she and Finn were going to try to make a go of things for Nia's sake.

He was made up for her, of course he was. He could completely understand that it was in Nia's best interests to have her father in her life, and he could also understand Rowena wanting to be with him. She had loved Finn once, and probably still did – hadn't he guessed as much? Huw had seen her pain first-hand when she'd told him about her ex.

How had he managed to fall so hard, so quickly? He'd not been in Foxmore two months yet, and he'd already had his heart broken.

Foxmore!

How was he going to be able to live in the same village as her after this? It would destroy him to see Rowena and Finn together, a happy little family unit with Nia at their centre. The thought of bumping into her at every turn made him feel sick.

He couldn't do it.

He *wouldn't* do it.

He had no choice – he'd have to leave.

–

'What on earth!' Betsan took one look at Rowena's face and pulled her into a hug. 'What's wrong? Is it Nia? Your parents?'

'They're fine,' she sobbed, as Betsan ushered her inside the vicarage and into the sanctuary of the empty living room, where she collapsed onto the sofa.

'What is it? Are you ill?'

'Nothing like that. It's Huw.' Rowena had been awake all night, tossing and turning and wondering how her life had come to this. On Sunday she had been happier than she'd ever been, but now her whole world had been turned upside down and her heart was breaking.

Betsan's mouth was a straight line. 'What's he done?'

Rowena fished around in her jeans pocket for a tissue and blew her nose. 'I think he's dumped me.'

'I don't believe it,' Betsan cried. 'Why? I thought you two were getting on like a house on fire.'

'So did I.'

Betsan rubbed her arm. 'Tea?'

'Got anything stronger?'

'It's nine thirty in the morning.'

'I know.'

'You've got work later.'

'I know.'

'You can have a cup of coffee,' Betsan informed her. 'I'll put two shots in.'

It would have to do, although the way Rowena was feeling she could have downed the best part of a bottle of gin.

'What do you mean, you think he's dumped you – has he or hasn't he?' Betsan demanded, when she returned with a couple of steaming mugs, setting them down on the coffee table.

Rowena hitched in a hiccupping breath. 'Finn is in town.'

'Give over! He's not! *Really?*'

Rowena nodded sadly.

'How? Why? I mean, is he here because of Nia?' Betsan's expression was one of shock.

'He's here on business, but he knows about Nia.'

'Start at the beginning,' Betsan instructed, so Rowena did, her coffee cooling untouched and forgotten as she relived bumping into Finn on the street, his realisation that Nia was probably his, his subsequent visit to her house, the revelation that he wanted nothing to do with his daughter, and the grand finale of Huw turning up at the worst possible moment. She finished with, 'He's not answering his phone or replying to my messages.'

'Back up a bit, lady, and park Huw to one side for a sec. Let me see if I've got this right.' Betsan counted off on her fingers as she spoke. 'You met Finn in the street and he tried to proposition you for old times' sake; he took one look at Nia and guessed she was his; he would have wanted you to tell him you were pregnant but only to talk you into having a termination... How am I doing so far?'

'Spot on.' Rowena blew her nose again.

'Then he told you to keep quiet about him being Nia's father because he is married; then told you he wouldn't pay child support – although we'll see about that! If he thinks he can shirk his financial responsibility to his daughter, he's got another thing coming. What the hell did you see in him, my lovely? What a scumbag!'

'That's it in a nutshell. But none of that matters because I don't want him in Nia's life now anyway, and neither do I want any child support from him. I'm doing OK by myself. Granny left me the house and some savings, and I've got my little job. I'm managing,' she insisted.

'Back to Huw. Are you sure it's over?'

Rowena's laugh was sad. 'I'm sure. You didn't see his face when he turned up on my doorstep and caught Finn trying to kiss me.'

'You've tried to explain, right?'

'I was going to, but he'd already left and now he's not answering his phone. I called around to his house after I dropped Nia off at school, but he wasn't there. I expect he's gone to work.'

'You have to keep trying. You love each other. Once he knows what really happened, he'll come round.'

Rowena dabbed at her eyes. Betsan was right, Huw was probably just in shock, and she tried to imagine what her reaction would be if she'd caught him kissing another woman. She could guess what it must have looked like, and in a way she didn't blame him for being cross. She'd wait until this evening, then she'd try to speak to him again.

She was about to ask Betsan if she'd look after Nia for an hour so she could sort it out, when she had a message on her phone and her heart lifted when she saw it was from Huw.

But when she read what it said, she promptly burst into tears.

'What is it? Is that from Huw?' Betsan asked.

Unable to speak, Rowena showed her the screen.

Betsan's lips moved as she read, then she looked at her with disbelieving eyes. 'He's breaking up with you and leaving Foxmore? But he's only just got here! You've got to talk to him. Surely this isn't just because your ex tried to kiss you?'

'Did you read the bit where he says he's moving to be nearer to his job?'

'Yeah, but Dolgellau is hardly Scotland, is it? Even if he does move, you can still carry on seeing each other.'

'This is like what happened with Finn all over again, but at least I'm not pregnant this time. I believe I've been here before. What is it with men dumping me because of their blasted jobs!' She let out a bitter laugh. 'Huw has made his feelings clear. It's over.'

Her heart was breaking. Had she just been a bit of light relief for him while he lived in the village? Had she known right from the start that he wouldn't be in Foxmore long? Rowena didn't for one second believe that this was a knee-jerk reaction on his part to seeing Finn last night. Huw must have been planning this all along, and she felt sick and lightheaded.

When her mobile buzzed again with another message from Huw, she read it wordlessly, then handed the phone to Betsan.

If she needed any further evidence that their relationship was over, this was it – he had only gone and asked a colleague to take over Rowena's co-op mentorship.

Abruptly anger replaced the heartache, and even though she knew the feeling was only temporary and the pain of unrequited love would take hold again soon enough, she grabbed it with both hands.

'I should never have got involved with him!' she cried. 'I should never have slept with him, and I should never have fallen in love with him. But do you know what I regret the most? Letting him anywhere near Nia. She adores him and now I've got to tell her that she won't be seeing him again.' Rowena grimaced. 'I should have stuck to my rules about not bringing boyfriends into her life.'

'Don't be so hard on yourself. It's not as though you have a different fella every month, or even every year. Huw is the first man I've known you to date since you came back to Foxmore.'

'Yeah, and there's a damned good reason for that. Men are nothing but trouble and heartache.'

'Aw, cariad, you'll find someone.'

'I don't want to find anyone, not after this. Nia and I were fine before we met Huw, and we'll be fine again. No more men,' she vowed, stifling a sob.

But when Betsan enfolded her in another hug, Rowena gave in to the hurt and disappointment she was feeling, and bawled her eyes out.

Chapter 21

Rowena's heart might be broken at this very moment, but her head was telling her that carrying on with the meeting in the church hall this evening was the right thing to do. If the zero waste shop didn't get the support she hoped for, then at least she would have given it her best shot. Because if she didn't, at some point down the line she'd regret not giving it a go.

In fact, having Finn turn up out of the blue had made her even more determined, in a grim kind of way. She wanted to make something of herself, not just for her sake, but for her daughter's, and if the shop didn't work out, she'd cast around for another opportunity. Nia was in full-time school now, so Rowena would try to get another job. The one she had was extremely convenient and it fitted in with school hours and the holidays, but it wasn't stretching her. She had been plodding along, quite content with things the way they were, but since the rally in Cardiff it was as though she'd woken up. She wanted more out of life than she was currently getting. She was a hard worker, she had a decent brain, she had passion – and she intended to find a job where she could use all three. Preferably whilst helping the environment at the same time.

Having given herself a pep talk, Rowena helped Nia get changed out of her scruffy clothes – the ones she wore for playing in – and into something more presentable. It was already six thirty and she would usually be making 'getting ready for bed' noises, but not this evening. Nia was coming with her to the meeting, and not just because everyone who Rowena would normally ask to babysit would also be going. Rowena wanted Nia up on the little stage at the front of the church hall with her and Betsan, because she wanted to make a point.

Nia was curious and bemused in equal measure. 'Is it like when I played an angel?'

'Not really. You won't be dressing up.' Nia had taken part in the nativity play last Christmas where she'd been cast as an angel. She had been most put out, because she had wanted the coveted role of Mary, although Rowena had been able to talk her round by pointing out that she had a much prettier costume than Mary's boring blue sheet.

'But you said I'll be on the stage.'

'You will, but it's not a play.' Rowena indicated that Nia should hold up her arms so she could pop the jumper over her head. Nia had managed to wriggle her way into her vest by herself, but the jumper was less stretchy. It was also getting too small for her, and Rowena would have to kit her out with new clothes soon – the child was shooting up like a weed.

'What is it then?' Nia asked, her brow creased into a frown as her head popped out of the jumper's neck.

Rowena knelt on the floor. 'You know that Mammy wants to open a shop?'

Nia nodded. 'A no-plastic shop. I told Miss Caldicott, and she says it's a good idea.'

'Well, I haven't got enough money to open a shop by myself, so I'm hoping people will help me.'

'I've got money in my piggy bank. You can have that.' Her little face was earnest, and Rowena's eyes filled with tears.

Hugging her daughter close, she said, 'That's your money, sweetie. But thank you for the offer, it's very kind. Mammy is hoping that people like Nanny and Grancha will give me some money out of their piggy banks to help me set it up.'

'Will it cost a lot?'

'It will.'

'More than ten pounds?'

'Much more.'

Nia thought about it. 'Twenty?'

'More than that.'

'Wow.'

Exactly – wow. Rowena knew it was a long shot, but others had done it. Since Mr Grimes had planted the idea in her head, Rowena had read story after story of successful co-operatives springing up all over Wales and the rest of the UK. If others could do it, so could she. All she had to do was to sell it to the residents of Foxmore.

'Are you going to ask them for money today?' Nia wanted to know.

'Yes, I am.'

'I'll tell them they've got to give it to you,' Nia said firmly.

'You do that!' Rowena laughed. Actually, that was precisely what she was hoping her daughter would do.

To Rowena's surprise, the church hall was fuller than she'd anticipated, and seeing many of the people that she had known all her life, plus some incomers to the village, made her go weak at the knees with nerves as she made her way onto the stage via the little set of steps to the side.

It wasn't much of a stage, but it had served Foxmore well over the years. The hall was now mainly used for jumble sales, the twice weekly mother and baby group, and Pilates, but it came in handy this evening. The stage itself was only about three feet higher than the floor, although to Rowena it felt more like ten. She was hideously conscious of everyone's gaze turning towards her, watching her progress and that of Nia and Betsan, as they took their seats.

A long trestle table and three chairs had been arranged on it, and Rowena's notes were already in place.

As soon as she sat down, she shuffled them nervously, then gave her daughter a reassuring smile. To her relief, Nia didn't seem in the least bit fazed. She was beaming widely, and every now and again she'd wave to someone. Her little legs stuck straight out from the chair and even with a cushion under her bottom, she could barely be seen over the top of the table.

She could be heard, though.

'My mammy is going to save the world from plastic,' she announced loudly, earning herself a ripple of laughter.

At least it broke the ice, Rowena thought, seeing nothing but indulgent smiles and kind curiosity on the sea of faces in front of her.

'Order, order!' Betsan shouted, banging a gavel on the flimsy table, which wobbled alarmingly. Rowena wondered where her friend had managed to find one of those. Betsan was grinning as she hammered on the table, so no one took her seriously until Nia screamed, 'Be quiet!' at the top of her voice.

A sudden hush descended.

'See, Betsan, that's how you do it,' the little girl said, gathering more titters.

'Thank you, poppet. What would I do without you?' Betsan turned her attention to the sea of faces. 'I know that most of you are here because you're nosey,' she began, 'but all of you are here because you care about Foxmore, and the world we live in. Although, I think Mr Stokes has only turned up in the hope of getting some tea and cake. Isn't that right, Mr Stokes?'

An elderly gentleman tipped an imaginary hat at her.

Betsan put a hand to her mouth and hissed to him, loudly enough for everyone to hear, 'Come to the vicarage later and I'll see what I can rustle up. Don't tell this lot though, because they'll all expect a piece, and a Victoria sponge will only stretch so far.'

More laughter. Rowena hoped the crowd's good mood would continue after she'd said her piece.

'We all try to do our bit,' Betsan carried on, in a more serious tone. 'I've got a compost bin in my garden, I recycle everything I can recycle, I turn lights off when I don't need them – but that may have more to do with how much Terry complains when I leave them on,' she added, to further amusement.

Rowena was awed at how well Betsan spoke and how adept she was at working the crowd. She'd be a hard act to follow, and Rowena swallowed nervously.

'However!' Betsan banged the gavel again, making everyone jump. 'We don't do enough. None of us do. And why don't we? Because we can't, that's why. And do you know why we can't?' She paused, and Rowena saw people shaking their heads, puzzled expressions on their faces. A few shrugged, and others glanced around to see if someone else had an answer.

'Because retailers don't let us,' Betsan crowed. 'How many of us have bought a toy, for instance, only to find it had so much plastic packaging around it that it took longer to get into it than your child spent playing with it? And what did you do with that packaging? You threw it in the bin, that's what.'

There were nods and murmurs of agreement.

'And don't get me started on all the unnecessary packaging you get when you buy a packet of cookies, or those little variety boxes of cereal, or – and this is my pet hate – the way they kind of glue plastic to cuts of meat. I nearly lost an arm trying to free a couple of sirloin steaks the other day.'

More laughter, but Rowena sensed that the crowd was ready for her to get on with it.

So did Betsan. 'Which brings me nicely to the reason this meeting has been called this evening,' she said. 'Thank you for giving up your time, and I'll now pass you over to Rowena.'

A smattering of applause accompanied Rowena rising to her feet, and she smiled to acknowledge it.

'Thank you, everyone,' she began, her voice higher than she would have liked. She cleared her throat and started again. 'Betsan has quite rightly reminded us of how much plastic that we – as a society, as families, and as individuals – use. I don't need to remind you of what a problem single-use plastic has become. It's damaging the environment, not just for us, but for our children, and their children.' She paused and gestured to Nia. 'I want Nia to live in a pristine world, an unspoilt world, and I'm sure that's what you want for your children and grandchildren. But that's not going to happen unless we do something about it. *Us. Today.* We can't afford to wait to see whether the government will pull their fingers out and make manufacturers and retailers accountable. We can't afford to stand by for years while we wait for the supermarkets to put the fate of the environment above their profits. We have to vote with our feet and our wallets – which is why I'm proposing we have a zero waste shop here in Foxmore.'

'If you want to open a zero waste shop, love, then go ahead. There's no need to have a meeting about it.'

Rowena smiled at the man who'd called out. It was Ianto Phelps, who lived on the next street to hers. He'd replaced her boiler for her, a year or so back.

'That's where you're wrong, Ianto – I *do* need to call a meeting, because I want this shop to belong to everyone.'

'Eh?' – 'What now?' – 'What's she saying?'

Rowena made out a few comments as several people started talking at once.

'Shush! Let my daughter speak,' Rowena's dad called, and gradually the noise subsided, apart from a couple of fellas towards the back who were holding a hushed conversation between themselves, which Rowena decided to ignore.

She sent her father a grateful smile, then carried on. 'I have a proposal for you. My dream is to open a co-op.' She glanced down at her notes, then hastily hurried on before anyone had a chance to interrupt her again. 'I expect you're asking, what is a co-op? Co-operatives are businesses or organisations which are set up, owned by, and operated by the members who run them. I'll give you an example,' she said swiftly, sensing that she might be losing the crowd. 'I recently visited a bookshop in Dolgellau that had been in danger of closing down. Several customers got together to save it and now it's being run as a co-operative by them. No single person owns it – they all do, equally. The members of that co-operative decide how the business operates, and anyone can join. It's a one member, one vote thing – everyone has an equal say. Members put something in – money, time, expertise or labour – and any profit that the co-op makes is shared equally between those members. This is what I'm hoping for in Foxmore.'

She sat back down, then quickly stood up again. She couldn't leave it there – she needed people to pledge their commitment to the idea, but before she could start speaking again, someone beat her to it.

'I thought we were here because of a new shop opening up,' a man called.

Rowena craned her neck to see who it was, but failed. 'We *are*,' she replied, scanning the faces in front of her. 'That's what I'm talking about – a zero waste shop.'

'But what about the new supermarket they're going to build on Aled's field? Shouldn't we be talking about that?'

There was a stunned silence for a split second, then the room erupted in a cacophony of noise.

The only person who didn't say anything was Rowena. She was too busy watching her dream go up in smoke.

Chapter 22

Despite Huw wishing he could stay at home this evening, he couldn't. It might hurt like hell to see Rowena and she might not want him there now that she was back with her ex, but he felt he had to be in the church hall to lend her his support. Not that she'd need it, because he had every faith in her, but if he could do anything to help her succeed, he would. Plus, although he'd handed mentorship over to Karen, she wasn't able to make the meeting tonight, so it was only fair that someone from Co-Op Cymru attended, and the only person available was him.

He'd waited until the meeting was about to start and had slipped in the back at the last minute, easing into a seat behind a tall, wide chap, and hoping the man's bulk would shield him from Rowena's sight. Not sure whether she'd appreciate him being there, he would only make his presence known if it looked like the meeting was going in the wrong direction and his two-pence worth might come in handy.

As the meeting started, bossy little Nia making him laugh, Huw gazed around the room, relieved to see there was such a good turnout. He was pleased for Rowena. Recognising many familiar faces, he tried to spot Finn but failed to see him anywhere. Aled wasn't there either, but

Huw wasn't surprised – the farmer was probably propping up the bar in The Jolly Fox. He seemed to be a permanent fixture there.

Huw settled down to listen, seeing the concentration on the faces of those seated near to him. The villagers seemed really interested in the co-op, and everything was going brilliantly: right up to the point where some chap asked about a supermarket and a sudden hush descended on the hall. Then all hell broke out as people began speaking at once.

Huw caught the words 'Cornerstone' and 'some smarmy git in a suit' and he froze, the skin on the back of his neck beginning to tingle.

'I want to know what's going on,' the man who had asked about the supermarket yelled.

'Don't we all, Bernie!' someone else shouted.

So did Huw. He didn't give a hoot about any new supermarket as such, but he did care about Rowena and how this might impact on her dream of opening a shop. If the meeting degenerated into a discussion about the supermarket, then people wouldn't be concentrating on her proposal to form a co-operative.

A man sitting behind Huw said, 'I'd better fetch Aled. I reckon he's got some explaining to do.' Huw swivelled around, the tingle becoming stronger, and he saw the man scramble out of his seat and head for the door. He had a bad feeling about this...

The hall had become a riot of noise, and Huw grimaced. Rowena, Nia and Betsan, who were sitting on a raised area at the far end of it, looked stunned. Nia appeared to be close to tears and her mother's arm was around her, holding her close to her side, so he was relieved when he saw an older woman step onto the stage and take charge of the little girl, hurrying her off the platform and out of the hall through a side door.

Huw decided he should step in, but as he got to his feet and moved into the aisle, the door behind him opened with a bang and Aled shouldered his way past.

And who should be following behind him? None other than Finn!

The tingle on the back of Huw's neck developed into a sledgehammer of understanding, as he abruptly realised why Rowena's ex was here. Aled and Finn were in cahoots! Finn, supermarket, field, Aled... It suddenly came abundantly clear to him what was going on.

A wave of pity for Rowena swiftly followed, as he realised something far more significant when he saw her shocked expression – *she hadn't known*. This was as much news to her as it was to everyone else, and at that moment he hated Finn for putting her through this. He hated him anyway because of his relationship to Rowena, but now anger accompanied his dislike. What sort of man treated the woman he loved like that?

Unless Finn didn't love her at all...?

Aled was spotted immediately, and a barrage of questions from the villagers made the farmer visibly flinch.

'What's this about a supermarket, Aled?'

'Have you sold your farm?'

'How much did you get for it?'

'When's it opening?'

Aled looked to Finn, and Huw saw Finn square his shoulders and paste a professional smile on his face. The man reminded Huw of a shark, with his too-white teeth and blank eyes. Huw could practically see the cogs whirring in the guy's head as he worked out how he might turn this fiasco to his advantage.

Finn strolled forward until he was in the centre of the hall and came to a halt in the aisle, then he held up his hands, turning slowly in a circle until one by one the talking petered out and all eyes were trained on him.

'Ladies and gentlemen,' he began. 'Sorry you had to hear about your wonderful new supermarket this way.' He glared at the stage before switching his 100-kilowatt smile back on. 'I'm sure you've all heard of Cornerstone?' He didn't wait for an answer, but ploughed on. 'I'm the company's property acquisitions manager for North and Mid Wales. It's my job to do due diligence on any locations deemed ripe for development and I was hoping to present it to you properly. But now that you *are* all here and interested in this brilliant new development for Foxmore, I'll happily answer your questions. First, though, allow me to explain why a branch of Cornerstone is such exciting news,' he carried on, without a pause, even though several people started firing questions at him. 'Let me just hop up here, so you can all see me,' he said, jumping onto the little stage without bothering with the steps.

Standing directly in front of Rowena, he held up his hands again as the crowd continued to call out, and he kept them raised until the talking died down once more.

'There, that's better, isn't it? Can you all hear me at the back? Excellent! OK, here's what we'll do: you hear me out, then we'll have some fun with your questions.'

Good grief, Huw thought, Finn certainly had all the buzzwords – wonderful, brilliant, exciting, fun… He was setting the villagers up to think of the supermarket as being the best thing since sliced bread, before they'd been told a single detail about it.

Finn clapped his hands once and scanned the hall. His gaze slid across Huw without the faintest flicker of recognition, and when Huw shifted his attention to Rowena, he saw that her eyes were on Finn, along with everyone else's.

Finn said, 'Cornerstone has long thought that the people of Foxmore don't deserve to have to travel for miles to do their weekly shop, so for a while we've been looking for a site that will be of benefit to the village.'

Huw didn't believe a word of it and neither did Rowena, he suspected, as he peered past the confident figure of Finn and studied her face. She looked devastated, but there was also resignation in her eyes, as though she'd never really expected her idea to get off the ground in the first place.

We'll see about that, Huw thought.

Finn was getting into his stride. 'We at Cornerstone know that Foxmore is an up-and-coming tourist destination. You've got an idyllic village, surrounded by beautiful farmland, and some of the most impressive hills and mountains in Wales. In the UK, even.'

'Too bloody right we have, so why spoil it with a ruddy great big supermarket?'

Huw saw it was Bronwen Jones who had spoken. The pensioner's mouth was set in a straight line, and she glowered at the stage.

'It won't be spoilt,' Finn said. 'But I'll come on to why not in a moment. Before that, let me share with you why we'd like to give Foxmore the opportunity to locate one of our stores here, although we have been, and we still are, considering other sites,' he added, his smile growing even wider.

Huw heard the implied threat that Cornerstone would easily go elsewhere if need be, and from the frowns on the faces of some of the people, he knew they had heard it, too. The fear of missing out was a very real fear, and Finn was playing on it ruthlessly.

'We know from our extensive research that Foxmore is growing as an outdoorsy staycation destination, which is one of the reasons why it has come to our attention. That, and the fact that the nearest decent-sized supermarket is ten miles and a half hour drive away.' He paused, as people nodded and murmured their agreement.

'We also know that although Foxmore's resident population is only 1800 at the last census, it becomes significantly larger when the surrounding hamlets are included, and larger again if you add campers, caravaners, cottage renters and second-home owners into the equation. That's a lot of people who are spending their money elsewhere and not in Foxmore itself. Little artisan shops are lovely, and Foxmore has them in abundance, but with the nearest proper supermarket a decent drive away, a great deal of business and *money* is being diverted away from the village. Cornerstone is here to make sure that doesn't happen.'

The smarmy git! Finn was making it sound as though he and Cornerstone were doing Foxmore a favour and that his company had nothing but the best interests of the village at heart, when they were clearly driven by profit. The company must have calculated that traffic, the catchment area, and footfall would make the site viable. Listening to Finn, anyone would think Cornerstone wanted to build a supermarket here out of the goodness of their hearts and for altruistic reasons only. Rubbish – absolute rubbish.

Finn spoke again. 'All of you know Aled, and you know his farm. He has kindly offered to sell Holly Field to us, plus the one next to it, to allow this wonderful opportunity for Foxmore to become a reality. As you are aware, these fields lie adjacent to the main road, and they are capable of housing a 70,000 square foot store, plus 480 or so parking spaces. It would be a big store, but not too big – a perfect size to ensure the village has the supermarket it so desperately needs and deserves, yet not too big that it would have a negative impact.' Finn shot Bronwen Jones a look that said, *see, we've thought about this*. 'We will widen the road leading to the site, of course, and put in a roundabout so the traffic will still flow freely, but the beauty of this store is that you'll be able to walk to it if you wish. If you've run out of bread, for instance, you won't have to jump in your car, you can—'

'Oi! What about me? I own the bakery. You'll be doing me out of business.'

'And me. I own the butchers.'

'There will be room for everyone,' Finn soothed, not looking at the two people who had voiced their concerns. Instead, he scanned the rest of the hall. 'Your products don't have to compete with those that Cornerstone sells.'

Huw couldn't be certain, but he thought the subtext to that comment was that it would be the artisan shops who'd have to amend the products they sold so they wouldn't be in competition with Cornerstone, and not the other way around.

Finn hadn't won over the crowd yet, but neither had he alienated them. If he was wise, he'd leave it there for now, to give the villagers some time to think it over.

But Finn had one last trump card to play, and he played it.

'Of course,' he said, nonchalantly, 'all this aside, you might want to consider the jobs that a supermarket would bring to Foxmore. All kinds of jobs, from cleaning staff to checkout operators, to shift managers, to back-office administrators, which would help the local economy enormously. But not only that, it would help *you* and your families.' He stepped back and Huw guessed he was done. 'I know I said I'd answer your questions, and no doubt you've got plenty, but I urge you to take some time to think this through. It's been sprung on you, and for that I apologise—' Finn's eyes flickered, and Huw had the feeling that the guy thought Rowena might have been responsible for revealing his secret '—but go home, have a chat with your family and your friends, and I'm sure you'll be as delighted as Cornerstone is to bring new life and new opportunities to Foxmore. Thank you, everyone.'

As the hall erupted around him, he leapt down from the stage and strode briskly to the door, Aled hurrying after him. The farmer wasn't as adept at dodging his fellow villagers and it took him twice as long to leave. When he reached the door he shot through it like a rat up a drainpipe, as Huw's grandad used to say.

Rowena hadn't moved, and Betsan looked equally shell-shocked. She had a small wooden gavel in her hand, and he saw her raise it, before slowly replacing it on the table without striking it.

Huw had to do something. Rowena needed his help, whether she wanted it or not. And even if he got nowhere, at least he would have tried. She mightn't love him, she mightn't want anything to do with him, but he loved her. There, he'd admitted it. *He loved her.* And he'd do anything for someone he loved.

After all, what did he have to lose when he'd already lost Rowena?

Rowena was too shocked to cry. She had honestly thought she'd been making progress and that maybe – just *maybe* – this scheme of hers stood a chance.

More fool her.

But how could she have anticipated that a new supermarket was being planned for Foxmore? And how could she have guessed that Finn would have something to do with it?

Feeling exposed on the stage with only Betsan for company (thank goodness her mam had the presence of mind to take Nia home) Rowena couldn't summon the energy to leave. No one was looking at her anyway, apart from her dad, who was being talked at by Mrs Moxley while sending Rowena sympathetic looks.

She almost laughed. She might have known Finn would be bad news. He'd already broken her heart once – although she wouldn't go back and change things for all the tea in China. Her daughter was the most precious thing in the world and Rowena couldn't imagine being without her. But he'd no sooner arrived in her life like a thunderbolt from the past, than he was ruining her future.

Just when she'd thought she had a chance of making a new life for herself and Nia, he'd scuppered it.

She blinked back tears, refusing to cry in public, but she nearly gave in to them when she felt Betsan's arm slip around her shoulders.

'You gave it your best shot,' Betsan said, and Rowena thought she was going to say something else, but instead she gave her a warning squeeze. 'Look who's here.'

Rowena had been so fixed on Finn and his departure that she'd not noticed a familiar face in the crowd, and her heart lurched when she saw who Betsan was referring to.

Huw was here, and he was heading in her direction.

Great, that was all she needed, the man she loved witnessing her fall. Both of her dreams lay trampled in the dust. Finn had waltzed off with the one, and Huw was stamping all over the other.

But she didn't have to think very hard to know why he was heading her way, a purposeful expression on his face. He was going to tell her that the co-operative wasn't viable now; as though she hadn't already worked that out for herself.

Betsan removed her arm from Rowena's shoulders, and Rowena sensed her friend moving away. Was everyone deserting her? She wanted to plead with Betsan to stay, but she couldn't drag her gaze away from Huw, who had locked eyes with her, his stare intense.

Rowena wished that she had never met him and she wondered if he felt the same, or whether he didn't care and all she had meant to him was another notch on his bedpost.

'We can sort this,' he said, leaping up the steps and coming to a halt in front of her.

Rowena was speechless. Was he here in an official capacity? And how on earth could he sort it? A little zero waste shop would never be able to compete with the likes of a giant supermarket chain. Anyway, everyone's focus was now on the superstore. She'd lost them for good.

'Do you want me to try?' he persisted. 'Or are you going to give in without a fight?'

Rowena shrugged. She didn't have any fight left in her. What was the point of trying to persuade people to invest in her shop when they would have everything on tap when a new branch of Cornerstone opened? It was the easy option; no effort on their part, no having to buy a share, or to help run it – all they would need to do would be to fill their trolleys once a week, pay for their goods and then go home.

'I'm not going to let you give in,' he snapped. 'I didn't think you were the sort of person to throw in the towel. You'll get knocks in this life, but you've got to get back up and keep fighting.'

'What do you know about knocks?' she shot back. 'What do you know about *me*?'

'I know that you can do this. You're determined and courageous, funny and smart.' He stopped abruptly. 'Is that enough?'

Rowena's laugh was bitter, and her voice was low as she growled. 'Yet you dumped me.'

'It saved *you* doing it,' he shot back.

'Excuse me?' What the hell was he talking about? 'Why would I dump you?'

'You could hardly keep seeing me now that you've gone back to Finn. I'm not stupid: I could see which way the wind was blowing.'

Rowena couldn't believe what she was hearing. 'I've not gone back to my ex. You couldn't be further from the truth.'

'But… I heard… I saw…' Huw stuttered to a halt and Rowena saw the realisation dawn on his face. 'You're *not* back with him?'

'No.'

'You *kissed* him.'

'Wrong. *He* kissed *me*. There's a difference, and if you'd hung around long enough you'd have found out that that was the last thing I wanted. I hate him.' She spat the last three words out with such venom that it should leave Huw in no doubt she meant it.

He stared at her blankly, and the meeting faded into the background as his face slowly lit up in one of the sunniest smiles Rowena had ever seen.

'My God, you don't know what this means to me—' Then he remembered where he was. 'Can we talk about this later? I meant what I said about not letting you give in. This lot will be off in a minute – we need to strike now!'

'*We?*'

'You don't think I'd let you do this on your own, do you? We're a team – if you want us to be?'

'I want,' she confirmed, hope trickling through the confusion in her mind, growing into a stream of cautious optimism that became a bubbling river of elation. 'Wait,' she said. There was a small point that she needed to clear up first. 'Are you really leaving Foxmore?'

'That depends on you.' Huw's smile dimmed and he gazed at her warily.

Rowena put her hands on her hips and gave him the kind of look she gave Nia when she was being silly. 'Huw Morgan, are you seriously telling me that I am the reason you were going to sell up?'

Huw hung his head and peeped at her from underneath his lashes. 'I thought you and Finn were an item. I couldn't stay here if that was the case. But Rowena, we can't talk about this *now*.'

Realising that if she intended to fight for her little zero waste shop she had to do it now, she shoved her feelings for Huw to the back of her mind. He was right. It was her shop, her idea, and it was up to her to win her friends and neighbours around. A little bit of support from Huw wouldn't go amiss, though.

'Team Sero?' She held up her fist to him and he bumped it gently, then she got to her feet and took a deep breath. She could do this. *They* could do this!

'Listen up!' she yelled, picking up the gavel and banging it.

Several people were already half out of the door, but they hesitated and turned around. Rowena knew she only had seconds to recapture their interest.

'If you want to talk about this new supermarket, then let's talk. I called this meeting because I believe in Foxmore, I believe in the people who live in it, and I want what's best for it. But I also want what's best for my child, and for all our children. I want to do as much as I can to make sure they have a world fit to live in, and I don't believe that will happen if we allow a big corporate chain who doesn't give a fig about you, or you, or you—' she pointed to several people, some of whom had resumed their seats '—to set up shop here. Despite what Finn

Bowen said, all he and Cornerstone are interested in is profit. Do you want to help a huge company like that get richer? Or do you want to have a say in how your *own* shop is run, have a share of your *own* shop's profits, and at the same time help make Foxmore a more sustainable place to live? If you don't want this, or think it's not for you, or you simply don't care, you should leave this meeting now. I'll understand. But if you do care, then you might want to listen to what I've got to say. Foxmore belongs to us, it's *our* village. Let's keep it that way!'

The cheer from the crowd was so unexpected that it took Rowena's breath away, and she had to sit down again for a second. Only a handful of people had actually left – being part of a co-operative wasn't for everyone, and not everyone was as passionate about the environment as she was, but if this project of hers did get off the ground, and if those people who walked away now, wanted in at a later date, she'd welcome them with open arms.

She meant what she said – the zero waste shop would be run *by* the people of Foxmore, *for* the people of Foxmore, and everyone would be welcome. Even Aled Harris.

Betsan was clapping along with the rest, and was smiling so widely that Rowena felt her face might turn inside out.

'Thank you,' she said, knowing Betsan could read her lips even if she couldn't hear her. If it wasn't for her wonderful friend, she wouldn't be sitting here now.

Even if she didn't get the pledges she so desperately needed, Rowena was determined that one way or another she'd open her zero waste shop. It might not be this year, or the next, but open it she would, because this was her dream and she refused to give up on it.

'OK,' she said, getting to her feet again. 'Let me explain how this will work...'

Chapter 23

'I thought that went incredibly well,' Huw said, as he escorted her home a couple of hours later.

Rowena wasn't as convinced. She'd managed to regain the crowd's attention, and many of the villagers seemed enthusiastic about her proposal, but...

'There's still so much to do,' she said. 'And people might have said they want in, but saying something and doing it are different creatures entirely.'

'You'll always get people who say they want to join and then don't,' he told her cheerfully. 'It's par for the course, but don't let it discourage you. Now that you've got an indication of pledges, you can present that to Co-Op Cymru when you have your next meeting.'

They'd reached her house, and Rowena hesitated. Her mam had sent her a message to say that she'd taken Nia home and put her to bed, and would babysit until Rowena got home. As much as she wanted to ask Huw in so they could have a proper chat, she wasn't going to be able to.

'We need to talk,' he said. 'And I don't mean about your shop.' He leant against the wall of her house and shoved his hands into his pockets. 'These past two days have been hell. I thought you'd gone back to Finn.' He grimaced. 'I wouldn't have blamed you – Nia deserves to have her father around—'

'But *he* doesn't deserve to have *her*,' Rowena interjected, her tone harsh. She forced herself to calm down and explain. 'When you came to my house the other night and saw Finn, we'd bumped into each other earlier in the street. I had Nia with me, and he put two and two together and realised he must be her father. I wasn't prepared to discuss it in public, and especially not in front of Nia, so I asked him to come to my house when Nia was in bed.' She blinked back tears at the memory. It still hurt to think that Finn, after seeing his gorgeous daughter, could even think that she shouldn't exist. 'He said I should have told him I was pregnant, and he's right, I should have.'

Her front door opening behind her made Rowena jump, and she let out a squeak of surprise.

'I thought I heard voices,' her mam said. 'Are you going to stand out there all night?'

'Huw was just leaving.'

'Hi Huw, I'm Tracey, Rowena's mam.' She put out her hand.

Huw glanced briefly at Rowena before he took it. 'Nice to meet you.'

'I've heard such a lot about you,' her mother gushed, and Rowena threw her an exasperated look.

'Not from me, you haven't.'

Her mam's reply was tart. 'That's because you never tell me anything, I have to hear it from my granddaughter, or Dee, or Mrs Moxley, or… anyone except you.'

'There's nothing to tell,' Rowena protested, but she wasn't able to look her mother in the eye, or Huw, for that matter, although she was aware he was staring at her.

Tracey shook her head. 'Hmm, that's not what I heard. Anyway, that's by-the-by – your dad told me what happened in the church hall after I left. That Cornerstone man sounds like a right piece of work, and I'm so proud of you for standing up for what you believe in. You can count me in for your shop, and your dad. Mrs Moxley said she wants in too, but that might be because she can't wait to get behind a shop counter again. Did you know she used to work in that very shop when she was a young woman? Then there's Bronwen, and the Powells, and Lowri and Lewis, they have all pledged their support. And—'

'How do you know all this?' Rowena interrupted.

'Haven't you seen? It's all over Facebook. Betsan has set up a page, and loads of people have commented and said they want to buy shares, or whatever it is, and you've had lots of offers of help, too. Ianto Phelps said if you need any plumbing done, he'll do that for free – although what plumbing the corner shop on the green could possibly need is anyone's guess, but it was nice of him to offer. Remember Ross Taylor? His mam used to live on Tawelan Street? Maybe not, he was about ten years older than you—' Tracey took a breath '—anyway, he moved to Chester a few years ago, but he's come back to Foxmore to live and he's offered to help kit it out with shelves and whatnot – he's got fingers in lots of pies, apparently. Then there's…'

Rowena had stopped listening. She was so astonished that all this had taken place in such a short amount of time that her brain had turned to mush. It was too much to take in.

'That's wonderful news!' Huw cried, catching hold of the top of her arm and giving it a squeeze.

Rowena nodded wordlessly.

Her mam narrowed her eyes. 'Aren't you pleased?'

'Overwhelmed.' That was about all she could manage.

Tracey sighed. 'Look, why don't you take a walk or something, and go and sort yourselves out? And before you say anything, I do have eyes in my head, you know. I can see what's been going on.' She turned to Huw and said, 'I've not seen her this happy since she came back to Foxmore to live. But these past couple of days she's been like a bear with a sore head. So do me a favour, and put a smile back on her face.'

Yet again Rowena was thunderstruck. 'But Nia—'

'I'm happy to stay here for a bit.'

'I'll bring her back at a reasonable time, Mrs Lloyd,' he said, grabbing hold of Rowena's hand. 'Come on, let's take that walk. It's a lovely evening for it.'

'You don't have to bring her back at all, if you don't want. I can stay all night, if needs be.' Tracey raised her eyebrows suggestively.

'Mam!' Rowena was mortified, but all Huw did was laugh.

He was still chuckling when they rounded the corner. But as soon as they were out of sight of Rowena's house, Huw halted, took her in his arms, and kissed her until she was breathless.

Before she lost herself in the moment, her last conscious thought for several long minutes was there was no way she was ever letting this man go.

-

The riverbank was deserted, the water calm, the breeze soft. The sun was setting, the air was still, and everything was bathed in a warm golden glow. As the shadows lengthened birds fluttered from roost to roost, tweeting and squabbling before settling, then taking flight again in a feathery cloud. Bats swooped silently overhead, dark, leathery acrobats hunting for insects, and in the distance a fox barked.

It was a beautiful evening for a walk. Strolling hand in hand, Huw led Rowena along the path, then left the well-worn track and headed for a majestically drooping willow. The branches formed a leafy curtain, and beyond lay dark dappled seclusion. Pushing several aside, he held them for Rowena to duck underneath, and when both of them were inside, he let the branches fall back.

'What now?' she asked, her voice as soft as the breeze through the leaves surrounding them.

'We talk.' As he sat down, dry leaves crunched under him and he patted the ground for her to join him.

Gracefully she sank to the floor and crossed her legs, her hands in her lap.

'It's all been a bit of a whirlwind, hasn't it?' he began. He knew what he wanted to say, but now that he had her on her own, he was scared of saying it. What if she didn't feel the same? He'd been to rock bottom once already this week, and although the events of this evening had given him hope, he was far from climbing out into the sunlight.

She shrugged. Her head was bowed, her fingers picking at her nails.

He took a deep breath. It was time to tell her how he felt. There was no point holding off; he wanted to know where he stood, whether there was a future for them. He hoped there was and that he hadn't misread the situation, but he had to know for sure. And if she didn't feel the same, then it was back to plan B – he'd sell up and move away.

He began, 'I fell in love with Foxmore as soon as I set eyes on it. The same with my cottage. I think I also fell in love with you the minute I saw you, too.'

She shot him a glance, her eyes wide, the last rays of the setting sun lancing through the leafy shelter and illuminating her face in dappled light.

'You might think that's ridiculous,' he carried on hastily, 'and maybe I didn't fall in love with you in the estate agent's office, but I think I most certainly did when you knocked on my door later.'

'You'd just moved in.' She nodded, remembering.

'That's right, I had. I remember thinking how lovely you were and hoping I'd see you again, but when I went to the church to donate some money for the repairs to the roof, the vicar mentioned that his wife had been out collecting signatures, and… You know the rest. But what you don't know is that despite thinking you were out of bounds, I couldn't get you out of my head. I couldn't stop thinking about you, you matter how wrong it was.'

'You couldn't?'

He took one of her hands in his and held it tightly. Her fingers were warm as she squeezed him back.

'No,' he confirmed, 'and I didn't like myself for it, but I couldn't help it. Then when I found out you weren't married, you don't know how happy that made me.'

Her soft laugh warmed his heart. 'And I thought you were married, too,' she said. 'When I saw you with Ceri…' She trailed off, shaking her head. 'We're a pair of numpties. Talk about jumping to the wrong conclusions.'

'I did it again, though, didn't I? When I saw Nia's father in your house, I thought you were getting back with him.'

'Not a chance.' Rowena huffed. 'I don't love him anymore, and he certainly doesn't give a hoot about me.' She narrowed her lips. 'Or about Nia. He doesn't want anything to do with her.'

Huw's mouth dropped open. 'You can't be serious?'

'I am.' Her expression was grim. 'In fact...' She paused and swallowed, and he sensed she was about to cry. 'He only wished I'd told him I was pregnant so he could have arranged for me to...' Her voice broke. 'How could he say something like that? His own daughter! He'd met her, he'd seen how gorgeous she is, yet he still would have wanted me to— Oh!'

Her wail of anguish cut him to the quick, and he scooted closer and enfolded her in his arms. What a jerk! Anger at Finn's callousness coursed through him. The man didn't deserve to have a daughter, and especially not one who was as wonderful as Nia. He didn't deserve Rowena, either.

'Shh...' he murmured into her hair, and gradually her sobbing slowed to a hiccupping sniffle.

'Sorry,' she said. 'It's just that it was such a shock seeing him. I used to go over and over in my head what I'd say if we ever met again, but I honestly never expected it to happen. And all he can think about is his wife not finding out.'

'Surely his wife will understand? OK, she might be a bit upset initially, but you had Nia before he and his wife got together.' He paused. 'Didn't you?'

'He was definitely single when I knew him.' It was her turn to hesitate. 'I think.' Rowena stared at Huw. 'Or maybe he wasn't,' she said slowly. 'It would explain a lot.'

'Do you think he should help with Nia's upkeep? She is his child at the end of the day, even if he doesn't want to be a part of her life.'

'I don't want anything from him!' she cried. 'And neither does Nia. She didn't take to him at all. Imagine if I told her that he is her father?'

'Will you tell her?'

'Not on your nelly. Not yet – she's too young to understand that her father is an arse.'

Huw guessed that someday Nia would want to know, but that was up to Rowena. Having never been a parent, he wouldn't have any idea how to deal with a situation like that. But even if he wasn't a father yet, he couldn't imagine turning his back on his own child, no matter how great the surprise had been.

'Nia and I are fine as we are. We don't need Finn Bowen.'

'I see.' His heart sank. Was she trying to tell him in a roundabout way that she didn't want *him* in their lives, either?

He felt her shudder against him, and he was about to release her when she said, 'But there *is* someone we need. If you'll have us. I know it's early days yet and I don't want to rush you into anything, but you are so good with her, and she adores you already, and...' Rowena ground to a halt.

Huw didn't know how he should respond. When she'd said that she needed him his heart had leapt with joy, but then it had just as quickly sank in despair. Had Rowena just told him that she needed him because of Nia? That the sole reason she'd want to be with him was because he was good with her?

'That didn't come out the way I meant it to,' she said, when he failed to say anything. 'I meant that Nia comes first. No matter how much I love someone, if he doesn't love Nia or if Nia doesn't like him, then it's not going to work. There has to—'

'Back up a second. Did you just say you love me?'

Rowena took a deep breath, pulled away and stared him in the eye. 'Yes.'

Huw didn't let her say another word. There was no need. They had both uttered the only words that mattered, words that would be the beginning of a brand-new life, ones that would bind them together, all three of them – him, Rowena and Nia, because Huw loved the little girl as much as he loved her mother. He'd be a husband to Rowena and a father to Nia, if Rowena agreed to do him the honour of marrying him.

But there was time enough to ask her. For now, all he wanted was to hold her and never let her go. And kiss her – again, and again, and again.

Chapter 24

'Are you excited?' Betsan asked as Rowena put the finishing touches to her outfit. She'd chosen it with all the care it deserved, because today was the start of the rest of her life. The zero waste shop was being officially opened this morning, and she was so excited and nervous that she felt sick. That the shop had gone from the seed of an idea all those months ago in Cardiff, and was now a full-grown co-operative, was a dream come true.

'I think I'm going to be sick,' Rowena said, swiping gloss across her lips with a shaking hand.

'You'll be fine.' Betsan was sitting on Rowena's bed, watching her get ready.

'Mammy, how do I look?' Nia danced into the room and did a twirl.

'Like a princess.'

'That's because I am one,' the little girl retorted with complete confidence.

'Do you have to wear fairy wings?' Rowena asked, stepping away from the mirror and slipping her toes into her comfiest shoes. No matter that this was a special occasion, she knew she would be on her feet for the biggest part of the day and she had no intention of getting blisters.

'Uh huh,' Nia said, nodding vigorously. 'Huw says—'

Rowena shook her head in mock despair. Every other sentence her child uttered began with 'Huw says'. Nia absolutely worshipped him, and in turn he adored her. In fact, sometimes Rowena felt like a spare part. Not that she minded: it was a great joy to her to see the two of them together, although sometimes she wondered which of them was the biggest kid. Nia might be five (as soon as she'd reached her fifth birthday, she had grandly announced that she was nearly six) but there were times when the child seemed older than Huw. He was often the one to instigate games, or come up with weird and wonderful ideas to keep the little girl occupied. His latest one had been to build a fairy trail in the graveyard (with Terry's permission, of course) and the two of them had spent hours painting river pebbles to look like fairy houses. It was his fault that Nia was now obsessed with fairies.

'Is everyone ready?' Betsan asked, getting to her feet.

Rowena checked the time and took a deep breath. 'As ready as I'll ever be. I can't believe this is actually happening.'

'You'd better believe it. Enjoy – you deserve it.'

Rowena wasn't so sure that 'deserve' was the right word, but she was determined to enjoy herself. She'd better had, because this was her future, hers and Nia's.

Holding her head high, Rowena stepped out of her front door. She could do this. With Huw at her side, she could do *anything*.

–

Rowena hadn't wanted a ceremony, or any kind of a fuss at all, really. She'd planned on opening Sero without doing anything to mark the occasion other than having a brew and a Jaffa cake before unlocking the door to welcome her first customers.

But the best laid plans had reckoned without her mother, Betsan and Huw, all of whom intended to make a ceremony out of it.

It was Betsan who had insisted that Rowena dress up. 'Wear something nice,' she'd instructed. 'Really nice. It's not every day you get to make your dream come true.'

'It's not just *my* dream,' Rowena had said. 'Half of Foxmore has had a hand in it.'

'That's why we need to make an occasion of it,' Betsan had argued.

Rowena knew her friend was right. She just didn't like being in the limelight too much, that was all, and the spotlight had been on her almost continually over the past few months, starting with that first meeting in the church hall. There had been many more meetings since then. As soon as all the pledges were in, setting up the co-operative had progressed swiftly, and with so much expertise and so many willing hands, the shop had been ready to open far sooner than if Rowena had gone it alone. There was the added bonus that she'd hardly had to dip into her savings at all, and because it was her idea and Sero wouldn't exist if it wasn't for her, the new co-op's members had taken the unanimous decision to employ one permanent member of staff – Rowena.

Despite all the goodwill and support from the wonderful residents of Foxmore, she continued to worry. What if she didn't get any customers?

Feeling silly, she immediately answered her own question. Of course she'd have customers. Half the village had shares in the co-op, so it was in their interest to shop there.

And more than half of the village had turned out this morning, she realised as she approached the shop on the corner of the green. There was quite a crowd and she spotted many familiar faces, some more familiar than others. Her parents were there, along with Mrs Moxley and her brood of daughters and grandchildren. Lowri, who was visibly pregnant, was there with her partner Lewis. Terry and their youngest child (the older one was backpacking around Europe) were smiling at her, and her own parents were beaming fit to burst. Karen, from Co-Op Cymru, was waving at her, and she also spotted Dee and Vaughan Powell, Bronwen Jones, Ianto Phelps, Bernie Williams, and Ross Taylor (who did indeed have his finger in many pies). Even Miss Caldicott, Nia's teacher, had turned up.

Aled Harris was the only sour face in the crowd. Rowena didn't blame him for not being happy about Sero: he held the co-operative responsible for Cornerstone pulling out of the deal to buy two of his fields. Rowena had a suspicion that the reason was more to do with Finn and their shared history, but she wasn't going to let on. The upshot was that the supermarket the villagers had been dreading (increased traffic through the village, fewer people actually visiting Foxmore's lovely shops, an eyesore in what had once been open farmland) had been relocated to further along the A470, and everyone, apart from poor Aled himself, was perfectly happy with the situation.

A round of applause broke out as Rowena came to a halt outside the shop's newly painted door and she smiled widely, revelling in the occasion. But even as she was thinking how wonderful it was that so many people had turned out to witness this wonderful moment, her eyes were scanning the crowd for the only person who she really wanted to see – Huw.

But he was nowhere in sight.

Deflated, she wondered whether she should say a few words. Would people be expecting her to? Should there be a ribbon to cut?

A noise behind caught her attention and she realised the door to the shop was opening. But how could it if she had the key and—?

A sudden hush swept through the crowd and she stiffened, then slowly, oh so slowly turned around, dreading what she might find.

Her sigh of relief when she realised it was Huw, swiftly turned into a gasp as he stepped towards her and got down on one knee.

What—? Rowena's thoughts were a scrambled mess as she tried to make sense of what was happening. Why had he opened up? Had he dropped the key? Why—

Huw cleared his throat. 'Rowena, I love you with all my heart and want to spend the rest of my life with you. Will you marry me?'

Rowena opened her mouth, but no words came out. To say she was shocked was the understatement of the year. This was supposed to be the day they opened the shop. Why was he on his knees, holding out a ring? What did he just say?

Realisation came crashing down.

Oh. My. God! Huw had just asked her to marry him, and now all of Foxmore was waiting for her answer.

She gulped and took a shaky breath. She wanted to say yes, of course she did, but there was something she had to know first. It wasn't just her own happiness she had to consider.

Gazing down at Huw, who was staring back up at her with his heart in his eyes, Rowena bit her lip, then turned to her daughter.

'Nia, are you OK with this? If you're not, I don't have to say yes.' Rowena ignored the collective gasp of the crowd – her daughter was the only person who mattered, her opinion was the only one she cared about. Apart from Huw. And she felt her heart breaking as she thought about what this might be doing to him. What if Nia said she didn't want her mam to marry him? Oh, Huw…

Nia stamped her foot. 'Of course I am, silly. Huw already asked me if he could ask you to marry him and I said yes.' She looked very pleased with herself, as well she might, adding, 'I'm a big girl – I kept it secret for ages.'

'Ages, eh?' Rowena laughed, relief making her feel weak.

'Five days,' Betsan piped up.

Rowena gasped. 'Were *you* in on this, too?'

'Why do you think I was so keen to get you into a dress?' Betsan smirked.

Rowena's gaze alighted on her mother, and she had a sneaking suspicion that someone else had been in on the secret, too: after all, Betsan hadn't been the only one who had urged her to have this opening party for the shop. 'Mam?'

'Yes, Rowena?' Her mother's face was a picture of innocence, but Rowena wasn't fooled.

'Come on, love, put the poor bloke out of his misery,' someone shouted, and Rowena's hand flew to her mouth.

'Oh, Huw, I'm sorry!'

He was still on one knee and he was still holding out the box containing the ring. His expression had gone from hopeful to pained.

'Ask her again, mate – I don't think she heard you the first time!' Terry called out, and when Rowena glanced at him, the vicar winked at her. Dear lord, they were all in on this.

'You did say that you can't keep anything secret in Foxmore,' Huw said, 'so I didn't bother trying.'

'You kept it secret from *me*,' Rowena pointed out, but she was smiling so widely that her cheeks hurt. *Huw had asked her to marry him!*

Huw grimaced. 'Rowena, for the love of all things holy, please will you tell me whether you'll marry me or not? My knees are killing me.'

'Yes, yes, a thousand times yes!'

'Thank God for that.' He took the ring out of the box and Rowena held out her left hand, her heart hammering madly and her legs shaking. When he slid it onto her finger, a huge cheer went up, and she began to cry. Her happiness was complete, and tears of joy trickled down her cheeks as he scrambled to his feet.

'I love you,' she murmured, and she saw her love reflected in his eyes.

'I love you, too,' he said. 'More than you'll ever know.'

When he swept her into his arms and his mouth came down on hers, the rest of the world faded into the background. Rowena melted into him, joy sweeping through her, her heart so full of love for this marvellous, wonderful man that she thought it might burst.

'Mammy? Mammy? Can I be a bridesmaid now?'

Rowena felt the tug of her daughter's hand on her dress and she giggled.

'Only if I can be one, too,' Betsan cried, and Ceri's voice shouted from the crowd, 'Me, three! I've never been a bridesmaid before. And if you still want me to buy your cottage, I'm game.'

When Rowena and Huw came up for air, it was to thunderous applause, whistles and shouts of congratulation, and she clutched Huw's hand on the one side and Nia's on the other.

Rowena felt on top of the world, with her friends, family, and the people she'd known all her life, here to share her happiness.

Then, out of the crowd, Mrs Moxley could be heard calling, 'Are you going to open this here shop or not, because there's a roll of bamboo toilet paper with my name on it...'